2

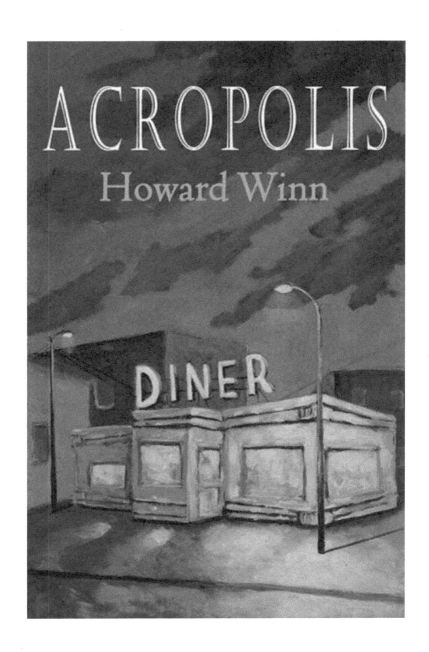

ACROPOLIS

Howard Winn

ACROPOLIS

a novel by

Howard Winn

ISBN eBook: 978-1-370-84988-8
ISBN Paperback: 978-1-387-09092-1

Propertius Press
Roanoke, Virginia
http://www.propertiuspress.com
email: admin@propertiuspress.com

PROPERTIUS
PRESS

This novel is a work of fiction. While the literary perceptions and insights are based on experience, all names, places, relationships, and events either are products of the author's imagination or are used fictitiously.

History

The Acropolis of Athens is a flat-topped rock which rises 490 feet above sea level. A temple sacred to Athena, Goddess of Wisdom, the Parthenon, was built there in the golden age of Athens under the leadership of Pericles (460 to 430 BC) and is considered the culmination of the Doric order. It is an enduring symbol of Ancient Greece and of Athenian democracy. Over time, it has been converted to a Christian church dedicated to the Virgin Mary, a mosque with a minaret added, and an Ottoman ammunition dump. It has been plundered of its ancient sculptures and is now considered one of the major tourist attractions of modern Greece.

It is also a Greek diner in Poughkeepsie, New York, U. S. A.

Contents

1935

"Just look at her. Just look at her. Pitiful. We have to do something. She has to go. There are institutions, public ones, our taxes already pay for. We can't easily manage this, this, what can I call her? A little better than a vegetable, maybe the mind of a puppy. Retarded. I have to work at the diner. The Acropolis feeds us. You have the house and the other kids. What are you thinking?"

He turned away from his wife and daughter and stared out the window at Conklin Street and the Karras house across from theirs. In profile, Mr. Christopoulos looked as if he could have been a classic model for the face painted on an ancient pottery shard from a Greek archaeological dig. A short man, he was sinewy and tanned. His hands were large. His hair was pepper and salt, cut short around the ears but with a stand-up brush-cut.

"How can you call her a vegetable? Insulting. Her own father to say that. She is only six years old," his wife said. She, too, was short but plump, and in body if not in face, she might have been drawn as a stout hedgehog in a house dress from a children's book. She did not look like some idealized Mediterranean woman gracing an ancient Greek vase, not with her hair pulled back into a bun and with her chubby hands caressing her daughter's head. "Only six years old. We can take care of her. We've got three big sons and one big sister to help. They can lend a hand before and after school. They are responsible children. We have brought them up right. They

pitch in. They have been doing that for the last three years, you've got to admit that."

"We have all tried, I do know that, for three years after she got well, if you can call it that. It is now nineteen thirty-five, six years, and she is never going to grow up. She will just grow older. I agree, retarded is a bad word. What would you use? You know what the doctor said. She won't even act like three anymore. An infant she is now and always will be." Mr. Christopoulos grimaced. "I loved her, too, but we must be realistic."

"And you think that the Hudson River State Mental Hospital will have a nursery for someone like Corry? Up there with those cottages for the mad men with syphilis?"

Mr. Christopoulos opened his mouth to answer and then shut it over clenched teeth.

"You said loved, not love. That is the problem. Past tense. You don't see the little loving girl that is still in there somewhere. Look at your younger daughter, look at her," her mother insisted, "She is still a beautiful child! And remember how sweet and darling she was until, until... You should have let me call for help sooner. Just the flu, you said. Meningitis it was!"

"I said loved because Corry is not really here any longer. Let it go, for god sakes," he said, "What's past is past."

"So you say, and yet you're still fighting the Peloponnesian Wars."

At that comment from her, he turned abruptly and left the room. She could hear the front door close. He did not slam it, but she knew he would have wanted to. She looked at her daughter and wiped the drool from her chin. She took the aimlessly waving small hand in her own and held it to her cheek. The child had the dark hair and regular features that could be found in the idealized illustrations on baby food jars; although, there was something just slightly out of focus about the little girl's expression.

"Baby, baby," she murmured, "I won't let him put you away. You can't understand, but I will not hide you somewhere. You will always be loved here." She continued stroking the little hands, restraining them in her own. "Right here."

ONE

1935

And that was the way it went. Corinthia – Corry – grew older. Her body changed as it must, but her mind was stuck in a damaged state so that she remained a baby, even less able than she had been when the illness stripped away the enchanting child she was. Her face gradually lost the sweet toddler aspect and the odd lack of focus in her expressions became more pronounced. Her arms and legs grew longer, still out of control. Her body began to fill in as she passed puberty, but in peculiar appearance, totally unlike the ways her older sister, Helena, had matured. Of course, some of the oddity was in the purposeless movement that seemed perpetual when she was awake.

"Grotesque, you know, retard," her brothers said to one another outside the hearing of their mother. They would not use such words where their mother or father could hear, nor would they use such language when talking to their school friends on the street who saw them often giving Corry her outdoor time. Then, they were either stoic in the face of unkind jibes, ignoring the pointed chatter, or they would take turns rushing at the taunting children to beat them about their chests with curled fists to drive them away. Neither response ever seemed to alter these exchanges. Was it cruel, this derision, or was it what growing boys did to make the reality of such an awful condition bearable? Could they even bring themselves to think about the terrible unfairness that lurked in every vision of the future? Mockery distanced them from acknowledging that possibility.

Corry was the monster of that street, a street populated primarily by Greek families, first and second-generation parents with many children. The adults were all sympathetic about the tragedy that had struck the Christopoulos family, but inwardly glad that it was not they who were so burdened. Some agreed with Mr. Christopoulos, and argued that the rational course was to institutionalize the child. It would be free of charge at the local state mental hospital. Others, mostly the wives, agreed with Mrs. Christopoulos about keeping one of their own in the family.

"Greeks support one another," said Mrs. Karras to Mrs. Dioderus. "Take care of your own, I say, particularly in this new place, but back home in Athens we learn this with our mother's milk." Two women of a certain age, gossiping over coffee in the Karras kitchen.

At other times, when Corry was out of view within the Christopoulos house, Jason, Nick, and Gussie Karras turned into their best friends. When Democritus and Timocrates were free after school and avoiding the care of their sister, they would go to the park where there was a baseball diamond and play with the Karras boys. Cleon, Jr., never came. As the oldest child, he was something of a loner, and apparently felt more responsible and able to help his mother more, as did their unaffected sister, Helena.

At the park, the six younger boys, together in the sixth, seventh and eighth grades at school, pretended they were big leaguers and threw high fly balls to one another in order to practice being outfielders. They continued at play for long hours, hitting grounders to one another through the infield and pretended they were first, second, third basemen or shortstops. For those moments, without the shadow of the disabled sister falling over their lives, the Christopoulos boys could live the lighthearted existence of boyhood.

They all hoped to play varsity baseball when they got to high school, where they would be starting in Nineteen Thirty-Six or Nineteen Thirty-Eight. This very serious game of practicing was to prepare them for this, if it could be worked in with the demands of the Christopoulos family business at the Acropolis Diner, and combined with the care of Corry. Small town high school sports were a big deal, and the Christopoulos boys were too small in stature to play football or basketball, so it was clear that baseball would be their genre. The other possibility was track, but that was also a Spring sport and would conflict with the more popular game of baseball.

The same could be said of the Karras boys. There were no Greeks in the big leagues, at least as far they knew. Maybe one of them would be that first player, although none of the boys ever said that aloud. But sometimes they thought about it, as they moved under a high fly ball or scooped up a hot grounder and then hurried home to Conklin Street to take care of the assigned household chores, except they did not always hurry.

***

All three of the Christopoulos boys were younger replicas of their father, with dark wiry hair that could never seem to be made to lie flat, even though they all doused it thoroughly with water when combing it every morning. One thing made Democritus different. His face bore the scars of acne beginning with puberty. Cleon and Timocrates had the smooth skin of their mother. In the family, it was accepted that poor Demi, the second son, was the unhappy one and his periods of gloom seemed to coincide with particularly harsh outbreaks of acne.

No one could say which was cause and which was effect. But then the gloom would vanish as quickly as it descended, and he would be as bright and funny as his siblings.

For the Christopoulos boys, chores also included various tasks relating to their disabled sister. When the two younger boys exploded through the front door, their mother would be there tending to Corry.

"Where have you two been?" she would say, "Playing, I suppose, while your older brother, Cleo and your sister, Helena, have been helping me in the house. You should be more responsible. Think about poor Corry and your tired mother."

If their father happened to be in the house, instead of at the Acropolis, he would say something about growing boys needing their exercise, even their fun.

"They pitch in," he might say, "They need a break once in a while, just to be children." He was not very often in the house when the boys came home, but if he was, he was likely to support them in this way.

And their mother, grumbling, might say, "Life is hard. Ask Cleon Junior. He has learned. They should learn it early," Then she would go to the kitchen, and their father would wink at the boys.

"Any double plays at the park?" he would say.

TWO

1936

"I guess playing for the Yankees would be the greatest," Demi said as they walked along the river after playing pick-up ball at the Park.

"Yeah," agreed Timi, "I think next best would be the Giants. Even the Brooklyn Dodgers if they just got a better team and a likable manager. I would want to stay in the East, close to the family in Poughkeepsie. I know teams go on the road, of course, but they do get to come home."

"Dream on," Demi said, as the two boys put down their gloves and then sat down on the hard surface of Kaal Rock. Wayward gulls from the New York City harbor sailed overhead, at times dipping close to the muddy surface of the river.

"Must be raining up in the mountains to make the Hudson look that way," said Timi. "Usually the water is clear here. We get tides up this far and sometimes it looks like the river is flowing north instead of to the ocean. See, that drift wood is going upstream."

"It looks unnatural to some, I guess, but if you live along the Hudson, you know what it is and what it does. I heard one of my teachers say it is more beautiful than the Rhine in Germany," Demi said. "I would love to travel and see that river. Comes down from the Swiss Alps, Miss Alpers said in geography class, clean and cold. Of course, this is really a Dutch river like this Kaal Rock where we sit."

"I'm not so sure I want to visit these days. Remember that newsreel, that *March of Time*, we saw just before that last Saturday movie matinee at the Stratford, with that raving German guy and all those Germans shouting - -what was it, 'Heil Hitler'? Looked really crazy to me." Timi shook his head in bewilderment.

"Oh, I don't know whether that will last. The German kid in my class, you should see him, he wore these funny suspenders when he first showed up, said most Germans were too sensible to fall for that baloney, he hoped. His parents brought him to Poughkeepsie early in the school year. Speaks real good English. Father was some kind of engineer over there and left to join Federal Bearings here. Swedish company, you know," Demi spoke confidently since he had this direct bit of information from a genuine German, "David Greenbaum. Nice kid but terrible when it comes to baseball. Always the last one picked at recess, I am afraid. He always looks so hurt."

"Well, sure I would like to travel to Europe later, if we could afford it. If Europe can get its act together. Pop says they have really not resolved the matters of the Great War, and that is what this is partly about. Screwed up the Armistice, he says. Read it in a book at the Adriance Library. But I would like to visit Greece, first, if that world does not fall apart, see the old home town Mom and Pop talk about, and maybe Italy, too. Greece, the cradle of reason, as Pop says, should survive."

"Well, you're going to be the designated college kid of the family," Demi pointed out, "Get the good job as lawyer or doctor, make a bundle, and take me with you on the tour."

"Wouldn't dream of going without you," Timi said.

"Good, just keep feeling guilty enough being the special one so you don't forget that pledge." Demi punched his younger brother affectionately in the forearm.

"And time to stop day dreaming and get on home," said Timi, "Before Mom has a fit."

"The dear monster calls," added Demi.

THREE

1938

The children grew older and moved on to high school. The two younger boys did, in fact, make the baseball team. Demi was the regular shortstop and Tim was the second baseman. They became famous in the sports pages of the local newspaper as *the Christopoulos boys, the double play machine.* Since there was only about eleven month's difference in their ages, they got to play together for three years in high school varsity. They were not great hitters, but both were adept at laying down the critical bunt when needed, and they could not be beaten as wizards of fielding. They were famous for stealing bases, including the occasional aggressive slide into home.

Often, when the team had home games, Mr. Christopoulos would play hooky from the Acropolis Diner. Someone else would handle all the food prep, and he would sit in the bleachers with their school mates and the other parents.

"My sons," he would explain unnecessarily to those around him, when the two executed one of their flashy double plays. "My two youngest sons," he would crow.

Helena and Cleo, Jr., however, would be at Conklin Street, helping out with Corry. Helena had taken the secretarial courses at school, and Cleo, Jr. had taken machine shop and drafting, very practical choices. They did not have time for extracurricular activities like sports. They both had seemed to grow up early, advanced beyond their years.

Demi was also taking shop courses since he understood that life after high school would mean he had to be gainfully employed, but he just had to make time for baseball and to be with Tim on the baseball diamond. Tim, on the other hand, was taking the college preparatory program to earn a State Regent's diploma. Their mother, with the support of their father, had decided that the youngest boy would be the first one in the family to go to college.

Tim's siblings understood the necessity of the selection and their part in making it work. A Christopoulos with a college degree – everyone would be proud. The other Greek families on the street would be impressed. It would be the American success story and all the others of the family could take pride in this singular accomplishment that was only possible with group support.

The parents talked of this plan at night, often in bed before they fell asleep. "Maybe a lawyer, or a doctor," Mrs. Christopoulos mused.

"Or a great writer," Mr. Christopoulos would add, for he was the one who read classic Greek drama in the original during the slow times between meal service, a habit that kept the employees of the Acropolis Diner a bit in awe.

"More money and reputation in law or medicine," would be his wife's rejoinder. In her mind was also the design to provide lifetime care of Corry. "He can write in his spare time."

"The Greeks invented money," said her husband.

And they would fall asleep on these happy, if slightly conflicting, plans.

FOUR

1941

Nineteen Forty-One came, and in December of that year the careful plans were interrupted. Of course, Demi and Timi were still too young to face military service and the Christopoulos family, patriots to the core, felt that perhaps by the time the boys graduated from high school in Nineteen Forty and Forty-Two, the war would have been won. They had much faith in their adopted country.

"They will go, of course, if the war lasts," said Mr. Christopoulos, "They will defend our nation. The Greeks have always been great warriors." He hung a flag from the front porch of their house on Conklin Street.

"I thought we were Athenians, not Spartans," put in his wife, but he ignored the comment.

The superior might of the United States did not quickly win the war, in spite of the Greek-American optimism of Mr. Christopoulos. The three boys grew older and their high school adapted to war time. Physical education was now conducted on make-shift obstacle courses, as if the students were taking infantry boot camp, overseen by paunchy physical education teachers, athletes gone to fat, who tyrannized the boys with shouts about getting fit to fight the Krauts and the Japs. Nothing subtle about these men. The three Christopoulos boys, like the Karras boys, small Greeks that they might be, were well-coordinated athletes, and took to that kind of exercise; even Cleo, Jr. , who did not play baseball like his brothers, excelled.

Of course, Tim and Demi continued to star with the high school lineup each spring during this period, with their double-play teamwork and crucial bunts at opportune times. Graduation and the turning point they would reach at eighteen years of age, however, loomed ahead. Some of their team-mates, older than they, enlisted directly after graduation. The star pitcher went off to the Navy and soon it was reported that he was taking flight training.

They talked with their parents about the draft, their ages, and the family needs. In these conferences, the boys talked of volunteering after graduation rather than waiting for a number to come up. Their parents considered what the family, with the care of poor Corry, would require, and everyone decided that Cleo, Jr., as the oldest, would apply for a deferment because of that home need as well as his machine shop work. The two younger sons would go, as they and Mr. Christopoulos desired.

"Fighting Greeks!" avowed the men on the street to each other, although most of the wives and mothers kept silent. War was a man's concern, as was the need to be trustworthy in wartime. That would be the answer to the popular canard about Greeks not being honorable. They all hated the joke, often heard beyond Conklin Street, to be wary of Greeks bearing gifts. But secretly, as all parents do, they hoped the need for their sons to go off to war would be over by the time of graduation. Wouldn't American military might certainly win the day against the Nazi regime?

Of course, it would. They believed in it fervently.

Surprisingly, the conflict did not end before the boys finished high school, and the consequences for the family had to be confronted. Cleon, Jr. got a deferment both as a necessary support for the family with a severely handicapped daughter, and as a worker in a vital war industry. His employer made carbines for the Army Air Corps. Cleo's shop training and his ability as a tool and die maker provided just the added evidence for the deferment.

As each finished high school in turn, Demi and Tim each decided to enlist rather than to wait in limbo for their numbers to be called. In order to get his enlistment date closer to his brother's, Timi doubled up some required courses for his Regent's diploma and graduated at mid-year, just a semester after his older brother. But because there was a six-month difference in their enlistment dates, they wound up in different infantry units.

"Infantry," said their mother, when Tim was home on his first delay-on-route after basic training in Mississippi, "I understood about Demi, what with his shop training and all. But couldn't they find an office job or something more befitting your pre-college program. Maybe even supplies? Officer training?"

"Ma," Tim said, "the army is not very creative. If you're first- or second-generation Greek, Italian, or Polish without a college degree, and they need able bodies to fight on the battlefield, into the infantry you go. It's not the Air Corps for you. Dog faces all. You should read Bill Mauldin if you want the facts. I'll send you some of his cartoons when I get back to camp. It's a dirty, grim world out there but someone has to deal with it and that turns out to be me and Demi, among others."

"So cynical for someone so young," said his mother. Her eyes were tearing up a bit. Such a smart, fine young man, her son was.

"The infantry makes you grow up quickly – it is not a high school baseball game, but don't worry, Ma. We're coming home as the great Greek heroes. We will take on the Trojans one more time," he assured her with a broad, confident smile.

"Beware of Greeks bearing gifts, Ma, but right out of the horse's belly to victory. Pa, Cleo Junior, and Helena will take care of you and Corry, and we will all celebrate when Demi and I come home for the ticker tape parade. It'll be the terrific double play again for the Christopoulos boys."

FIVE

1945

The Ardennes Offensive began December 16th, 1945. It was a major German attack in the craggy regions of the Ardennes Mountains in Belgium, and later became known as The Battle of the Bulge. There were 84,323 American causalities – 19,276 killed, 41,493 wounded, and 23,554 captured or missing.

Those figures are in the history books. One of those killed was Timocrates Christopoulos, blown away in the 75th Division, and buried in Europe.

Democritus Christopoulos survived with only a wound in his thigh but he had one of his squad members die in his arms with his guts hanging out on his combat boots. A Purple Heart and a Bronze Star for him. The British had 1600 casualties, 200 killed and 1,400 wounded or missing. With the Allied losses totaled, the Germans had an equal number of casualties, 84,834 with 15,652 killed, 41,600 wounded and 27,582 captured or missing. Those figures are also in the history books.

It was the grisliest battle for the forces of the United States. The family learned later that Tim and Demi had been less than ten miles apart in those bloody mountains, as the Germans launched their plan, *Unternehmen*: *Wacht am Rhein*, German codeword for the operation known to the Allies as the Battle of the Bulge, to split the allied forces and destroy four armies. It failed after the most furious fighting, from which the Germans never recovered. Bradley, Patton, Hodges, and Eisenhower together prevailed.

Demi eventually came home with his Purple Heart and his Bronze Star. The Christopoulos family tried to recover. Demi hung around the house at first, sometimes spoon-feeding his damaged younger sister, sometimes reading the sports pages about big league baseball, sometimes helping out at the diner, sometimes sitting in his father's Lazy Boy lounger and staring into the middle distance silently. FDR was dead, and Harry Truman had taken over the responsibilities of Commander-in-Chief, promising to bring no changes but successful outcomes to a war-weary America.

The Russians destroyed Hitler's troops in the snow, beating them back to Berlin. V-E day had come. Yet, the Christopoulos family could not really celebrate, since it only reminded them that Tim was not coming home, ever.

Then somewhere in that other war zone, first the Enola Gay with The Great Artiste following behind to observe, then Bockscar, took off from North Field runway Able, on the island of Tinian in the Western Pacific, and the war was over.

The Karras boys had come home, one by one, as their discharge numbers came up; Jason, Nick, and Gussie, wearing various non-com stripes and the gold bars on the sleeve signifying overseas service.

They all felt that the good guys had won.

SIX

1946

The other Conklin Street men eventually celebrated with Demi at Nick Rossi's Italian Restaurant on Main Street, with a toast in Chianti to Timocrates Christopoulos, who gave his Greek life for his country, as Gussie said. Gussie also said it was perverse of them to be eating Italian, even though it was great food, nearly as good as the authentic stuff he had eaten in Italy.

Cleon, Jr. was not there. He was helping their father at the Acropolis Diner. Besides, as a civilian, even one who was contributing to the war effort at his factory job, and had therefore sat out the war at home, he did not really feel he was part of the gang.

"A change from all that Greek food," said Demi, and the Karras boys agreed. Gussie, who had fought in Italy, noted that he had become enamored of Northern Italian cuisine, although he did not use that word, just as he had become enamored of nubile Italian women while there. He even talked of finding a way to go back, as a civilian.

"Go to college on the G.I. Bill," said Gussie, "And get a job that takes me back to sunny Italy, a dark-eyed Italian signora, and the high life of Rome. I checked into the possibility and found that New York State is creating some new colleges to take the overflow of us returning vets. There will be one in the North Country near Lake Champlain. Going to look into it. Practically free tuition, with the G.I. Bill, living stipend to boot, and in the meantime, I plan to join the 52-20 club until next fall."

Gussie, the youngest of them all, was the operator on the street. He looked for the angles and the odds and played them well. He usually succeeded.

"So, what's the 52-20 club, smart ass?" asked Demi.

"Part of the vets' benefits. Just go down town to the New York State Employment Office and register. Take your discharge papers to show you belong. Sign up as looking for a postwar job, check in every week, say you haven't found the right thing yet, and get your twenty dollars per for the next whole year, or until you get that job or leave for college. Perfect scheme, if you ask me." Gussie smiled around at his fellow veterans, polished his finger nails against his shirtfront and blew on them. "All legal and above board for our boys returning home. They told you at the discharge center, if you just listened instead of rushing to get home."

"And suppose they actually find you a job, one you could do or are trained for?" Jason, his brother asked.

"You think we grunts from the infantry were trained for civilian jobs? How about, as a sharpshooter, and I have the badge to prove it, you are offered an entry position as an assassin or hit man? That likely, huh? Maybe the Mob has an internship in killing, you think? Come on. Besides, they tell me that the job interviewers, dumb old ladies or 4Fs from the war, bend over backwards to be nice to the fighting men back from the front. Don't knock it. Use it." Gussie sounded so sure of his position, that his brothers and Demi could only nod in acceptance.

"Don't talk so loud. I heard that Nick Rossi has to pay-off the mob to stay open, and to buy only their booze," Jason said in a stage whisper behind his hand, "Don't antagonize a member of the Family, in case one is listening."

Gussie's plan did sound logical to Demi. And if the Army had taught him one thing, it was to game the system, if you could, without harming your buddies. One for all and all for one, but particularly one for one in this dog-eat-dog world. Demi had added a postscript to the code of the Three Musketeers. He'd read the book for tenth grade English class. In fact, he had enjoyed the story, much as he thought he would not, since it did not seem written for shop kids. Then again, maybe it was.

Here was a romantic at heart, an outsider might have surmised upon hearing about his juvenile interest in literary French derring-do. But like father, like son, it would appear. For Demi, a love of literature, however unrelated to the demands of the practical world and not part of his expected role in life, seemed to be part of the family DNA.

***

He ducked below the edge of the foxhole. The rain was just a mist that cooled his face. His back ached from holding still. He did not want to disturb the other dozing soldier. Hearing the regular breathing told him the other man was probably asleep. Two in a hole, sort of like two eggs in a pan of water for coddling. One could rest or dream, he thought, while the other stayed alert, if he could.

Did make it cramped, even intimate, he thought. When his companion awakened he knew he would see fear return to the second man's face. The look of repose was only temporary during a stolen nap. The pure fright would be visible for the first moments of awareness, and then it would be hidden behind the bravado expected of a hardened fighter.

"Sheeit, it's calm for a bit," the smaller man said, "Guess I fell asleep." Looking up at the darkening cloud cover, he began to search his clothing for cigarettes. "Gotta get a smoke before real dark comes," he said, "Jerries could see a spark of light and know where to shoot. Zap!"

"Inhale it fast, if you need that nicotine," his companion said, "Lulls like this never last, believe me."

SEVEN

1946

Much as it might have seemed to be a kind of freeloading, which Demi normally abhorred (because you always paid your way with labor in the Christopoulos family code), he confronted the 'dumb old ladies' and 4-F civil servants at the State Employment Service, discharge in hand. It all went as Gussie had described.

Forms were filled out. His discharge information was noted, as well as his CIB badge and status as "Combat Infantryman," although that did not seem to be a relevant civilian job category, as Gussie had jokingly noted.

"Perhaps you could try training as a typewriter repair mechanic. That is a trade that will become important in the post-war world. I see you were a shop student in high school before the Army, so you probably are good with your hands and with small tools and machinery." One of the 'dumb old civil servant ladies' looked up from his papers.

Demi thought she looked really concerned, and rather motherly, as she watched him. Maybe not so dumb, he thought, as just provincial. How could she see the world through the dim vision in those small-town eyes, and not, in fact, conclude that boys who found their way through the shop wing of the local high school simply could not be material for higher education, or the professions?

Most especially if the boys were Greek, or Italian, or Poles.

"Thanks," he answered, "I need to think about it for a while longer. I just got discharged, and I need to think about it. That okay?"

"All right for now," the maternal woman nodded, her wattles jiggling, "Just don't wait too long. This aid program expects you veterans to adjust to civilian life sooner rather than later and the money is to keep you going for a while until you decide. Get re-established in civilian life. Check in next week. There are other training or apprentice programs you can consider. International Business Machines, which is expanding locally, has something starting soon. It is a growing company with great opportunities and wonderful benefits. They pay really well, higher than the other local concerns, even while you are learning. Can't beat that arrangement. Very paternal, is I. B. M." The woman emphasized the separation of the letters distinctly, as if showing respect.

"Yes, I have heard good employees stay for life, nearly," Demi said as he picked up his papers.

"Give it serious thought," the woman said again as he turned to go, "My son works there on the South Road where they made those rifles, or carbines, as he calls them, for the military during the war, and now he is being retrained. They do take care of their own. They have a great apprentice program. Very practical."

"Thank you, thank you. I will keep it in mind." *Got to escape*, he said to himself, and he glided away, even as she seemed primed to continue talking.

***

"So, what are you going to do, just sit on the porch steps and brood?" Rebia Karras, standing on the sidewalk in front of him, grinned saucily.

She watched him carefully, brown eyes under her lashes steady on his face. Taking a step up, she stopped and leaned back against the railing of the porch in a way that pulled her thin blouse tight across her breasts.

"Aren't you going to get on with life? The war is over, you know." Rebia was thin, but not too thin, and she was very pretty. Her dark hair, always neat and clean, shone in the sunlight like polished wood. When she laughed, it seemed childishly gleeful, as if she had gotten the joke and it was not on her.

The same age as Corinthia, she was in her last year at the high school, another secretarial student like Demi's sister, Helena, before her. Probably going to work after graduation, Demi thought, taking shorthand from some local lawyer until she gets married to an auto mechanic or someone with something similar, and starts having babies. She would likely want to live on Conklin Street, near her parent's house. Or move with the mechanic husband to the new suburbs. Then the thin body would thicken, like his mother's, and the laugh might not be as youthfully spontaneous, because by then the joke might be on her.

Life's prank on the young of the working class.

"Just thinking about the future," Demi said.

"So what is it in your future exactly," said Rebia, stretching her arms over her head in a gesture that pulled the blouse even tighter. She seemed to be imitating the Greek movie star, Katina Paxinou, in some film made from a Hemingway story.

Oh, what the hell. "Want to go to the movies tonight?" he said. "How's that for the near future? Some action here. Good movie at the Rialto, I hear, and I have that 52-20 cash to splurge." What the hell. Nothing better to do. And Rebia is kind of cute, if not very smart, and awfully young.

He knew instantly that the ancient warrior pose he was projecting was partly phony. He was not that much older than Rebia, but he had been in England, Belgium, and France. Hunkered down in troopships. Downed warm ale in an English pub, and Vin de Pays in France. He felt a generation older than this young woman, while at the same time feeling that old urging in the groin. *What the hell! Go for it, whatever.* Women matured sooner than men, he had heard. Check it out, buster, he thought.

"Meet you right after supper and we can go to the early show. Maybe go somewhere after."

On the other hand, it was a first date and Rebia was saving herself, as she said, for marriage, at least for the moment. After the film, he had a beer and she had a Shirley Temple at a tavern on Cannon Street. Demi sipped his Dutch lager and Rebia held a mouthful of her ginger ale and orange juice stained with grenadine. She swallowed and then snagged the cherry, sucking it into her mouth while watching Demi through shuttered lashes.

"This has been fun, better than high school," she said later at her door on Conklin Street, "We can do it again, now that you're home and in society again?" It was a first date, so there were just polite good nights between them, and nothing more.

He would never have considered her as potential rendezvous material before he went away to fight a war, but she seemed to have grown up in the meantime, so he thought there would probably be more dates. She seemed eager, he thought, and right across the street. Nothing permanent was planned for the moment. He had to get his life back in order and under control. There was still help needed at home with Corry, and he was disturbed at how old his mother and father looked to him, now that he was home, particularly his father. The gap in time filled by the war had made them both seem so aged when he returned, as if time had sped up for them while slowing down for him. They had wrinkles now, and often looked tired and harried. He did not remember things that way before he left. Maybe he was just too self-absorbed as a kid. That was it, he realized, how life was school, baseball, and joking around with brother Timi.

The relationship between his parents also looked more strained than he remembered. Things had never been good, not after the contentious decision supported by his mother to keep Corry home and not put her in an institution; but now it seemed worse. When his father was not at the Acropolis, he was usually not home. He walked about the downtown area, looking in store windows or chatting with old friends on the street. He appeared to know hundreds of local people after all these years of running the diner, or so it appeared to his younger son.

His brother and sister agreed, when he could get them to talk about their parents. Mostly his siblings kept to themselves, their jobs, and with help around the house. In fact, Demi often felt like the odd man out, not exactly a full-fledged family member, just an observer who ate meals with them. If Tim were alive, he supposed they might have talked together about the war, if they felt up to it, as well as the family tension, because they had been the double-play team and felt particularly close. Christopoulos to Christopoulos and out at first, whoever was covering there, it had been. No longer.

"Jeez, Tim," Demi said out loud, "Why didn't you duck?" No answer to that, and Demi looked around to see if anyone had heard. He was alone, thank goodness. They would think him goofy for talking like that to himself or to the absent Tim.

But to whom could he talk? Not to Cleo, Jr. He was too involved in his tool maker's job, his buddies downtown, his golf on weekends, and the war was not his business. He had sat it out, stateside. He did not talk much anyway, even on the golf course, according to the men who played with him at the public course on College Hill, next to Morgan Lake. Not Helena, either. She was just as involved with her secretarial work, taking shorthand from her senior partner lawyer employer, mooning about the younger W.A.S.P. associate who did not know a Greek secretary existed, and coming home to diaper Corry, or feed her with a spoon.

His parents? They were still grieving over Tim. He was really odd man out. He felt more kinship with Gussie, in fact, than with his family. They had shared a war.

He could talk to Rebia, he supposed. She listened with an intensity he did not know was genuine concern about him or just what young women did when wanting to feign interest in a potential mate or merely a possible sexual partner. Perhaps it was just curiosity about an "older man," except he was not that much older. He wondered why war and combat did not prepare him to understand women, but he knew the answer.

It did not prepare you for anything but murdering someone.

They never used that term, but that was how he now saw it. Once you kill someone, things are never the same, even for a "good war." As to preparing one for women, the military confined its wisdom to posters in the PX saying things like, *She may look clean but….*

Thinking about what he'd learned in the Army, scenes from training films floated before his eyes, about disabling a less than human enemy with your combat boots. Rake down their shins and break the bones in the foot. Slam them in the Adams apple with a rifle butt. Jab the bayonet into the gut and twist and tear sideways. Shoot them in the face before they do you in. Get the upper hand and keep it. Are we going to fight face to face? Be prepared, boy scout.

Talking to Rebia did actually help, though, he discovered with some surprise. He did not go into the gory details of the past. It was the present and future that mattered; although, later he learned that the past is never past. Literary types clued him in, when he came to them. Talking to a relative stranger seemed to be easier for him than talking to family, even though he had grown up on this street; he remembered watching Rebia go from little girl, hanging around her brothers through elementary school when he was aware of her at all –and then re-discovering her on the edge of womanhood.

This young woman was now the stranger who listened to him.

I could have invented her, he thought. Maybe that is what we all do, invent the people we need and find a person to embody the invention. Sort of a benign Frankenstein's monster, animated by our desires or needs. Better not tell her that, however, since it did not sound complementary, exactly.

I am becoming introspective, he added silently. Is that actually a Greek thing, I wonder?

***

He massaged the small of his back. It didn't help. "So, settling in as a veteran of three weeks?" he said, trying a hearty if fake smile. Can't really put him at ease, he realized. "So, what bothers you now?" Get a hold of yourself, he thought.

The other soldier did not respond with a grin. His eyes traveled over his companion's face but not meeting the other's eyes. "Aren't you scared? I mean, aren't you…?" He looked down at his hands.

"Who knows what that is?" the other said. "Fear? What the hell." He straightened, and looked over the edge of the foxhole. "Too shit eatin' quiet," he said, and ducked down again as there was one mortar burst several meters to their left. He made himself breathe normally. That was hard.

"So, it was calm for a bit. The usual quiet before the storm, as the saying goes."

"Christ, oh, Christ!" The second soldier's voice wobbled as his shoulders trembled. "Christ," he said again, "Don't this scare you at all? How the fuck do you…? I don't think I am a coward, but… oh, fuck it."

"So, stuff it." The first soldier gripped the other's shoulder. He raised his head again over the edge of the hole and peered into the shadows.

EIGHT

1946

Gussie Karras stopped him one morning in June. His round and smiling face reflected his satisfaction. "Well, I did it," he said, "I filled out the application and got the high school guidance office to send my grades. Going to Champlain College upstate. Just opening up. Cheap state resident tuition and the G.I. Bill will cover it all. Come on, join me, buddy. It will be a ball. Bunch of vets and some young kids just out of high school. Eager small-town pussy everywhere, you know, and you can lay off my sister. She thinks you're serious, you know. Why don't you look into it?"

Demi shrugged. "Aw, my grades were okay but outside the basic courses, I was mostly shop. Did okay there, too, but what college is going to care that I passed Print Shop or Drafting with A's. So, I got B plus in required English and A minus in U.S. History. What kind of college admission office would value that? No languages, except Greek, which came with the territory. I think those liberal arts colleges expect you have had Latin in prep school. Think about all those college prep types. I know about them. You know, the dentist's and lawyer's kids wearing their tweed jackets. Girls in sweater sets. Living in the Eighth ward on the south side of town, going to Krieger School or Quaker Oakwood. Tim's classes were not mine, but I knew what they were. I even looked through some of his textbooks once. Didn't know what the hell the Chemistry was all about, those flippin' tables to memorize. And the Trig he had to take. I sort of got some of it, but then it got beyond me." Demi shrugged again.

"Oh, shit, Demi. You're the closest thing to a war hero on the street. At least, still alive. How can they not bend the rules for the medals? Give it a shot."

"Hero shmero. I'll think about it." Demi wanted to shut down the conversation. It only made him think about his dead brother and the war. He could even hear the sounds again. Explosions. Whistling fire. Shouts and some screams. Waiting and silence, too. Enough already.

But he did think about it. It would be a balancing act. Go to college, absurd as the idea would seem for a shop kid, or stick around, go to work for Standard Gage or IBM like Cleo, and help the family with Corry and the Acropolis Diner – still open twenty-fours a day, seven days a week. The neon sign out front promised it, and the same went for Corry as well – needs help twenty-four hours a day, seven days a week. It was grinding down his mother, alienating his parents. All the time he was fighting for flag, country and Chevrolet, Helena and Cleon, Jr. were more than holding down the home front. They were postponing their lives.

Maybe forever, he thought.

"Go to college and stay here," Rebia told him when he brought it up with her. They had been to the movies on Market Street and were splurging in the Regatta Room at the old Nelson House Hotel across the street from the theater. Another one of those 52-20 checks coming in handy. He wondered if the President and the Congress had in mind supporting an expensive date with that money. So, he was using it to adjust to civilian life, just what it was for.

He looked up at the graceful sweep oars crossed over the bar. No doubt cast-offs from some Ivy League school, where rowing was the big social deal and connections were made that lasted a life time. Boat houses on the Hudson River bank just south of Hyde Park for Columbia, Syracuse, Yale, where the elite made their connections.

The stretch of the Hudson River at Poughkeepsie was where the International Rowing Regatta was held every year. It was at this Hotel where FDR celebrated his election and re-election, in a place and county that never went for him in any election. What an irony. The Christopoulos family voted for him, nevertheless, although Mr. Christopoulos never talked about his politics at the diner.

"Not good for business," he told his family and his employees, "Not in this town."

"I read in the local paper that Vassar College was going to accept veterans temporarily because of the crush on acceptances with all the returning service men getting out in '45 and '46. Some deal with the State University of New York," Rebia went on with her report for Demi, "You get to live at home, there will be no dormitory time for you men, Demi; you can take classes and be on deck for your family. And me, of course." She giggled.

Demi did think about it, and made a decision. What did he have to lose, except making an ass of himself and bringing dishonor on the Christopoulos name with his failure?

Go for it. Over the top, he thought, or some crap like that. And there would be Rebia for relaxation and amusement. Was he being a cad, as one of the required English novels he read in high school would have put it?

Who cares? He thought bluntly, laughing at himself. Who cares?

NINE

1946

"I am going to college," he told his mother and father, and explained what he had learned about Vassar College, without mentioning the information came second hand from Rebia, and the decision that the administration and trustees had made. It was good public relations for the college, he explained to them. The gesture would bridge the town-gown divide that was significant for this parochial little city and the exclusive institution, and it was also an act of good will for the local returning war veterans.

Everybody wins. Patriotism triumphant. Good politics.

"Fine," his mother, "You can do it for Timi."

"I am going to do it for myself," Demi said, "For myself. Tim isn't here any longer and is nowhere that he can care what I do much as we all wish he could. This is my time, Mama, a chance in a million I never would have thought of and I am not going to let it go by. Maybe I'll fail. Maybe I won't. I will give it one hell of a good shot."

"Don't blaspheme, Demi," his mother said, "Your brother is in Heaven and watching over us."

"Tim lies a-moldering in his French grave, as the poet says, and can't give a... damn." Demi nearly slipped into an infantry profanity but stopped himself in time.

"Oh, son, how can you say that? What will God think?" His mother touched his shoulder. "Salvation is through his name, as the Bible says. Despotes knows and cares, as you learned at Greek school."

"Kurios or Despotes, take your choice of name. Despot is more likely. Tyrant. Oppressor. And what God is that, exactly? The one that visited his wrath on a three-year-old child and turned her into a monster? Did he

38

mistake her for Job? The god that watched over the deaths of thousands of men in the late lamented war? If there is one, he doesn't give a flying fuck about humanity." This time the profanity came out. "I would rather believe it is all some myth, just like the Greek gods, and you know something – I would rather believe in Zeus, or Apollo, or Hermes, or maybe Athena for her wisdom. We seem to have been worshiping Aries these past few years, anyway. Why not go whole hog and take on the bundle of them. They are ours, after all. Jehovah seems like some mean bastard who would kill his son to make a point."

"Blasphemy, Demi! War has changed you." His mother looked stricken. "What did you learn in the Greek Orthodox Church?"

"You go to college, Democritus, and do yourself proud." His father stepped in and stopped the exchange between his wife and his son. "You have been reading poetry, Demi? Good for you. And you know your Greek gods, I have to say. So, go to college and learn more. Things that will make your life better, both the practical stuff and the impractical. Both are important. There are two kinds of people, Demi, the strong and the smart, the Romans and the Greeks. Use your smarts." His father nodded expectantly, ignoring, or perhaps condoning, the strong language of his son.

"Yes, you go to college," his mother said, "It is your chance and maybe it is God's will that things have made it possible." She could not give up her beliefs, the beliefs that had gotten her through the two tragedies of Corry's illness and the death of (dare it even be thought) her favorite son. She turned away to hide brimming eyes.

***

"I did it," Demi told Rebia a few days later.

"Good for you," she said, nestling against his shoulder on her parents' sofa. "Now, just don't you get too educated that you forget me. Remember I told you to do it. I expect gratitude, you know."

"And how will I show it?"

"Just kiss me before my parents come in from the kitchen."

"What are you two young people up to in here?" Mrs. Karras said as she came through the door from the dining room, followed by her husband, "How about we play four-handed canasta?"

"Going to college, eh? Just like Gussie, he tells me," Mr. Karras said, as he dealt the cards, "Good for you both. Better yourselves, I say. Don't wind up flipping burgers in a diner, growing old tending a machine, or something worse. Wish I had had the opportunity. The Land of Opportunity, they called it when Theodosia and I arrived at Ellis Island. Work hard and be rewarded in this life."

"Life has been good enough to us," Mrs. Karras said, "Good kids, food on the table, roof over our heads. What more would you want, I say."

"Well, maybe more," said Demi, "Leave some mark besides kids, not that this isn't important." He added hurriedly, "but do something that makes life better for people. Make a contribution that's lasting. Change society."

"Listen to him," said Mrs. Karras, "An idealist. You got to admire that in a young man who has seen such terrible things."

"I want people to know that Sophocles, for example, more than two thousand years ago, laid out why war is inhumane, or why General Sherman said that war is hell, and no one learns." Demi felt himself getting worked up and that embarrassed him. It sounded juvenile to his ears and he did not want to talk like some wet-behind-the-ears adolescent, like some jerk know-it-all, to these good people. After all, he had been around in the larger outside world of war. He should be a serious adult with an adult perspective. Besides, this was not proper social card game chitchat, even with neighbors as close as the Karras family.

He realized he was just working out these feelings and beliefs. He knew that in the victorious atmosphere of the triumph of good over evil that had followed V-E day, the bomb, and then V-J day, pacifist notions of this sort were out of sync with the mood of most of the nation. He himself believed that a great good had been done. Photographs of emaciated corpses piled up like driftwood on a beach after a storm could not let you think otherwise, or of vacant eyed scrawny zombie-like people staring at camera lenses as they stumbled out of death camps. Balanced against all that for him was the unseen shattered body of one Greek kid in the Battle of the Bulge.

Tim, why didn't you duck?

He wondered what had happed to that German kid that came to his grade school so long ago, David Applebaum, who could not play baseball. What of him? Too much to think about. Too much. He took the discard pile and melded them all with his hand. He then put down one final discard and said, "I win." At canasta, if the cards fell right and you play what you have shrewdly, you could win. Maybe in life? Or was he just getting too sentimental? Life was not a card game. It was life. Sometimes life was played like a card game, though.

Sometimes, in spite of everything, you win.

TEN

1946

"Say, guess what?" Gussie said a few days later when they were shooting baskets at the park. "I went up and looked at this Champlain College. Weren't no real college, as they would say in the street. Decommissioned army base. Going to put us great warriors in old barracks. What a friggin downer. I found out the college president was a technical high school principal in an earlier life. Probably a coach before that. Bet the teachers are mostly retread high school teachers who couldn't keep discipline in the nine to twelves, as well. I don't need a recycled B.O.C.E.S. guy telling me what to study or how to live in a barracks. Been there, done that."

"Oh, it can't be that bad, but then what are you going to do?" Demi said, as he faked Gussie out of position and drove in for a lay-up.

"Go to a real college and get a real education, that's what. Do just what you did. Go to Vassar. If you can do it, so can I." Gussie one-handed a long looping shot over Demi's head and watched it swoosh through the basket. Demi was smaller and more agile on the court, but Gussie was taller and could always lift the ball over Demi's head and waving hands. "Maybe we could get Vassar to sponsor a basketball team and we could play other vets at some other college."

"That's great, and it will be good to have men there I know, but it won't be sports that I will be going to college for," said Demi, "I doubt that they have a baseball diamond, anyway, maybe soft ball for the girls, and hard ball is what I am, or was, good at." But no Tim to take the double play throw and relay it to first.

"I know, I know," said Gussie, "Me, too. I want to learn stuff and get away from this street, but you got to have some fun along the way, you know."

"You absolutely sure you can get in?" Demi held the ball a moment as he asked that important question.

"Done deal," answered Gussie, "Went to see some Dean or other, and the Admissions Director. Anyway, in the main building, discovered the secretary in the outer office was a girl we went to high school with. Cute girl, Irish name. O'Connell, I think. All grown up with a job, yet, while we were fighting a war. Probably took the secretarial courses. Maybe I will look her up when we become students."

"Already you are looking for diversions from getting an education," Demi laughed.

"And then how about you and my sister? She is really serious about you." Gussie made a mock frown. "Leading the poor little girl along, are you, you dastardly villain?" He laughed. "Tie her to the railroad tracks if you can't have your way with her?"

"Come on. She is too young to be serious, and my life is too indefinite and unsettled for now. Give me some time to get an education under my belt, will you – or under my hat, is more like it."

"You better make that clear to Rebia. I don't think she sees herself as too young. Not the way a senior girl in high school these days understands it, particularly one who does not see a college education for a woman planning on marriage, and certainly not on this Greek street. Marry young and make your fucking legal, if you will pardon my French, even about my sister, and I love her dearly, like a sister." Gussie laughed again.

"Oh, it will be all right. I am being careful. Learned that in the Army. Nothing actually very significant going on there anyway. A sort of delayed high school romance, you know, for me. I wasn't much for dating then. Too busy getting ready for war and pitching in with Corry." Demi shrugged. "Speaking of, got to go help with Corry. It's feeding time at the zoo and they will be expecting me home any minute now."

***

"Hey, guys." The sergeant's voice was muted and guarded.

"Holed in here," the first solder answered.

The sergeant, crouching, came to the edge of the foxhole. "Both of you men there?"

"And where else. Something up, Sarge?" Men, that's what they were here.

The sergeant knelt at the edge of the hole, breathing hard. "You guys ready? Everything ready?"

"Depends on what you have in mind," the corporal responded, "Our mutual friend here has been bellyaching about the tranquility. Hard to sleep without that battle lullaby, he says."

The sergeant grunted. "We just got a job." He paused a minute, but there was no answer from either man, so he continued. "Kill some people." He moved his weight to the other haunch. Some pebbles fell over the edge and rattled into the hole. "Battalion asked for a squad to knock out a tank. Lieutenant says this is the squad."

"Brown-nosing bastard. Those West Point types. Thinks he's in training to be the next Eisenhower or Bradley. If we aren't always the ones. Why us again? He burns me, that mother fucker. Every time there's dirty work, it's our squad. Where will he be?"

ELEVEN

1946

The Dean of Faculty stood at the front of the lecture room in Rockefeller Hall. Her short, doughy figure was at the side of the lectern, since if she had stood behind it, her head would have appeared as if severed and placed on the polished wooden stand. No dean would want to appear to be only a talking head, lopped off at the neck, particularly somehow with that iron gray hair in a stiff perm. It looked as if it had been poured, red hot, into one of the molds used to create a machine part and then allowed to cool to that permanent shape. Her tight mouth could have been shaped of rust-reddened steel.

"I am Dean Winifred Thomas," she began. "It was not my idea to have you here as students," she said with a hint of a southern accent. "Your presence conflicts with the whole spirit of this college for women as envisioned by Mr. Vassar. But it has been done and here you are, so you will follow the rules the College has in force, or you may be asked to leave. You will also need to keep passing grades in your courses, naturally. The College has had the regulations and requirements separately printed and you may pick them up on your way out, after the meeting."

The assembled men sat in silence and waited. There was a slight rustle of bodies moving in the rows of seats. There were about a hundred of them, Demi saw, as he waited for the next compliment from this starchy academic.

"You have all registered for your first semester courses with your academic advisor who will also be available to help you with any further questions or problems during the year. It would be wise to check his or her office hours."

She turned to go. "Oh, and the best of luck," she added from the door.

44

"And we will need it. That was one jolly welcome," said Demi to Gussie.

The men stood about in front of the classroom building, a few sitting on a mill grindstone that, for some reason, was enshrined by the steps leading up to the doors. Something to do with Vassar history? Part of the beer making process, mashing the beer barley? Would they ever know why?

The group did appear motley. Some men wore left-over pieces of military uniforms – wrinkled olive drab or khaki pants, a few field jackets, one Eisenhower jacket with the insignia taken off, khaki shirts, olive drab wool shirts with insignia of past military assignments on the shoulders, blue jeans worn with chambray blue work shirts in a kind of naval look. A couple of the men did wear blazers and pressed trousers over combat boots. They must have been reading about postwar styles in Esquire Magazine. The Bold Look.

"A bitch of a meeting, if you ask me," Gussie said, "Really made you feel welcome. She might as well have said that she sure as shit didn't really want us low class types here, we would probably fail, but since we are allowed through Main Gate without cars, of course, we had better toe the line, shape up or ship out. Boy! Creepy as shit."

"I don't know," Demi said, "She was playing it straight, after all, and a few of these guys are kind of scary. Not exactly the sort you want to meet in a dark alley, considering what they might have done overseas. Not dressed like Princeton men, either, except for a couple of those freaks."

"What do you know about Princeton men?" laughed Gussie.

"Not much," admitted Demi, "but I did read *The Great Gatsby* in high school."

"Hey, a real intellectual," said Gussie, "Like that sort of stuff, do you?"

"Yeah, I like to read good stuff when I can fit it in, just like my father," Demi acknowledged. "The public library, a great invention. Try it, Gus, you might like it."

"I heard there are a couple of women vets but I didn't see any in that group. No WACs or WAVES at that meeting. Maybe they are camouflaged in sweater sets. For men only, obviously," said one of the others, a shorter blond man wearing a silver earring in one ear. "I'm Ted Collins, by the way. I was on the high school track team with your brother, Tim, when he could fit in track meets with the baseball schedule. Busy kid, he was, and speedy."

"Probably they would have just merged with the regular female students," said Demi. "Practical move to make. They'll be getting the regular Vassar degree, after all and can stay the full four years. They want to boot us guys out after a year or two, I heard, when there should be room in other places. Start planning, you dog-faces," said Demi. "Glad to meet you," he added to Ted Collins, without responding to the reference to his dead brother.

"Maybe different rules for the females, vets or not," Gussie put in, "Got to keep an eye on all us sex-starved military males, you know. Can you imagine how a good campus scandal would rock the boat here. A certain kind of Poughkeepsie native would love the scandal."

"I certainly fit that description. Name is Evelyn Smith," said another of the men in the group, "Funny name, I know; long E as in Evelyn Waugh, the British writer. Blame it on my English mother. Thought maybe I would become a famous writer by name connection. Dreamer, Mom. Friends and relatives call me Ev, short E." Shorter than most of the men except Ted and Demi, he was dressed in blue jeans and blue work shirt. "Not one of the Poughkeepsie Cough Drop Smiths, I am afraid, although I did date Ginny once before she went off to a select Miss Somebody's classes in New England, which meant a Girls' Finishing School, I learned. Cream of the crop, but it turned out she was not smart enough for a good college despite the best efforts of the spinsters at The Classes, so I hear she wound up at Bennett Junior College in Millbrook, that holding tank for rich girls waiting for the boyfriend to pass the bar or finish his medical residency. I am just an ordinary run-of-the-mill Smith, not a Sm-y-th or Sm-i-t-h-e," spelling them out, "but here I am at Vassar. She would be green with envy."

"Hey there, Ev," said Ted, "Long time no see. We went to grade school together eons ago," he explained to the others.

"Good old Governor George Clinton School, better known as Number Eight," said Ev, grinning. "Where the self-defined elite went before they left public education for Oakwood School after the eighth grade. The Quaker school just outside of town," he explained for the benefit of the veteran outlanders who lived beyond the reach of Poughkeepsie. "We public school types had to stick out the city system even if we all did reside on or near Academy Street. That is where a lot of the relative big-bucks nineteenth century families settled in, like those cough-drop Smiths I mentioned, or the Coughlin's and Averill's who owned the Nelson House Hotel, where the elite meet to eat. There were the Hinckley ladies who inherited the trolley system better known as the Wappinger Falls Poughkeepsie Railroad, or the Rhodies who heated all of Poughkeepsie with their patented anthracite Blue Coal, and the Van Kleeks who ran the Poughkeepsie Saving Bank. Residue of the Patroon system of the Hudson Valley. They had a good-looking daughter, too, the Van Benschotens, another Dutchman, the first Dodge dealer in the world or maybe the US, according to his newspaper ads. I forget which. There you have the Readers Digest version of Poughkeepsie society for you non-locals, leaving out the beer baron, Matthew Vassar who dropped dead while reading his farewell speech to the college he founded with half of his alcoholic fortune. How about that?"

"You seem to be up on the good-looking daughters, Ev, as well as the important people, and the public schools were not so bad in those days," said Ted, "We thought Oakwood was for the sissies, then, I am afraid. Narrow of us, I am sure. They had stopped playing Poughkeepsie High School in football because they used to lose to us at 57 to 6, or scores like that. Amazing how we cared so much at the time."

"What's with the silver disk hanging from the ear? Mean something?" asked Evelyn of Ted.

"Just a little memento of wasted time in the Western Pacific while waiting for my discharge number to come up and to go home. Got used to it, for some reason. Means absolutely nothing except that it made me out of uniform. I will retire it right away. Kind of forgotten about it. Don't even feel it anymore."

Ted reached up and loosened the decoration from his ear lobe. "Put it with the ribbons and the wings," he said, "as an insignia of the past from the piece of war we probably did not need to fight, if it hadn't been for the racism and imperialism of Teddy Roosevelt, cozying up to the Japanese in his time who, I believe he said, should expand, take over Korea, and be the United States of the Far East."

"What are you, a history buff? And the mustache? Don't remember that from high school. Does it go with the contrarian history about the famous rough rider?" Ev laughed. "Where did you learn that anti-official history stuff, anyway?"

Ted made the motions of twirling the ends of a blond mustache that was barely a wisp on his upper lip. "That came from the same place as the silver earring – boredom while waiting for my discharge number to come up on Tinian, North Field, Runway Able. No beards in the 20th Air Force, but at the time you could get away with a mustache, even one with handlebars, particularly if you were flight crew. I have minimized it considerably since I came home. My mother hates it, even with what is left. Her little boy with a mustache, she complains. As for the info about that great white hunter, that is from the radical literature I found in the library that tells me about the feet of clay."

"On the other hand, the next thing you know, as you adjust to conventional civilian life, could be a purchase of a civilian suit at Brocks Haberdashery or even Schwartz's Men's Department Store," replied Ev, "and the revolutionary vanishes in the double-breasted bold look. At Brocks, you might run into Rose who is working for her father part-time while taking nurses training at St. Francis Hospital. Don't know how she works it all in."

"A suit and Rose, both at the same time. Have to give it some thought," Ted laughed. "I read that same article in Esquire Magazine, where it says that is the new look for the late nineteen forties with the return to civilian life of service men sick of uniforms. Been reading Esquire to catch up with civilian life and the Petty girls, Ev? Still need pin-ups?"

"Don't we all," said Ev.

"Phil Costello," said another one of the men. He was wearing neatly pressed khakis and a bronze-buttoned blazer. He was tanned as an outdoor worker would be, and dark haired, worn long. His work callused hands were apparent to the others, who nodded him into the group.

"From blue-collar Beacon down the river," he added, "and the only important things about the town is National Biscuit makes boxes in a big factory along the river and the town is the home of the famous Melio Bettina, at one-time light heavy weight boxing champ of the world. I never played high school football, I have to admit, or baseball. On the other hand, speaking to an earlier observation, I can see temptation all over the campus. Give us a warm September and the shorts come out. Hard not to be distracted by all the great naked legs. Some girls are already sunbathing on the lawns outside the dorms. I wonder if we can join them."

"Hard is the operative word, I would say, pun intended," said another one of the men. "Richard Forrest, refugee from the line at IBM," he introduced himself, "Afraid I never heard of this Bettina. Never followed boxing except for Joe Louis. Could not miss him."

This veteran was tall and blond with an early receding hair line and thinning hair, marking him as one of the older men. He, too, was dressed more formally than most of the others, with a white dress shirt open at the neck, and tie-less under a sleeveless sweater vest. He was wearing neatly pressed khaki pants but incongruous brown wing tip shoes appeared below the cuff-less pants legs. IBM could leave lasting habits, hidden brands to establish who owned the cattle in the herd.

"I would not try sunning with the girls just yet, Phil. Check the rules Dean Thomas gave you. I bet there is something there that speaks to that," advised Ted Collins, "I also bet that that southern lady has thought of lots of things you had better not do or even think of doing. Maybe there are some hints there of forbidden pleasures. She seemed the type."

"Chris Wohl," said another. He was also taller than most, a thin wiry handsome young man wearing a leather flight jacket. He had one foot up on the grindstone that graced the front walk down the steps from Rockefeller Hall.

"Wohl?" said Gussie, "Any relation of the Poughkeepsie Police Chief Wohl?"

"Uncle," said the vet, "Don't hold it against me. Can't pick your family, as they say."

"He seems like a good enough guy from what I read in the paper," said Richard Forrest, "Always read the local rag and keep up with what's new in Poughkeepsie, although it is usually not much. Mostly about local high school sports, in fact, and local politics or the society page. A real hoot about the latest wedding or some local variant on a debut party. And the

Neanderthals who write letters to the editor, they are worth a read to get the flavor of Duchess County."

"For a cop he's okay," said Chris, "He really wanted to be a lawyer, but the Wohls couldn't afford law school. He did well on exams for cop, so he worked his way up. Lots better than that political creep, our local J. Edgar Hoover, who seems to have the Sheriff's job locked up. He doesn't know shit about real law enforcement. But of course, that position is all local politics. You pay your dues to the Republican party here in the Mid-Hudson Valley and you can go on being re-elected until you are trundled off to some retirement home in Florida. Cops at least have to pass tests like civil servants and you can't fudge those results."

"Well, welcome to the institution where who you know and whose palm you grease will not be a factor. You heard the Dean. Here the Meritocracy prevails," Ted laughed, but he was serious.

"And I prefer it that way. Brown-nosing as a way of life never appealed to me," answered Chris.

"Know some of you guys from high school," said a heavy swarthy man, "although I don't think anyone here played on the football team with me. Dominic Calenti, for the unfamiliar. Former Ranger with the badges to prove it, and before that, fullback on the football team at Poughkeepsie High."

"Hi Dom," said Gussie, "Somehow I thought you had a football scholarship to Syracuse and I didn't expect to see you here with us."

"I did have the offer," said Dominic, "But it seemed like with the G. I. Bill I could get a real education in my own backyard without getting my butt busted for good old Syracuse. Who can get an education playing varsity football? And being a pro after college never seemed so attractive, if I made it that far. Get knocked silly for a few bucks and finished before you are thirty, probably. Besides, I got my final fill of football playing for the Second Air Force team when I was stationed in Lincoln, Nebraska. What a shaft for the rest of the G. I.s, putting us football players on exhibition to liven up the home front, while others were fighting a real war. Couldn't stomach it after a while, so I volunteered for Ranger training and became a real soldier. Some of the upper brass, colonels and majors mostly, didn't like it. They enjoyed the football competition as if that was war enough for them. Besides, I discovered there are attractions here. When I went to apply I found a girl I had dated in high school – a cheer leader, in fact— was now the Dean's secretary. Great looking Irish Catholic girl and I thought we might pick up where we left off. She seemed available."

"Oh shucks, and that was the girl I mentioned to you, Demi," Gussie put in, "Guess I will have to look around since I would not want to butt into a fellow vet's picking up on a potential love life, and besides, he is bigger than I am." They both grinned.

"Both of you sound noble and admirable for different reasons," said a thirty-something thin but tall man, also with a premature thinning spot on the crown of his head.

"Leroy Freer. Glad to meet you all," He stood at the edge of the group, dressed in faded khaki trousers and an equally faded khaki shirt. "From New Paltz. My father is the Chevy dealer in Highland with some cars coming in to sell at last, now that G.M. is converting back to civilian production. I thought that Dean really laid it on the line and I guess I prefer that approach to some sentimental drivel about helping the boys when they come home, like those war time ads about fighting for Mom, Apple Pie, and Chevrolet, even if my old man believes that the sun rises and sets in good old General Motors land. Detroit, the car capital of the auto world is his Mecca."

"Never owned a Chevy," said Evelyn Smith, "My first car was a 1934 Ford V-Eight. Pisser of a car. Went fast and had terrible brakes. It was a wonder I didn't kill myself showing off for the kids at school who didn't have a car."

"I used to sell those in the used car lot for him before I was drafted. Hot engine, actually, but with those outdated mechanical brakes. I think FDR drove one that was modified for hand controls. Anyway, I never gave a thought to college, although the old man used to say I could just go to New Paltz and become a grade school teacher. Good clean profession, he would say, but I never could see myself in front of a bunch of fourth or fifth graders keeping order and putting them into snowsuits at the end of the school day, but sometimes when trying to sell a used car to some Highland moron that kind of life seemed more attractive, and I suppose fourth and fifth graders can actually put on their own winter wear."

"Another one reprieved or repositioned by the G.I. Bill, I would say," interrupted Evelyn Smith.

"Right-O," responded Leroy Freer, "Freed from used car bondage and ready to study real subjects that will get me an even cleaner job in this post-war world. Don't need an academic advisor to make that call. Sometimes I had to fill in for a mechanic in the shop and that put grease under my finger nails. That grease I am escaping as well. Hated tune-ups, although working on an engine that couldn't talk back was sometimes better that dealing with a car customer who wanted to cajole a really low price out of you. Hated that because you had to keep smiling while thinking 'you cheapskate bastard, I have to make a living, too'."

"Don't be so hard on the mechanic's life," put in Demi, "My older brother is a machinist, tool and die maker. Oily dirty work, true, but skilled and exacting, you know. An honorable profession, in fact, important in our twentieth century, as an apologist for the industrial revolution might say, and maybe one of the jobs that helped win us a war."

"True enough," responded Leroy Freer, "although I notice you are going for the clean work here at Vassar."

"I also plan to keep my nose clean, hit the books, spend what leisure time I have in the library, get as good grades as I can manage, and go home to downtown Poughkeepsie when the day is done. And take my local girl friend to the movies when I have the money," Demi asserted, "And listen to my academic advisor even if I think he doesn't know which end is up."

"Who did they give you?" Gussie asked, "They sent me to the Chaplain. In the Army that was where you went with personal problems, so it felt a bit funny to go to him here for academic advice and picking a schedule. He seemed an okay guy, I thought."

"A man, you dummy, a real honest-to-god man. Didn't you figure that out? They sent me to a physics professor and I have no interest in taking any more sciences than are required, but he was a man," Demi snorted. "Actually, the freshman year course selection was no big deal. Anyone with a few more brains than a clam could figure it out from the catalogue."

"Funny chapel, though. Somehow, I expected stained glass windows with saints, and an altar. No saints. No altar." Gussie made a surprised face, raising his thick eyebrows in wonder. "And he, Mr. McGiffen, said that he was a Unitarian. I know my mother would say that he wasn't even a Christian. No Holy Trinity for him, if I understand Unitarianism."

"If you read your cheat sheet from the Dean, you would find that Chapel is not even required, although there is an hour in the day's schedule for it. Wonder what they do, pray to Ralph Waldo Emerson?" said Ted Collins.

"Huh?" said Demi.

"Emerson," replied Ted. "Big guy in American Lit. Learned that in eleventh grade English. Thought highly of Walt Whitman, although all the thighs, semen, sweat and such embarrassed the hell out of such a proper New Englander. Think I'll take a course in American Lit here and get the scholarly take on Emerson, Thoreau, Whitman and company. My high school English teacher was not exactly a free thinker when it came to some of the literature. Not a bad old girl, but careful and inhibited. Otherwise, I liked her English classes. Got to read some neat stuff," Ted finished.

"You got to be careful in a small town high school, I suppose," said Demi, "For example, politics and religion are definitely no-nos. I wouldn't blame her, but it sure does skew what the kids think they know. I am hoping we get the straight stuff here in college. No futzing around with what is or isn't – just the honest facts."

"You think literature, or even history, is just the honest facts?" said Ted, "It is all fiction, even the non-fiction. Winners get to write it. William the Conqueror, big deal. King Harold who lost the battle of Hastings and died in the process – who he? Richard the Third, bad rap from the royals that beat him. I learned that in world history. Now there I had a teacher who told it like it is. Nice guy, pretty guy, like to swim at the Y, body build, a little peculiar. Like to squeeze the arms of some of the boys in the class when they went out the door. Maybe queer. Went into the Navy to keep from being drafted, school scuttlebutt had it, not long after and became a Seal. Macho stuff, I suppose. Got killed somewhere in the Pacific. Being macho."

"They killed you whether you were macho or queer or pretty or not," said Demi, "I sure know that."

"Didn't give 'em a chance to kill me," said Ted Collins, "Take the right courses in high school, qualify for the ASTP program, and go to school. That was my plan, if I had a plan, which I didn't actually have. I made it up as I went along. But that is how it nearly worked out. Put in the Air Corps for basic in some hell hole in Mississippi where Yankee soldiers ranked just below the local Negroes in social status, and then I was sent to tech schools in the benighted middle west in a bible belt dry state, to learn about plane armament," he continued. "Funny thing, I started out with B-24s and B-17s and then the B-29 came along and made the older planes redundant for the Pacific. So back to another school to learn about Central Fire Control and early computers of a sort and then instructing in that school, it looked as if I was going to have an easy ride. Then somebody up there decided they needed more B-29 armament technicians in the Western Pacific, and off I went to the edge of a war zone, following the Marines who did the really hard work, but that is another whole story, a real bore. What do you plan to major in, Democritus?"

"I thought a double major. Seems you can do that here. Sociology and English. Soc for the practical life since I can become a licensed social worker eventually, and English for the pleasure of it, since I like to read and write. Be a bit harder for a Greek proletarian like me, but I just want to do it," Demi grimaced and then turned it into a grin. "Who knew I would get the chance?"

"The name's Daleo," one more man spoke. He was short and dark-haired with black bushy eyebrows. "Carmen Daleo. My family runs a grocery down near the railroad station in the Italian ghetto we call home. Sells genuine Italian stuff. Olives, pasta, sauce, right from the old country. Even homemade gelato. Drop by and browse. We're right across the street from the greatest Italian bakery on the East coast, and the coffee there is the best."

"My family would dispute that," said Gussie, "Nothing like genuine Greek style coffee. Have to eat it with a spoon. We should have a contest sometime." He reached over to shake Carmen Daleo's hand. "Loved the beat-up Italy that I saw in the war, by the way. Good looking girls."

"Probably," said Carmen, "I like blonds myself."

"Welcome aboard," said Demi, "See you in class."

"Right," said Carmen, "Only no jokes about my first name, either, please. I can sympathize with you, Mr. Smith. Out of the ordinary first names in our good old U. S. of A. can cause confusion. Had enough of that in the Navy, I am afraid. For some historic old country reason, we give that name to both boys and girls, so I don't want to be confused with a real Vassar girl, if you don't mind."

"Never," said Gussie, "although in the Navy it might really be misleading. Sorry, that will be my only joke for the duration."

"Apology accepted," replied Carmen Daleo, laughing.

"I can identify with that problem," put in Evelyn Smith, "There is enough to worry about these days without gender confusion."

TWELVE

1946

Walking to the Main Building in search of an elusive men's room on this campus for women, Gussie said to Demi, "Male teachers and administrators must pee and shit somewhere on this campus! And what do you make of this Ted Collins? Putting on airs about his learning and connections, you think? Talks really radical. Different from us ordinary grunts."

"Probably not. Just trying to establish identity in a different situation, like a new kid in school. We're all new kids on the block, when you come right down to it, even if some us spent time together in Poughkeepsie High School, and if it comes across as sort of pompous, so what. More likely feeling a bit insecure, as we all are. Cut him some slack, is my advice. We will be getting to know the whole bunch better as the semester goes along. Now where is that men's lounge and the facilities?" Demi turned into the door of Main. "Ah. Here it is," he smiled.

"Where the Yale men wait for their weekend dates, I heard, and now kindly turned over to the male vets, I understand. So, we will be spending a lot of time here, I would guess, between classes. Wonder if they found another place for the visitors," Gussie held the door to the lounge. "Where will they put the Yale and Princeton guys now? Probably not want them to have to mix with riffraff like us. I understand that Vassar girls do not usually even date West Point men, even though they are so available, because they tend to come from working class families and going to West Point is a step up in society for them. Still makes them working class, though. Hard to tell social class visually when they are in those cute operetta uniforms."

"Don't be a reverse snob, Gussie. They all mean well, as my mother would say. Besides, this is a great location for us, and don't forget – we will be hanging about and relaxing in historic surroundings. This building, with the exception of this excrescence where we are right now, is a historic replication of the Palais de Tuileries." Demi bowed in mock thanks for his friend's door holding courtesy.

"How very impressive. *Mais oui, mon capitaine,* or Corporal, as the case may be. Impressed by my French? I can also say '*Que voulez-vous chewing-gum?*' That is how I got around after V-E day before coming home." Gussie smirked.

"Such a cosmopolitan," said Demi.

The men's lounge that the college had transformed into the veteran's home base was in the front of the Main building, in that later addition which had ruined the French image of the original architecture. Some practical administrator with no sense of history or balance had grafted the space on where it did not belong. The room contained worn leather couches and chairs, and a battered coffee table upon which were various copies of the student newspaper, *The Miscellany News.* Some copies were yellow with age and some were pristine white. Maybe the gray-haired White Angel women in their smocks that seemed to be omnipresent in all dorms, who policed the premises and guarded the doors, were responsible for shifting the reading matter.

The walls of the lounge area were an institutional pale green, above dark wooden paneling that reached a third of the way up. Minimal windows let in a little light from the front of the building and under the shadow of the porte-cochere. It was not exactly a home away from home, as it was originally planned as a holding tank for visiting males, forbidden to enter the residence proper, who were waiting for Message Center to inform the Vassar girl dates that a man was waiting. But, as Demi and Gussie looked about the room, they agreed that it would do.

The sound of a flushing toilet came from behind a closed door, and Phil Costello came out.

"I heard you guys. I just pissed where only Yale men and perhaps Princeton guys have gone before; although maybe 'guys' don't go to Princeton. Ain't that somethin'? And your French skill leaves something to be desired, Gussie. Now me, knowing Eye-talian from my grandparents, I picked up a more workable version of French. More than just chewing-gum conversation. More cigarette and chocolate bar, you might say. In fact, I have already decided to major in foreign languages, having such a head start on it, and maybe teach French or Italian or try German or all of them. Ought to be a soaring demand for that sort of skill as the good old USA angles for world business and financial dominance against the USSR, although Russian is a whole different thing. I don't know about trying that, but Vassar has a good Russian department, I hear."

"Always thinking ahead, Phil," said Demi.

"That's what they taught us in Ranger training. Think ahead, look at the lay of the land, anticipate your enemies' moves, plan your own, go quickly and quietly. Don't give any mercy. It's a battle to the death."

"Oh, good grief," sighed Demi, "And I thought we were just going to be college students."

"I hear they grade on the curve here, so it's a battle all the time. All those smart-ass girls with high SAT scores, and school valedictorians in every class who know the language of success so thoroughly they don't even have to think about the vocabulary. It just comes out automatically." Phil looked around after this outburst, cocking a brow as if daring anyone to challenge him on this point.

"What are you talking about?" Gussie interrupted.

"Hey guys," said Ted Collins as he entered the lounge, "Reconnoitering before the charge, are you?"

"Getting ready for the new President's address to the vets, I guess. You hear she is going to welcome us? After the welcome by the Dean, this has to be friendlier; but this welcome will be to the whole Freshman class, us included, so it should be less pointed. That is what they use that Chapel time for, apparently."

"My father's cousin who lives in Lexington knew her there," Ted Collins said. "I don't know exactly how, but this cousin was the music supervisor for the Lexington school system when Sarah Bloomer was Dean of Women at the University of Kentucky. Maybe Miss Bloomer likes jazz. This spinster cousin of my father had a small jazz group and she played honky-tonk piano in it. Doesn't sound very school teacher-ish, does it? "

"Sounds like you might have an 'in' here if you pursued it," said Phil.

"I don't plan ever to mention it," Ted said, "I heard she started out as a gym teacher. Female gym teachers, I stay away from on principle. Male ones are bad enough. The assistant-principal of my high school had been one and he was a big shit administrator, or more accurately, a little shit."

Demi protested, "Don't be so bigoted, Ted. Some are okay. The baseball coach that my brother and I played for was tough but fair, and he could turn out great teams. On the other hand, female scholars who plan to be college presidents in this time and place would most likely have a tough time being taken seriously for that top job. Think of P. E. as a possible door opener."

"Well, I am glad we are exempt from the P. E. requirement here and we can escape that kind of stuff. Had enough organized exercise in the service, Admissions said, but I think that it was just they couldn't figure out how to have us men in that female-focused gym. They don't have segregated locker rooms, showers, or any urinals, I bet, and all the gym teachers are those short haired female jocks."

"Sort of men-women," noted Gussie. "Tough girls."

"Don't you be so conventional and bigoted," Demi said, "But I think the term is butch."

"And here I was going to see if the College would sponsor a basketball team for the vets," interrupted Richard Forrest, "As I would like a little organized sporty exercise and some competition, and I am going to go ahead and pursue it. Any others interested?"

"Competition? Spoken like a true IBM business man," said Phil. "I know a guy who is going to Skidmore the way we are doing here at Vassar. He wanted to know if Vassar Vets would like to play them in football."

"I don't think Vassar would cotton to that," said Bernard Black, "Expensive, no coach, and no real equipment or facilities, my father says, and he hears stuff at faculty meetings."

"I'll sign-up for basketball," said Chris Wohl who had entered the room during this conversation, "Center? Forward?"

"Put a sign-up interest sheet on the vet's bulletin board," suggested Gussie, "See what happens. Only about seventy guys here now to draw from. Down from the original hundred."

"I didn't come to college for sports. Besides, I'll be pumping gas and tuning up engines when I am not in class or studying. Going to look for a campus job eventually." Ted picked up a text book and riffled through. "Poetry book for first year English 105, but no authors listed. Wonder what educational philosophy is behind that gambit? Probably so the poet's name and reputation won't get in the way of the new criticism, I suppose."

"Whatever that is," said Demi.

"Someone will tell you eventually," Richard Forrest suggested, "I think they always do."

"Anyway, time to hit the road for Conklin Street," said Demi, "Got to clock in with the family. Help with the sister. See you all tomorrow for those classes coming up. Come on, Gussie. Got to catch the bus at Main Gate."

"They had trolleys there when I was really little," said Ted, a bit wistfully as he waved at the two who were leaving. "So long, guys."

***

"So what happens with Dartmouth and your future in electrical engineering?" Mr. Collins looked up from the car engine he was working on and slammed down the hood. "Vassar seems a reasonable stop-gap solution, and I suppose you can get the math and science for pre-engineering if you select carefully."

"I'm not so sure about that choice any longer," Ted acknowledged.

"No?" said his father.

"Well, I have had too much experience with Sperry bombsights, with B-29 Remote Control Turrets and those G.E. computer remote 50 Caliber machine gun sights. I could do it out there, and knowing it after those Air Corp schools kept me out of combat, but it was no real challenge after a while." Ted looked at his father as he wiped the grease off his hands with a kerosene dampened rag. "It was just following the tech manuals some tech writer engineer put together. Boring, unoriginal job."

"Well, you were saving democracy, you know, out there in the Pacific. We were proud of you, your mother and I."

"So they told us, but technical skills were really mechanical applications of someone else's brilliant mind. It didn't take brilliance to do what we were doing. An Air Corp Armament Specialist, even with flight time, is no creative person. Tricky stuff that required know-how and skilled hands, but not creative." Ted shook his head. "Just high tech ways of killing people."

"Okay," said his father, "Maybe what you were doing was mechanical and not original, but if you went on into real engineering at Dartmouth you could be original, and electronics are the coming thing in the post-war world. Just look at that Heath Kit TV we are putting together. Soon there will be many broadcast channels, not just that Dumont experimental one. Get in on the ground floor, Ted."

"I suppose you are right, Pop. I know radio had been your thing for a long time. The ham station, the Signal Corp in the Great War, the whole hobby of sound reproduction, and now this building a TV receiver from parts. I know it has been a big thing for you."

"I thought once," his father said softly, remembering, "When I had just got out of high school, and was working in the local assembly plant where Fiat was converting schematics from metrics to feet and inches for the American market, that when I got enough scratch together, that I would go to the University of Michigan and study electrical engineering." Mr. Collins polished the fender of the Pontiac that he had been working on, removing some invisible lint from the protective cloth he had used while working on the engine.

Ted knew that story. It was something his father had talked about when Ted was still in school and the two of them sat together in his father's radio shack behind their house in Poughkeepsie. That was where his father explained ham radio to him. It was Ted that he took there, because his older brother did not have any interest in electronics or the hobby. It was girls and football for him, and his paper route where he was saving money for bigger things and entertainment.

"Didn't work out, of course," said Mr. Collins, "Married your mother out of Vassar, had your brother, and went to work as a salesman for my uncle Jacob selling men's pants on the road for the Duchess Trouser Company."

"I know that one, Pop. Ten cents a lost button, a dollar a rip. I remember the slogan from my childhood. Seems pretty cheap by now." Ted laughed. "And the story about how the company turned down the chance to be one of the first to use a zipper on the fly." Ted laughed again.

"Right," his father agreed, "Just too risky for the male anatomy, our sales manager thought. Might just zip off the man's pecker, he said. Not in mixed company, of course."

Ted knew his father was a very proper old-fashioned person when it came to using 'offensive' language, so his comment was a bit jarring, even considering it was between father and son. Not the usual. Ted listened a bit more intently now.

"Your mother's family was unhappy over the marriage, you know. Vassar had a rule, may still have it but I doubt it now, that no married woman could be a student. So your mother never graduated with her class of 1916. Her family, particularly her mother, your grandmother Emily White, was angry. They were both teachers, you know, graduates of New Paltz Normal School for Teachers. That was what it was then. They had planned for your mother to get a B. A. and teach in a high school, and she was their whole focus after her sister, your Aunt Carole, died in the World War One flu epidemic."

This was another old story for Ted, but somehow his father often needed to repeat it, particularly when the two of them were alone together in the radio shack.

"Didn't work out the way we planned it," Mr. Collins said, "Your brother had no interest in either teaching nor engineering. All business, you know, and so he majored in economics at that Tennessee college and IBM has been a natural match for him. Your sister, now, she is the literary one and no engineering for a woman."

"Maybe not yet, Pop, but give it time." Ted had to put that comment out there for his father.

"Maybe," Mr. Collins answered, "Still, she had no interest in math or science. Literature and history at Vassar was her thing. And it was that way from grade school on. Not even the music that your mother plays and loves. Some teacher, or maybe teachers, told your mother at a Parent Teacher meeting that your sister had a real flair for writing. Your mother has always been enthusiastic with the Parent Teacher Association for all you three kids."

"Actually, I think one of my high school teachers told Mom the same thing about me," Ted needed to say.

"You could be right. I just don't remember that, I am afraid." Mr. Collins stared into the middle distance at something unseen. Perhaps it was another memory, Ted thought, just beyond the dark blue Pontiac.

"That brings me back with what I am, or think I am, going to do now that I am home and in college, even if it is Vassar and not Dartmouth." Ted took the opportunity to return to the subject of their talk from the beginning of this conversation. "I have a short story in the English 105 magazine that Vassar puts out with the creative work the Freshmen are doing, and my instructor says, in so many words, that I have a flair for writing."

"Did you bring a copy home, Ted? I would like to read it."

"Mom has it right now."

"What is it about?" his father asked.

"Making a sort of brandy out of the dried fruit bars that come in K-Rations. Illegal, of course, but it was done when time hung heavy between B-29 armament servicing on the flight line."

"War time stuff, I see. When I was serving in the Signal Corps down on the Mexican border we had that kind of off time, too, but I don't think anyone ever thought to distill liquor while we waited. Didn't have the ingredients, I think, or the ingenuity. You must know, as a veteran, how much military time is spent just waiting." Mr. Collins made a wry face.

"Hurry up and wait, I suppose in both wars," Ted agreed, "I have a couple of poems coming out, too."

"You write poetry?" Mr. Collins asked, "I don't think I knew that. Does your mother know that?"

"I believe so. I wrote some for high school English classes, but did not talk about it much. They were for assignments. I thought writing them was interesting." Ted smiled at his father. "So I think I will just deep six Dartmouth for the moment, anyway; stick with Vassar and tentatively make my major English; although declaring a major this early is not absolutely necessary, particularly if you take the required distribution of entry level courses. If Vassar boots us out after two years, Dartmouth is still my fall back, if I can find a place to live up there in icy New Hampshire."

"Well, I guess you know yourself best, and you are a grown man who has been to war, so I think you should know what you want to do. It is not always just age that determines such things, but it sure helps, as it is experience." Mr. Collins punched his son gently in the shoulder. "I have known some pretty dumb old people in my time. So, you going to write the great American novel, son, or the epic war poem?"

"We'll see, but whichever I think I will find it more satisfying than playing with the circuits, even if engineering might be more sophisticated than what I was doing on Tinian. More positive than oiling up the war machine, anyway. I could even make Mom happy by following the White tradition and turning to teaching. You never know," Ted acknowledged.

"You're a smart boy, Ted, and will make a success of whatever you choose. It will be your choice, and not ours. It's your life."

"Right you are. I will take full responsibility."

"And it will keep your hands cleaner than this," his father said, tossing into a garbage can the oily rag he had been using to wipe his hands, "A lot cleaner. On the other hand, this family has survived two world wars and the great depression. Something said for hard work."

"Nothing really terrible about dirty hands from doing honest labor, Dad." Ted returned the gentle punch to his father's shoulder. "Got us where we are, you can say."

"Could be," answered his father, "But you do have to use the brain or it can wither."

THIRTEEN

1946

On a brisk October afternoon when leaves were just beginning to turn to brilliant colors, fall, and blow about the campus, a group of men collected in the lounge, with one addition. Jack Wyzinsky had turned up in the lounge for the first time. Somehow, he had been absent or unnoticed at the Dean's meeting with the vets. Blond Pole, wearing a tweed jacket and khakis. Hair carefully waved back in an ample pompadour. Dirty buck shoes. He came in and looked around for any familiar faces, and spotted Ted Collins.

"Hi there, Ted. Sort of like being together again at that long ago high school election for class president. I do believe I was canvassing for votes."

"You must have been successful at it. I do believe you won. The beginning of your long and brilliant political career, no doubt." Ted grinned.

"You can joke if you like, but I am planning to go into politics. Law school after Vassar and whatever, local politics, pay my political dues and move up. Maybe a judgeship. Nice sinecure. Or, if I am lucky, maybe something on the state level. When I do, I'll be happy to take care of anything you might need in the political way. Who knows what might come, and I will be playing the veteran's card without shame. Local war hero seeks political office. I have been planning this thing since I was serving in Europe. Should be good for something after all the excrement I had to put up with in the service."

"Think it was politically wise to skip that orientation meeting with Dean Winifred?" Gussie asked.

"Didn't really think she would know whether we were all there or not, and I knew I had signed up for the right courses. Some more important connections to re-establish, you might say. I hate to put up with more of the red tape feces, even here." Jack wrinkled his nose as if he smelled something bad.

"Didn't we all, don't we all," said Demi, "but I would think local politics would be equally shitty. And exactly what was the heroic action of which you speak?"

"Surviving and coming home in one piece. And maybe a bit dirty," Jack acknowledged, "A little black market on the side, but the payoff should be a hell of a lot better, if you play your cards right."

"Not me," said Demi, "Get my undergraduate education and then most likely head for California and graduate work. I'll have enough G. I. Bill time to take me through the four B. A. years with some left over for a couple of graduate semesters. If I do well, maybe then I can get a scholarship or something like that for the rest of the time."

"What? You want to leave the good old Hudson Valley and the Queen City for the wild west?" Gussie joined the conversation. "I know you hate the smell of roast garlic and lamb that wafts out of those Greek kitchens on Sundays, but I didn't think it was strong enough to drive you all the way to the other coast."

"Hey, it isn't that it's Greek garlic. It's just that it's strong garlic and gets in my clothes and hair."

"Right. You just want to smell nice for my sister. She planning to go with you to California?" Gussie raised an eyebrow.

"This has nothing to do with Rebia. I don't think I have even told her about my possible plans, because nothing is certain in this life. Life is what happens after you make plans, you know that. Wars come along, for instance, and before you know it, the cold war is a hot war. And I did a dumb thing and a smart thing when I was discharged at Fort Dix. I signed up for a three year hitch in the inactive reserve. Some smooth Army guy said I could protect my rank, seniority and M.O.S. in case of whatever, although the M.O.S. did not seem like something I wanted to protect."

"So what was the smart thing, or was the reserve the smart thing?"

"The smart thing was signing up for the American Veterans' Committee, the liberal alternative to the American Legion, or the Veterans of Foreign Wars. 'Citizens First, Veterans Second' was the slogan that convinced me. The dumb thing was the reserve, but the smart talker convinced me at the time that I would be getting three more years of military service on my record. Now, I don't see the point, but too late."

"Not the slogan for me," said Jack, "As I said, use the weapons you have, in politics."

"I was impressed by the vets who started it. People like Burgess Meredith, the actor, Cord Meyer, Bill Mauldin. Now there is a good man who tells it like it is. His cartoons kept me going overseas, to exaggerate a bit. The AVC is chartered by the U. S. Congress, so it has to be on the up and up."

"There is a Mid-Hudson chapter, you know," Ted Collins added, "I was buying records at a local shop and the owner told me about it. They meet in a room over that bakery on Main Street. Brad's Bakery, I think it's called. Drop in at the store, Arts and Gifts, and ask about it, if you are interested. I thought I might go, in fact."

"Lefty stuff," said Jack, "Watch out. This is going to be a conservative country from now on, Truman or no. Lucky that Henry Wallace was dumped as Vice-President before FDR died. Duchess County is right in the conservative mainstream. FDR never carried his home county, you know."

"Maybe things will change," said Ted, "You heard what Chris Wohl was saying about his uncle, the cop, and the political sheriff. Want to buy into that old-boy system, do you?"

"Amen to the first," said Demi.

"I doubt it," said Gussie, "Fundamental change here seems like an impossible dream."

"I am not for change, and doubt we will have to worry about it," echoed Jack, "and a good thing, too. Who runs this Arts and Gifts place, by the way?"

"Guy named Ettinger. Went to high school in my brother's class. A commissioned officer, it seems. Served in England. Harvard guy."

"Harvard guy!" said Jack, "and one of this town's Jewish mafia I'll bet. Maybe a Marxist. Why would a Harvard guy open up a little store in this town? Lots of that extended family here, of course. Clothing stores, car dealers, fuel oil suppliers, junk yards, bakery goods wholesalers. Probably why the lefty group is meeting over a bakery."

"You are some piece of work, Jack," Demi said, "Even a touch anti-Semitic, perhaps?"

"Well, you won't get me there, and don't say I didn't warn you." Jack sounded hurt. "And some of my best friends in the service were Jews."

"Did you hear that old personal protest? Can't you be original, Jack?" said Demi.

Ted tried shifting the conversation back. "I like him. He knows about music. He is a real encyclopedia of classics, folk songs and jazz. I think he knows the Swann Catalogue by heart. Books. Art as well, and he is a local history buff. His wife seems to know a lot about art and crafts, too. She buys prints and gifts, and they have original paintings and photographs from artists of the area. Their three-year-old kid was playing around their feet."

Ted was getting excited about this source of cultural activities for Duchess County. "Just what this parochial place needs. He talked about starting a series of live performances. Pete Seeger from down in Beacon.

Martha Graham's dance company from the city; Josh White, art films. Wake up Poughkeepsie."

"Sounds like a Commy, if he is having Pete Seeger or Josh White, and I wonder where he will put all these shows on," said Jack.

"Hey, Pete Seeger and Beacon go together like ham and eggs," protested Phil.

"Pardon me for saying it, but you are some kind of Neanderthal, Jack. Vassar may turn out to be a shock to your system," Demi shook his head. "Advice for you, take political science and avoid economics. I heard the Polit faculty are quite conservative in general, even sending one of their faculty to the state assembly as a Republican, and the latter is a pretty liberal department. Some were active members of FDR's New Deal, in fact."

"As a future lawyer, I think Polit would be my meat anyway, if you are right. Maybe with a dash of psychology,"

"My father knows the Public Defender. Probably went to Poughkeepsie High School with him," Ted said, "and he told my father that he found literature was very useful in arguing cases. Nothing like throwing into the legal argument a quotation from Shakespeare or Robert Frost. So there you are, mine the literary world too."

"I am taking no more than the required courses in English. I already speak it. Speaking of which, I have to go to English 105 right now. See you all later," Jack said as he swung out of the door.

"Are we going to have to put up with that sort of crap for the next year or two?" Demi asked.

"Maybe we can subtly urge him to transfer somewhere for right-wing pre-law," Ted replied, "How about Fordham? Good Catholic college. Just the place for Jack."

Demi shook his head. "I wonder. Jack has been overseas in the military but at heart he is an indigenous Hudson Valley type and might find the big city daunting. But where else would he go? No local law schools. Up to Albany? Big frog in little puddle, as my father would say, and happy with it. Did you register his plans for his resident future? And besides, being an enlisted man in the service where somebody is always there to tell you what to do and where to go hardly prepares you for independent action."

"Hey, if comes to that, I will take him by the hand and lead him to the Bronx myself. Maybe I could lure him with a Yankees' game." Ted Collins laughed. "As a future all-American small town politician, he will have to be devoted to baseball and basketball. I wonder if he can alter his history to make himself a star for the Poughkeepsie High School when he never went out for any sports as a student. But as a dedicated politician, facts should probably not stand in his way as a valuable career move."

"Too bad I won't be around then to call him on it," commented Demi, "I prefer the truth."

***

"So, here's the job," the sergeant said, "There's a fuckin' tank over in the Third Platoon sector. Got 'em pinned down. The Jerries come up over a little climb at random moments and lets 'em have it with an 88.; C. O. says get it. Gave the job to the lieutenant and he has handed it off."

"Oh, Christ Almighty," said the second soldier. The older one was silent. They both thought the lieutenant was a friggin' West Point bastard. Just a second looie out to prove something as long as he was safe. One of these days some dog face would get fed up and let him have it. There were spare grenades around, after all. He had sweet-ass favorites, this gentlemen, but no scholar.

"So, how many doggies you got here?" asked the sergeant, "Two in the hole on your left, correct? How many on the right?"

"Two guys in two holes. Six, counting us."

"Okay. Six is enough. The rest stay."

"What kind of tank, Sarge?" whispered the younger soldier.

"Tiger. Big fucking Tiger."

"Oh, Christ on a bleeding bicycle," said the younger soldier.

FOURTEEN

1948

Mrs. Christopoulos raised the spoon of baby food to Corry's lips. "Open, sweetheart," she said, probing her daughter's closed mouth, "Here we go, nice creamed spinach."

Demi watched, his fingers laced tightly together on the table before him. "How are things going at college?" his mother asked, wiping her daughter's chin with a dish towel she had draped over her shoulder as though it were ready to burp a baby.

"Okay," said Demi, "Holding my own. I can do this, you know. Just a question of paying attention, doing the reading, and remembering the right stuff. Of course, this double major involves lots of work, but I like the combination of the practical and the theoretical."

"You are spending a lot of time there," his mother noted, "Not seeing as much of Rebia Karras, I guess, at least according to Rebia's mother who tells me Rebia is feeling neglected."

"Hey, I just don't have the kind of time that I had the summer, before I started classes. Besides, I have no obligation to jazz up Rebia's social life or anything like that. We just saw some movies together and had a hamburger and drank some coffee together a few times at the diner."

"Here, you feed Corry for a while. I have to finish making the *dolmades* for our dinner." Mrs. Christopoulos handed the jar and the spoon to Demi.

"Right," Demi replied, taking both and looking at the greenish mush in the jar.

"Jeez, looks like vomit," he said.

"Don't be so disgusting," his mother said, "Just feed her. You know we have to get things she won't choke on, and she seems to like that brand of baby food."

"Anyway, I love your dolmades, Ma, just go easy on the garlic. I really looked forward to them when I was eating mess hall chow. Nothing like greasy hamburger in a white sauce on toast. But I got to go back to the library to study after dinner and I don't want to stink up the stacks when I breathe."

"You never complained before about the recipe, but I'll try. Although your father might complain if they are not just like the ones his grandmother made for his mother and that he makes for the Diner. But don't try to change the subject from Rebia and what she thinks is going on with you and her. Maybe you should be clearer. She may have some expectations for when she finishes high school next June."

"Okay. Okay." He shoved the mush laden spoon at his sister's face and smeared some creamed spinach on her upper lip. "So not to exactly change the subject, I been meaning to tell you and Pop I have this Greek Psychology professor in the Intro to Psych. Her name is Dr. Adonia Labropoulos. I thought you might be interested."

"So that is a real Greek name," said Mr. Christopoulos, coming in the door, "That first name is the female version of Adonis. Means 'my lord.' Is she a looker?"

"Hardly," snorted Demi, "Short, fat and with a slight moustache. Gives Greek womanhood a bad rap, I am afraid. But she does lord it over us men. And you know what she told us in class? That some academic survey where ordinary people were asked to rank in order of preference what ethnic group or nationalities they would not want to live next door, and this fat, squat, hairy Greek of a professor says that Greeks came out as the most objectionable. Actually, she started her lecture by standing there and saying, 'The questionnaire shows you would not want to live next to me.' She must have been addressing the young upper class women. What do you think of that? Didn't she notice me? How about the Eye-talian guy sitting next to me?"

"I think we don't have to worry about that on Conklin Street, since nearly everybody is living next door to a Greek and is Greek. The Italians live closer to the river." Mr. Christopoulos laughed. "Ever hear about self-hating Jews? I guess there must be self-hating Greeks, particularly when they wind up teaching at a cream of the crop Episcopal college like Vassar. Or maybe it is just a clear-sighted view of how the melting pot does not always melt some people."

"I don't think Vassar is an Episcopal college. In fact, I think the first president was a Baptist, and maybe Matthew Vassar was, too. Anyway, the

Chaplain who was assigned as Gussie's academic advisor turns out to be a Unitarian," Demi pointed out that evidence.

"Maybe," said Mr. Christopoulos, "but Episcopals are running this country right now and have for a lot of years. Sometimes well, sometimes badly. FDR was an Episcopal, for example, and he did a good job, and then there was Chester Arthur and Franklin Pierce, but I haven't noticed any members of the Greek Orthodox Church running things."

"I guess," said Demi, "How come you know these things, Pop?"

"I just decided an American citizen of Greek background should understand American history. The public library is free, you know. Simply get a card. I don't cook *all* the time. And sometimes I just have to get away from the griddle or from this house." He ended the sentence *sotto voce*.

"Okay, so anyway, I was sort of hoping having this Greek teacher for psych would be a good thing for me. Sympathetic, you know. Now I am not so sure. I get hostile vibrations to men in that department, at least from the three older women I have seen. They seem to resent having men in the group."

"Vibrations, yet," said Mrs. Christopoulos, "I suppose it is merely that they just aren't used to having you men there. Maybe not having men in class is why they came to Vassar to teach. Be tolerant about the poor things."

"Well, I can feel the difference in the Economics class I am taking. The woman teaching that session actually seems to value the opinions of the vets. Of course, she is a real liberal sort and worked in the New Deal at one time. So, you see, I get the opposite vibrations in that class."

"You have to put up with all kinds in this world," said Mr. Christopoulos, "You learn that even running The Acropolis Diner. Particularly running the Acropolis. Or reading in the public library."

"I get it, Pater. Let's have dinner because I need to go back to the library and do some looking up of stuff. 'Go to the original sources' is the slogan of my classes, and maybe of the whole college. Sure, not like high school where all I ever needed was the encyclopedia and the text book. I think Corry is finished. She keeps spitting out the food when I get it into her mouth."

"She can't talk but she has her ways of saying no. It is the yeses that are hard," his mother spoke from the kitchen.

***

"Gussie says you were talking about going to California for graduate work after finishing the B.A. here in the East." Rebia looked over her coffee at the Diner. The plastic table top glistened in the artificial light. Sugar grains spilled from the shaker sparkled. The Acropolis was not very busy in the middle of the afternoon and Rebia had stopped in on her way home after school. Demi had taken a break from library work since she had said she wanted to talk with him. "You have plans for that far ahead?"

"Just talk, to kill the time in the Men's Lounge. Can't keep talking about the war and the past, you know. Gets really repetitive and why bore one another with stuff we all know pretty well. We are there in college to make a change, not harp on the past. Talking about classes can't be the only other topic, so our plans for the future keeps coming up, and I can tell that most of the guys are just speculating. We don't really know whether Vassar will let us stay to the end, or where we would go if they didn't. One guy has already applied to Cornell for transfer. So I am just hypothesizing, not speaking to the inevitable. I think California would be interesting. I read somewhere that everything starts in California and migrates east, so why not be where it all begins." Demi stirred more milk into his coffee. "Strong stuff that Pop puts out. Anyway, beginnings appeal to me, since I feel as if my life has been on hold during the war."

"Well, I thought we had something going here, beginning, you could say, and I would like to hear about your plans." Rebia pushed out her lower lip and stared into Demi's eyes. "Just don't use so many big college words, if you please."

"Just idle talk among the guys right now. I'll let you know"

"So, a little break from the scholarly world, you two?" Mr. Christopoulos in a white apron appeared next to the table. "How are your parents, Rebia? You would think I would see them more on the street, but I am either here, or getting supplies for the Diner, or reading the newspapers at the library, or something. Occasionally I get the chance to walk down to the river, think about what I've read. You know you can get all the world news in the periodical room at the library. I like to keep up." He smiled down on the two young people.

"They are fine, Mr. Christopoulos. Really proud of what Gussie is doing at Vassar. Demi, too, of course. First Karras to go to college, Gussie is."

"That's the ticket, getting an education. That G.I. bill is something else, and better than just a token money bonus like in World War One -- even then, the veterans had to march and protest for their promised five hundred bucks handout. The Republican president sent General MacArthur to chase them away with his troops. Imagine, the American Army used against the American veterans! Did you young people know that? Probably why the Republicans wanted MacArthur to run for President later. Thank God for FDR and Harry after him. Good people who cared, those two men."

"Yes, I did read about that in my high school American History class last year," Rebia said.

He nodded approvingly. "Good. Learn your American History. And remember that some of the founding fathers knew their classics, too, at least Jefferson and Adams did. Maybe Franklin, but I am not certain about some of the others. Much of their ideas came from the Greeks, you know," he nodded significantly.

"You might say that I actually bought this educational largess," said Demi, "With my blood, sweat, and tears, as the misquoted Winston might have said, as well as with my time. I don't think of it as some free ride. Pardon my getting corny."

"Right you are, son. Just keep making good use of it all." His father turned away. "Got to get back to the grill and get ready for the evening rush."

"And I should get home," Demi said, "to take up the slack with Corry and Ma, until Cleo and Helena get home from work to help out. Tough for each of them with an eight hour day, and then dealing with Corry, particularly for Cleo, working at the machine shop. Precision work and well-paid for Poughkeepsie, but hard. Helena has it easier, doing her secretarial thing for that pompous political lawyer, but both can get really physically frazzled by the jobs combined with taking care of Corry before and afterwards. They see Ma just worn out at the end of the day. I cannot be all that helpful, although I try, because I have to spend so much time in classes or in the library, or I will waste all this 'largess' from the government and ruin what I want to do with the rest of my life. Taking this time here is probably not a good thing."

"So, go already, and chuck the guilt. You, you and I, maybe that is, have a future to think about." Rebia waved him toward the diner door. "Get moving, man."

***

The echoing *punk* of a fired mortar came floating to them as a remote innocent and harmless sound, followed at once by another. A few moments later there came a rush of footsteps from the top of the ravine and two figures stumbled down the bank toward the foxhole.

"Sarge got it, Sarge got it." one of them blurted. He was breathing hard.

He looked into the older soldier's face. "Guess you're the squad leader now. Sarge got it when the two last mortar hits came over."

"Is he bad?"

"Dead duck," the other answered, "Not pretty. Guts spilling out. Not a good way to die. Medics took him, but he was a goner, you could tell."

"Oh, Christ," breathed another young soldier, "Medics available?"

"For God sakes, is that all you know – "

"'Oh, Christ?' You think He is listening somewhere?" The older soldier was contrite as soon as he said it, and saw the expression on his comrade's face. What the fuck, he was too edgy. Taking a deep breath, he steadied himself.

The sergeant was dead. That made him squadron leader.

He thought how proud he had felt when they made him a corporal, the assistant squad leader. Now he found himself resentful of these other men who would not be called on to lead, no matter what.

Stupid response, he knew. Where was the fucking blowhard lieutenant?

FIFTEEN

1948

"You know what happened back on the first day of German class?" Phil Costello said, settling into the worn leather couch against the wall of the men's lounge. "In a reasonably loud voice, one of those uppity bitches said to the girl next to her, and the room at large, that when she accepted the Vassar offer for the class of 1950, she didn't know she was volunteering for the U.S.O. I should have said something like, 'Merci, mam'selle. Would you care to dance?' but that is the wise-crack you always think about saying later. Then again, I probably would not have said it anyway, if I had thought of it at the time."

"Pretty good line, though," said Ted Collins, "Save it for when the opportunity ever arises again. Otherwise, how goes it now, with some weeks under the belt?"

"Well," Phil drawled, "Okay. I can dig learning another foreign language. I always liked being able to talk to my Italian grandmother in Italian. Only thing, the instructor is a really young German, not much older than me, I think. She has got this really blonde hair, platinum, I guess you would call it, cut in a short mannish way that reminds me of some of the young German P.O.W.s I saw in France. Gives me a kind of creepy feeling. Her being female and looking as she does. One of the *Herrenvolk*, you know. Kind of unsettling, but she is sexy in a kind of icy way."

"Androgynous, she sounds like," said Demi, "Just ran into that term in my Sociology class."

"Well, whatever it is, I sometimes first see her as this teenage German P.O.W. and sometimes, when she wears a short skirt to teach, or shorts in warm weather as she does, I think with those legs she could be Marlene

Dietrich. Got to get my mind off that sort of stuff and concentrate on vocabulary and grammar." Phil shook his head in disbelief.

"She wears shorts to teach?" said Ted Collins, "Incredible."

"She did quite regularly in the warm days at the beginning of the semester. You know, lederhosen is the Deutsch national costume. Perhaps she was being nationalistic or subversive," Phil laughed. "Now she doesn't wear them so much, but believe me, when she sat on the edge of the desk and waved those calves and thighs at us, and I am the only man in this class, I wondered if this was higher education or a peep show, and was the show for me, for the girls, or all of us."

"Always take a look, I suppose, when you are given the opportunity," said Gussie, "Consider it is just aesthetic appreciation, and if the view actually means anything, follow up."

"To change the subject from sex – always an interesting topic but we can overdo it – let me tell you all what I am going to try. Something a little different for me," said Richard Forrest. "I'm taking the Intro to Economics and the teacher is this great guy. Huge fellow. He acts in student plays because they are always in need of men to take the male parts. He stopped me after class and suggested I might like being in one of the student productions. A Shakespeare play. Said I had a good voice. And I said to myself and to him – why not. It would be different for me and it could be fun. I have always sung in my church choir and this could be a bit like singing in public. I figured to give it a shot. Gone to rehearsals already and have a part."

"So, if you feel the need of a claque, we can all come and whistle and shout when you get on stage." Ted Collins laughed.

"You guys, no horsing around. It would just embarrass the girls," protested Richard, "And make me look like an ass."

"We were kidding. We were kidding." The others protested.

"The drama students take themselves very seriously, and some do go on to be big deals. One of them told me she hopes to go to Yale Drama or someplace like that when she graduates from Vassar. I think she will have to be a character actress, though, because she has a kind of long horse-like face, but she really gets into it on stage. Probably will make it if conviction and ambition, along with talent, has anything to do with it. Actually, I like her." Richard sounded very sincere, but he was a serious, IBM type and it was hard for some of the others to tell for certain.

"Well," said Demi, "if she makes it, you can always go backstage, remind her that you and she were in student productions together. A little Broadway glamour might rub off."

"Only trouble is that she is also big on horses. Brought her own horse and keeps it at some riding stable south of the campus. Greenvale Farms, I think is the name. Couple of brothers run it, she told me. One is actually

74

Master of the Hounds at some ultra-social group that call themselves The Rombout Hunt Club." Richard laughed. "They actually ride in a fox-hunt up county somewhere, appropriately near Red Hook. Red Coats and all, Harriet says. She doesn't do that, Sympathy for the fox, I guess. Anyway, she goes riding early in the morning and comes directly to the English class we are in together wearing her riding gear, the whole works, boots, riding jacket and the hard hat, even, and as the room in Rocky heats up, it is exactly like being in a stable before they shovel out the horse shit."

"Look out for those arrested development horse loving girls," Ted commented, "The fascination with horses seems to start just before puberty, the story goes. Sometimes, apparently, they never grow up to be a normal heterosexual woman, or so I have heard. Or maybe it is one of those male myths. Men don't always get, even if they try, which that blow-hard Norman Mailer does not."

"I don't know about this Mailer guy, but she seems normal enough to me, otherwise," said Richard, "The question is, should I say anything about the barn odor, or not?"

"I think it would depend on how seriously interested you are in this young lady – I assume that with riding to the hounds and all that, she is a *young* lady," Demi advised, "It may all seem so usual to her that carrying the horsey smell doesn't register. Or a concern for your own odor absorption?"

"Or you could take up horseback riding yourself," Dominic Calenti broke into the conversation. "Then you can really be rank together." He laughed.

"I thought you guys were here for an education and not for the girls," put in Leroy Freer, "There is more to life than chasing down willing pussy. Service time corrupt you?"

"Yeah?" asked Dom, "What? Why not a well-rounded life? Here I am trying to get an education and also to get it on with Mary O'Donnell, the Dean's secretary. Lot of work. She is Irish and I am Italian. Our families are both Catholic and go to Saint Mary's, and yet they both think we should be dating according to our 'ethnic heritage,' as my father put it. What crap we have to put up with. What would the Pope say? Wonder if his holiness has an opinion? If so, it would be infallible, of course, on this kind of 'mixed marriage' if it comes to that."

"There is the rest of life," went on Leroy, as if Dom had not spoken. "I'm older than you fellows. I know. I have a wife who is working as we speak on the books at Dad's Chevy dealership. She's an accountant. While I was in service she worked for my father, obviously. She wants to quit when I finish the B. A. and I get that good job afterwards, so we can have kids and a house with a lawn, a dog. Sarah says she wants pets and a baby or two or three, and me pushing a lawnmower in the front yard. *That's* what else, Dom."

"Sounds dull as dish water," snorted Dom, "And what I want right now is the prospective in-laws to talk to one another and recognize our Italian Irish American kids when we have them, if and when it comes to that."

"See," replied Leroy, "When it comes right down to it, you're buying into the American Dream, too."

"But with inter-ethnic heritage sex," laughed Dom.

"Right, Leroy. Some of you fellows are just too crude for words," said Bernard Black, who had been standing in the doorway to the lounge listening to the repartee. Bernard was a 'faculty brat' whose father was a professor of religion. He did not frequent the vet's space in Main much, since he had a family home just off campus to go to when he had extended time between classes.

Bernard knew he could have gone away to school, of course, since he might have claimed a Princeton legacy from his father and his grandfather, but apparently the other vets, when they thought about it, which was not often, had observed that perhaps he was too attached to home and hearth to go away when his parents' house was so conveniently placed. Or perhaps he was too much of a mama's boy to leave bed and breakfast.

Or maybe the war had left him with some kind of stay-at-home fixation.

On the other hand, the professor's son dressed as if were actually going to Princeton – genuine Irish tweed sport coats, khakis, and dirty white buck shoes. The word in the Vet's group was that he dirtied them himself with Fuller's earth, but that might just have been a tale told in reaction to his preppy clothing style. The other vet students tended to wear the casual clothing of left-over military life – field jackets, combat boots, khaki shirts, some with military insignia left in place and others just sporting a few stray threads where the badges had been removed. Occasionally, in cooler temperatures, an Eisenhower jacket would appear on the vets from the European theater, but that kind of gear was often too heavy for the steam-heated classrooms.

"So, you actually talk to us," said Dominic. "I thought that condescending to the riff-raff would be out of character."

"Just what do you mean by that?" Bernard said, his voice rising, "I come around. I contribute to the conversation. I report college gossip, you know. I have an in. I don't think that I am that different from you all." His voice had gotten husky as if he might cry, which made the men uncomfortable at this unpredictable possibility.

"Aren't we all just a little too rough and ready for your tea party and raised pinky world?" Dom seemed to be just getting going, surprising the rest of the vets with his vehemence.

"Oh, knock it off, you guys," said Demi, "We are all in this together, and who has time for this kind of crap when there is learning to do?" He felt a bit like he did during the conflict, settling a squabble between two soldiers in his squad. The thought made him shudder slightly.

"'Coarse," said Bernard, turning on his heel and disappearing into the hallway.

"He's okay, really," said Phil, "Just an uptight lonely kind of guy. He likes art. Even paints, apparently. We had a conversation accidentally over coffee in The Retreat. I also heard that he thought about being a CO when the draft caught up with him and then decided to be a medic. Somehow I connected that choice with his father being a Professor of Religion and all that. Big ethical questions, as well as the social status thing, and this riding him. Give him some slack."

"But he can sometimes come off as such a snobby prick," said Dom, "Gets under my skin, you know. Glad he doesn't come to the vets' lounge that often. I suppose he can piss and crap at home."

"As my late father would have said, a putz, nomenclature he learned from his father-in-law. Or to go Italian, *il pistolino*. There is nothing like being the mutt offspring of an Italian father and a Jewish mother. Gets you a good vocabulary," Phil laughed. "Got to be something positive out of that mix, besides inter-family friction, particularly at Christmas and Easter. The Italians wouldn't speak to the Jews until the first baby, which was me, was born. You could say I was the reconciler," he added, laughing again. "I brought the family all together."

"The Greeks have their own word for that kind of fool, *boutsokefalos*." Gussie observed. "A bit longer, you all will notice, but saying it gives you a chance to really draw it out to enhance the effect of the insult."

"So beware of Greeks bearing multi-syllabic insults," laughed Ted.

"You could say that, but in the long run I think I prefer the spitting out of the Yiddish with lots of saliva. Putzzzzz!" Phil said, "That part of the family tended to be more laconic and to the point than the goombahs on the other side who tended toward the stereotypical Mediterranean excitement and fervor."

"I think you had better let it go about Bernard. Live and let live, and all that, as my grandmother would say. She also said things like 'less said, soonest mended.' Full of old Catskill Mountain wisdom with which you academic psych majors will disagree I am sure. Right?" Ted turned to Demi.

"I'll get back to you on that," Demi laughed. "After I take some more advanced courses. But for now, I would agree, most definitely. Let Bernard go his way. It could be that he is just shy."

"Okay, so let's change the topic under discussion. Hey, Demi, I see that you have taken an interest in one of our classmates in the Statistics course." Phil said.

"Well, it is such a dry subject, I have to find something or somebody in that class when my mind begins to go blank under the weight of numbers and formulae," Demi responded, "I know I will need that information for my future profession in Social Work, if I get there, but I find it difficult to keep my attention. Besides, this Nancy smells good. Better than the barn odor you described about the budding actress, Richie."

"I would say she looks good, too," Phil said, "Tall, willowy. Maybe a bit taller than you, you compact Greek. And the perfume is probably at least a hundred bucks an ounce. I would not count on it being just from soap. Not something you pick up at your local drug store."

"I wouldn't be buying her any of that," Demi said, "That will have to come out of her Daddy's allowance for college expenses. Maybe a beer at the College Pub, if I work up the nerve, would be more like it."

"Big spender," said Gussie, "I won't mention this new attraction to Rebia, even though I should have some loyalty to the family."

"It turns out she is some distant relation to William Sloane Coffin. I guess I should have heard of him. Funny last name but big in New England and New York, it seems. I tried looking up Coffin in Who's Who at the library. Bunch of them. Sloanes, too, in fact. Probably a bit rich for my blood, in fact, but she seems down to earth and interesting. She likes to talk about social issues, ethics and politics, in fact. Sometimes seeming a bit off-the-wall in her ideas, but definitely not boring."

"I am afraid I would have to say that Rebia is out of that intellectual league, even if she is my baby sister," Gussie acknowledged.

"My advice is not to get mixed up with high class Vassar girls," Jack Wyzinsky put in, "Stick with the simple local girls. I am. Daughter of a local mortician, she never went to college and doesn't plan to. Women like that don't expect as much. They would know how to fit in here in Poughkeepsie as a married woman, certainly they'd know where to get the best deals on household necessities, groceries, and the like. And hey, maybe they would even be grateful for the chance to be connected to someone who attended this noble institution," Jack gestured around them and they all shared a laugh.

"What are you looking for, a cut-rate embalming job when you need it, keep death in the family?" Demi snorted, "And who said anything about marriage, you dog?"

"Whatever," said Jack, "But just remember my advice. After these high-class Vassar women experiment a bit with the locals and then leave them behind at the Log Cabin Tavern when they graduate. They'll more than likely set out for the expensive Westchester or Connecticut suburbs and the marriage of the century with some conservative banker, lawyer, or whatever."

"Oh, you are just a reverse snob, in your perverse way, Jack – believe it or not. Enough already. Got to go prepare for midterms in the library. Maybe I will study with Nancy Coffin, how about that?" Demi gathered his books and left the lounge.

"Infected," said Jack, "Some kind of social virus has gotten into him."

"He is right and you are wrong," responded Ted Collins, "Give the girls a break. For many, this situation is not covered in the etiquette books or the rules at the posh all-girl prep-schools. The situation is just not like their experience at summer camp where the girls get to play awhile with the boys from the camp across the lake under grown-up supervision, and then everybody goes home and that is that."

"We are outsiders, outlanders, and it is best to know it," said Jack, who was getting red in the face.

"Let me tell you about authentic outsiders," Ted answered, "There is one Negro girl here now as a student. *One.* I knew her in high school because she was the only Negro in that grade level at that time in what the school referred to as the "fast track" classes. I think her younger brother was in the same kind of classes, but a couple of years behind. Her older sister had been, too, and she had gone on to Smith College. They were all smart kids; she was really brainy in the English and history classes that we happened to be in together."

"Is this going to be long?" Jack asked, pretending an elaborate yawn which he covered with a dismissive hand. "Are you bragging, by any chance? One of my best friends is colored, sort of thing?"

"That was your line about Jews, remember? Give me time to make my point, you goon, and be educated. I got to know her in high school and we worked on the yearbook together just before I was drafted. In fact, we occasionally corresponded for a while after that while I was away. Anyway, back in high school, there was one particular English assignment. It was to write a poem, sort of in the style of some prominent poet in our text. Not an imitation, exactly, but at least in the spirit of the original. I tried writing a blues lyric derived from Vachel Lindsay's *The Congo*, but following the pattern of authentic Negro blues instead of in Lindsay's bombastic style. We had to read our adolescent efforts aloud to the class. I was pretty proud of it because I had a record collection that included a lot of Victor Bluebird releases in what they called the 'race series,' and I figured I knew what the model was."

"Come on, Ted, speed it up. I have things to do," Jack said.

"Shut up, I will. Anyway, I read this thing and as I finished this girl, Nan Jefferson, in the back of the room, exclaimed, how dare you try something like that when you know nothing about it, and you think Lindsay is so great with his sneering white-man put-down of the African experience.' And I was just flabbergasted. Miss Finnegan, the teacher, was speechless for what seemed like a full minute, and then went on as though nothing had happened. Others read, and that was that."

"So, tell me, Ted, what is the point you are making?" Jack began to collect his books and notes.

"Well, actually I, in my adolescent way, was trying to imply exactly what she said about *The Congo* and Lindsay, and how it did not speak to the real condition; that it was all phony drama, but I just subsided into my seat. But the thing is, I ran into Nan Jefferson recently in the library. She is a junior here now, having gone from high school right to college while I was in the service."

"So?" Jack was edging toward the door.

"And over a cup of coffee in Main dining room, we continued, sort of picking up from our written conversations." Ted put his hand on Jack's arm to detain him. "She told me again how it has been, once more being the only student of her color here at the moment. Her older sister went to Smith, where there were only a couple from the same sort of background as her. She repeated that students either ignore her, or act as if she were really incapable of handling the work, even though she is doing well in her classes. Some few teachers also apparently reflect these student views. Funny thing, she said that if she had been a foreign student from Congo or Ivory Coast, she might have had a more welcome reception as an exotic, but that as an American she was treated as if she were out of place or invisible, except when she sings in some musical group, apparently,"

"So?" said Jack.

"Now, there you have a real outsider, Jack, and in comparison, you are one of the in-crowd and so are all of the white male students. In comparison. And this place is a bastion of liberal attitudes. Go figure. And it is the 1940s and Harry Truman has just done away with racial segregation in the armed forces. How long does it take for the Civil War to be over, even in Poughkeepsie, New York?"

Jack was silent, but glaring purposefully at Ted, who continued. "Funny thing, she told me, her mother won't let her touch her own hair. No washing, no combing unless done by her mother. How important is hair? When she graduates she is making tracks to New York where maybe her music can be an in of some sort. Or law school, like one of her relatives has managed to do. You and she might be classmates again. What do you make of that? "

"Nothing. I got no more time for this topic, Ted, not if I am going to be prepared for classes tomorrow. Try someone else with the soap box. See you around, unless I see you first," Jack left.

"That Jack is from another universe," said Richard Forrest, who had come into the lounge and listened to the last part of Ted's story, "Although you were getting a bit heated and preachy there, Ted. There must have been some students and faculty who could accept this woman as an individual and not as some, what, interloper or something from the untouchable caste. There are many free-thinking students here, you know, as well as faculty who are enlightened about social issues. You yourself have talked about economics and sociology faculty members who are left-overs from the New Deal."

"Right," said Phil Costello, who had also come in after his class. "Did you happen to go to that debate between the two editors of the Vassar *Miscellany* and the two Yale conservatives? Now that was a show. I felt sorry for the two girls, in fact. Their earnest liberal views were just no match for the malice and sarcasm of those two guys, particularly the short one with the plummy accent. The taller guy with the red hair seemed brighter, but he could be just as nasty and condescending to the point of being personal in his arguments."

"Buckley and Bozell," Ted said, "Yeah, I went. I have heard there was such a thing as a Harvard accent, think F.D.R., but I never heard of an accent like the one Buckley has, would you call it a Yale accent? Or maybe it was because he's from Connecticut. I think the Buckleys live in Sharon or Greenwich or some such expensive enclave. Oil money, you know. He sounded at times like an opera singer or dramatist, all those elongated vowels and soft-trilled r's. It seemed designed to throw the women off the curve, and very superficially affected," Ted observed.

"I don't know about the upper crust accent, but I do know that those two guys were using the British form of debate. That is more attack-dog style than the American approach, which is building a logical argument in as dispassionate way as possible," Richard explained, adding,."I used to be on the debate team in high school."

"Whatever the source of the accent, I kept thinking of the P. G. Wodehouse character Bertie in the Bertie and Jeeves stories. When I was in the eighth grade I read all of them in the local public library," Ted confessed, "when I should have been reading serious literature. This Buckley reminded me of the twit, Bertie Wooster, only meaner. Supercilious, arrogant, and pretentious, in fact. Here we have just come back from defeating fascists in Europe and the Far East, and I get to listen to a homegrown one, some kind of racist crypto-Nazi with the accent of a pseudo-British twit. It was criminal how the two of them put down two well-meaning Vassar students."

"Blessed be the twits," said Phil, "for they shall inherit the earth."

"Buckley and Bozzo," said Ted, "I understand that Bozzo is dating Buckley's sister, who is a student here. Birds of a feather, I suppose. If she is anything like her brother, I'll bet she is a real suburban Connecticut chahhrmer, as Buckley would say it," said Ted.

"I think you are probably doing Bertie Wooster an injustice," Richard said, "Wodehouse portrayed him as well-meaning, if a bit shallow and vapid, but certainly not as a nasty right-wing snob or Nazi-in-training."

"This has certainly been an enlightening bit of conversation," said Ted, looking at his watch, "but it's later than I realized, and I have to go finish up some work for class before I get ready to take someone out to dinner downtown."

"And who would that be?" said Richard.

"Nice girl I met in class. Also from Connecticut, so there is appeal in that state, after all. Actually, she was one of the first few to speak to me. Asked if I had trouble getting to campus after that big snowstorm we had awhile back. Then we talked about the readings for our class, and that led to my inviting her to dinner. Which we will be doing this evening. Sara Bauer."

"Still waters run deep, as my grandmother used to say," said Phil.

"And that means, exactly?" Ted countered.

"I just mean we see some other hyper-hormonal guys drooling over girls, most of whom are not interested or available, and here you are quietly taking a gorgeous one out to dinner. That's what I mean. Under the radar, so to speak."

"Gorgeous maybe, but she is also a really nice girl, smart and interesting to talk to. Liberal perspective, considering her father is some kind of big shot executive at United Carbide." Ted settled into his chair. "Besides, I doubt that you even know which one she is, so how can you comment?'

"Don't get your shorts in a tangle," Phil said, "I meant nothing at all about it. Let's go to the library. We have assignments to do."

"Don't we always," came Ted's answer.

SIXTEEN

1944

"West Africa," she said, "Ghana, I suppose. Or Senegal. My ancestors were clearly West Africans, anyway. You can tell from the wider facial bone structure that pops up on some of us Jeffersons, but not all, until we got modified by the blend of English, Scots, Welsh genes. Moon-face, I call myself when I don't feel that good about being me." She laughed. "At least no connection that we know of with the Squire of Monticello who loved to cohabit with his house slaves."

"Really?" he said, "Is that why you and your sister don't look that much alike?"

"That or my mother was fooling around, and that is not likely. Not my church-going choir-singing mom." She smiled at him. "Those plantation owners, you know, even historic figures like good old Tom Jefferson, they exercised their rights. Lucky my ancestors got sent to the U.S. instead of one of those sugar plantations in the Caribbean, bad as the cotton hoeing must have been, otherwise I might be illiterate, living in a Dominican hovel and eating out of dumpsters."

They were making conversation while waiting for the movie to start. It was *To Have And To Have Not* based on the classic Hemingway story which they recalled having read in their third year English class in high school. Their reminiscing had begun when they started to recall the classes they had taken together, simply to make conversation. Somehow the heated discussion after the reading of Vachel Lindsay's poem *The Congo* in Miss Finnegan's English class had morphed into an exchange about her family connection with the infamous slave trade.

"That poem really pissed you off, as I remember," he said.

"It was so, so, so ignorant and white. Not even the noble savage sort of thing, in fact. Worse than Conrad's *Heart of Darkness*, you know." She frowned. "And it was part of the English curriculum, after Lindsay had been critically praised for his rhythm, his language, his imagery."

"An insult then?" he said.

"Boomlay, boomlay, boomlay, BOOM." she whispered. "*A History of the Negro Race.* Give me a break. Worse than an insult, defamation of character. Made me realize we need an Anti-Defamation League just like the Jews."

"Give it time," he said, "It will come. It has to."

"Long time a-comin'," she said mockingly. "Just my first semester at college, the only brown face in my class of '48, and those preppy girls, when they notice me, act as if I were some rare tropical bird that had gotten blown off course and landed in the Hudson Valley."

"Your sister get the same reactions when she got to Smith?" He watched her profile.

"Well, sort of, except the lesbos thought maybe she was some exotic homosexual and the skin color seemed to excite them into tentative overtures, which only her boyfriend on a visit from Amherst could eventually put a damper on."

"So, that is no problem like that for you at Vassar, Nan, I would suppose, there being no such Smithsonian tradition there, in spite of Elizabeth Bishop, since there is always the counter push from the Mary McCarthy and Edna St Vincent Millay devotees. Sex pots of a sort, you have to admit." He snorted.

"Think this movie will ever start?" she said. She seemed ready to let the subject drop, and he gracefully silenced that avenue of conversation.

At that moment, it did. They watched it in silence. "That Hemingway," he said, as they inched their way up the theater aisle behind the other movie goers leaving the building, "Great writer, I guess, with direct, simple written prose but sometimes the hairy chested thing gets a bit too much. Relief from Henry James, though." He knew he was sounding a bit pompous and maybe a little affected. What did he know about cinema, really? And he had only high school English to draw on. And the free paperbacks the Army put in the rec hall.

"Wonder how he would feel about his movie in a theater named the Bardavon with its Shakespearean echo and that mural over the screen," Nannerl commented.

"Given his large ego, he might think it fitting, since he could see himself as the Twentieth Century version of the bard. Although I think Bogie is not the muscular type I visualize for a Hemingway tale. Maybe the terse dialogue, I guess," Ted said, "And the young female lead would fit in a Hemingway-drawn world, I guess." He knew he was sounding pretentious.

84

"You like that kind of bitch?" Nannerl asked.

"How about a beer at the Pub?" Ted replied, turning the subject away from his likes or dislikes to something simpler.

"You have a beer. I would settle for a Coke," she answered.

He got the drinks from the young woman behind the counter and brought them to the booth by the window. It was dark outside the Pub but the lights of the campus dotted the blackness from down the hill and across the avenue. The headlights of a city bus made slow circles of light as it swung into the space before the main gate to the college.

"I don't really like the taste of beer," Nannerl confessed.

"Acquired taste," he said. "I didn't drink it much until I was drafted, and then everybody drank or smoked and beer was dirt cheap at the P.X. It might be a marketing plot to get us G.I.s all hooked on beer and tobacco, since I can see all the guys I am with – kids, really, eighteen, nineteen years old – going back to civilian life to drink and smoke. That is, if they make it home at all."

"Kids?" questioned Nannerl.

"Well, in basic training, that is." He laughed, mostly to himself. "There was one guy drafted late for some reason, about thirty, and we all called him 'Pop.' How about that. I expect it may be different at my next assignment. After this fifteen-day delay en route, that is."

"What's next?" she asked.

"School," he said, "Near Denver. Going to be better than Mississippi, I hope. Biloxi was an eye-opener for this hick from Poughkeepsie. Only folks lower on the social scale than draftees from the North were the local Negroes." *Should I have said that*, he thought to himself.

The two were quiet for a few minutes. She sipped her coke through the plastic straw and he swallowed three gulps of his beer. The silence was nearly physical.

"Yes," she finally said, "I would not want to live there."

"Neither would I," he said, "Unless forced to by the Army, and then I might go AWOL eventually."

"School," she finally repeated, "What kind?"

"Technical stuff related to machine guns and bombsights on big new bombers, the B-29. Going to blast Japan right out of the water, they tell us, or burn them all to cinders with saturation fire bombs."

"Sounds just lovely," she said. He remembered she was famous in their high school English class for biting ironic statements like that. Particularly about that Vachel Lindsay poem.

"I guess I got chosen because I had been accepted at Dartmouth and R.P.I. before the draft got me. Supposed to be hush-hush, of course. G.E. and Sperry have developed electronic controls that almost think when the right info is entered so even dummies can be smart gunners. Computing sights, they call them. Now, don't leak this to the enemy, Nan." He smiled. "We could both be in deep shit, if you will pardon the language. Army life has infected me, I guess, this hick from Poughkeepsie."

"Okay, I have heard worse," she said, "Not from my parents. They are so resolutely middle class to escape social stereotypes, but I hear worse from the kids in the area around Pershing Avenue." She shook her head. "That is what Vassar is supposed to do for me, and what Smith is doing for my sister, Clara Ann, get us up and away from that neighborhood."

"Into the wild blue yonder, like the Air Corps song," he said.

"More or less," said Nannerl, "Speaking metaphorically."

"Which you do a lot of, actually," he answered.

"You know where my parents got our names? Of course not. Let me tell you. Clara Ann is named after a poet, a Negro woman, Clara Ann Thompson who published a volume titled *Songs From The Wayside* in 1900. Came from Ohio. Somewhere my father and then my mother read about her and then read her writings."

"Okay, so they're literary. Good have to have literary parents," he said, "Encourage literary talents."

"More likely law school, to follow in the footsteps of my mother's cousin, who is some sort of juvenile court judge in New York City. Dad said to me that he wanted better for me than working for the post office, which is what he has done. He got high scores on the civil service tests, and it doesn't matter the color of your skin or your name when you get the top scores, according to my father. You will get the job, even if you don't really want it. He had to settle to bring up three kids in Poughkeepsie. I could have used a more ordinary name, if you ask me, but I am stuck with the name Mozart's family gave his older sister. Unusual nickname and at times a pain." Nan shrugged. "Kids in school make fun of different names. Anyway, Nannerl it is. Mother, being the musician in the family, just liked it and Dad's name is Earl, so I guess I get it. Original, she would say. Makes you stand out, as if there weren't more reasonable ways to stand out."

"So, you are Nan to most people, anyway." He cooled his fingers on his beer glass. "So?"

"Not on official class rosters, for one," she said, "In case they missed the skin color, which is unlikely, the name grabs their attention, at least with some of the first year instructors who actually take attendance."

"Piss you off like the Vachel Lindsay assignment?"

"I try not to let it bother me, and the instructors who don't know what to do with the first name, not their fault, I suppose, although I could do without the raised eyebrows from a couple of them. Particularly my Italian professor with the kinky African hair, those Italians are in a state of denial about their Mediterranean connections, and the English prof. That Miss Turnbull can turn 'yes' into a two syllable word, 'yeah-us,' with a southern drawl. When she talks to me in class she always looks just over my head and not at me," Nannerl sighed audibly, but gently. "I expect better from them."

"Why? Some are as parochial as the sheltered students they teach, considering their upbringing and their education. Old money, some of them, so they can teach here at the lowly salaries they pay and still live very well. Trips to Europe first class and all that. Lily-white, from segregated schools. I supposed it is not Biloxi or Gulfport, Mississippi, or Barksdale Field in Shreveport, Louisiana. One of the permanent cadre at Keesler Field in Biloxi told me about the white country club atmosphere there when he was on that base." Ted shook his head in disgust.

"Maybe," said Nan.

"And did I just imagine it, or did your parents give me a kind of fishy-eyed look when I came to pick you up for the movie?" Ted looked uncomfortable when he said this, and it was on impulse. He had decided not to mention it, and then it popped out.

"Well, what did you expect? First white boy ever to stand in our living room who wasn't delivering something, while I got my things," Nan looked him over her Coke glass. "In some kind of fly-guy uniform to boot. But I did explain that you and I had been editors for the yearbook and that when you graduated at midyear and then got inducted in April that we communicated for part of the Spring about finishing up the book for the printers before you went away. They got it."

"Right. Gave me something to do while waiting for the physical and all that other draft board stuff. Nice to have something on my mind besides following the war in Europe and the Pacific. Thanks, Nan."

"Oh you know, support our boys in uniform and all that patriotic drivel. Besides, we got to continue our conversation about hokey Lindsay, the real blues, other music, and lit. It was fun. Is fun." Nan smiled. "My parents are liberal but very old school. Lots of ambition for their kids but the need to keep them safe and happy."

"I can agree with that," he answered, "So, I should take you home, if you are finished with your coke. I have to catch a train for Denver in the morning. Go up to Albany and then change to cross the country for those technical courses in how to kill people at a safe distance."

"You are being melodramatic, Ted. Cut it out." She stood up and pulled her cardigan around her shoulders.

"Okay, I can do that if you promise we can go on writing to each other. I can give you my A.P.O. number. No other addresses allowed, for security." He stood up and shook his car keys that jangled in the quiet of the pub.

"Can't find a nice girl from high school who would write to a lonely G.I. and support the war effort?"

"Isn't that you, Nan? I suppose Angela Winters may be around, but the last I heard she was dating some older 4F gambler from Saratoga. When we dated in groups in my car because I was the only one with a car and a license, Angela was sort-of with me." Ted grimaced. "On the other hand, she was a dope and couldn't really talk about anything but clothes and movie stars and movies. I think she lived the magazine *Seventeen*. You always have something interesting to say."

SEVENTEEN

1945

It was a green and lush Spring in 1945. The war seemed like it had always been part of his young life. Since 1939 and then 1941. Getting closer and closer. Forever when you are in your teens. Now it had caught up with him.

"Travel orders," said the MP, holding out one hand.

The young soldier pulled them from the inside pocket of his olive drab Eisenhower jacket and handed them up from his seat.

The MP looked them through. His companion MP read over this shoulder.

The two looked at each other.

"Probably going to get you into Salt Lake City about eight hours late. Going on to Kearns?" the first MP asked.

"Military bus pick-up, I guess," answered the young soldier, "They take you out to the Repple Depple, I was told."

"Okay," said the talkative MP, "Tell 'em late trains, missed connections. After all, it's war time. It'll be okay. You should have started earlier, you know, but hard to leave home on these delay-in-route orders. Happens lots of time. Eight hours ain't exactly AWOL, of course. Good luck, soldier."

The two MPs moved on down the railroad car, toward other men in uniform.

He knew he would be late when he started, but his mother and father wanted him home as long as possible, he had arranged to take a girl to the movies on his last night. That was self-indulgent, he knew. He could also tell himself, and it would be true, that he was afraid his father would have another panic attack, thinking he was having some kind of heart problem.

Watching the younger son – only eighteen – leave for the overseas replacement depot outside Salt Lake City was not easy for either of them, but his father seemed the most affected. Odd thing it was his father, not his mother, the young soldier thought. Maybe it was because only about twenty years earlier, his father had gone off, leaving a young wife and a child at home, to serve in World War One. That child had been his older brother, also now serving in the Army Air Corps, in a cushy job as a supply sergeant in Atlantic City. He also had a wife and daughter but lived in an off-base apartment with his in-laws.

"The war to end all wars," his father had said, "What a load of nonsense they sold us back then, and I voted for that blasted southerner, Wilson. It was all about empires, Africa, the far east, India."

"Oh, Albert, he was all right," his mother had protested, "There have been a lot worse since. Think of Coolidge, or Hoover, and that Harding was a crook."

"Right out of high school, yet. I knew I should have paid off that Frank Trumble, two-bit lawyer in town. Look what he did for the Cavanaugh kid." His father was not to be diverted from his rant.

"Oh, Albert, there you go again," his mother had said

"Well, get the Cavanaugh family to buy a bunch of sheep from someone he knew up in Columbia Country and put them out to pasture on their golf driving range as though it were some kind of farm, and then Trumble gives the kid, that one that went to Sunday School with Ted here, a farmer's exemption. What do you call that, but a kind of buying preference? Wonder if the sheep herder gave Trumble a kick-back."

"Legal, I am sure," his mother had said, 'Frank is a lawyer, after all."

"Big difference in being legal and being ethical," his father had returned.

And the young soldier had just wished all that talk would go away, and he would leave for the oversea replacement depot and get on with it, whatever it was to be. He had finished all the appropriate air force schools in G. E. and Sperry computer gun and bomb sights, so get to the next step with the Twentieth Air Force in the Pacific.

He knew that would be it.

The M.P.s had moved on from his car and he settled back in the seat. He was sharing it with a young mother who was anxiously watching the seat facing them where her young husband was sitting with a child on his lap, a little girl of about four. Next to him in their seat was a cloth covered cello that he was protecting as much as he was his child. Perhaps more.

"I'll take Molly," the young mother said.

"Okay, for a while," said her husband, handing over the child, "Got to keep protecting the cello. Too bad we could not put it in the baggage car, but that would wreck it, I am afraid."

The young soldier had seen the couple and their child, who was obviously tired and fussy, waiting with other civilians in the train station in Chicago.

Military personnel were put on one side of a rope barrier and civilians on the other side, because the military got to board first. He thought it was not very chivalrous to do that to the women and children, but who was he to question patriotic favoritism at such a time. After all, he was fighting, or soon would be, to preserve motherhood, apple pie, and Chevrolet or some bullshit like that.

Our way of life, the slogan everywhere, came into his head, along with *Lucky Strike Green has gone to war.* Each hardly made any sense to him. What did, at the moment, he wondered.

He had settled himself in when the ropes were dropped in the station and the civilians streamed aboard. The young couple, child, and cello had appeared at the door of his car, making their way down the aisle to his seat. A sailor sitting across from him moved to another empty seat, so that the couple, child, and cello could sit together. This act was appreciated as there were not too many vacancies in the car by then.

Chivalry is not dead, the young soldier thought, although he himself had not moved. He also could not help thinking that sailors' suits were ridiculous. He supposed he was glad he was in the Army Air Corps.

A bell rang. The train began to move out of the station. The terminal walls seemed to slide backwards, as if they were moving and not the train.

"Look, look," said the little girl, pointing out the window. "The station is moving backwards. Look."

"Just an optical illusion," the young soldier explained, without thinking.

The child turned to him with a questioning look.

Trapped into a conversation, the young soldier went on. "It only looks like the world is moving when it isn't. We are moving. It all depends on where the observer is. If you were on the platform, you would see the train going past you."

All relative, he thought. *Sort of Einsteinian, maybe. Everything is positioned only in relation to something else. Connection, that was it.*

"Oh," said the little girl, and the young soldier wondered if she were old enough to get it.

"Hard to understand that sort of thing when you are only four," laughed the mother, "I find it difficult myself, not to trust what seems to be what I see."

By then the train had burst out into the sun light and buildings rushed by at an ever increasing speed. Another train whooshed past, whistle blaring, going in the opposite direction. "Me, too," replied the young soldier, "but I learned differently in high school physics."

"Not so long ago, I'll bet," said the young father, "If you will pardon me asking, but how old are you?"

"Eighteen," said the young soldier, with some embarrassment at revealing his youth.

"Oh, Lord," burst out the man, "This war has become a Children's Crusade!"

"Hush, honey," said his wife, "Where are you going, if it is not a war secret?" She had turned to her seat mate.

"Well, after Utah, some place in the Pacific, although we don't ever know really until we get there. Wouldn't send you to Europe from the West that way. Some place where they have B29s, since that is what I work on. That's no secret." The young soldier shrugged. "So it will be the Pacific, and you all are going where?"

"San Francisco," put in the man, patting his cello, "Got a string spot with the San Francesco Symphony. Drafting some of the musicians for the war effort gave a less experienced guy like me an opening. New York is probably a better place, but Frisco isn't bad. Up and coming out there in the Wild West. Pierre Monteux is the conductor and he is an innovator."

"Oh, honey, I don't think San Francisco is the Wild West, exactly," his wife put in, "Particularly with Monteux conducting. He is a serious man."

"Maybe not wild, except in some of the musical choices. Anyway, the orchestra has a reputation for playing more modern music, and I dig that." The man patted his cello. "So does Rover, here."

"Rover?" asked the young soldier.

"I named it that," said his wife, "Since it is like his faithful hound, Rover. Loves it nearly as much as wife and child." She laughed. "A man and his loyal cello can't be separated. You can tell that by just looking at us, sitting here with a seat just for Rover."

"So you like modern music?" queried the young soldier, interested. "You mean like Stravinsky? Shostakovich? Prokofiev?"

"Not just the Russians. Ives. Cowell. Schoenberg. Copeland. I love that stuff." The cellist laughed.

"So do I," agreed the young soldier, "My mother, who plays the piano, doesn't. Mozart. Bach. Chopin for her, but I buy records of those other guys and my mother puts up with them. Bartok, Milhaud. I would like to go see San Francisco sometime. Maybe I'll come back through there after the war," Ted continued. "I got to actually see Kansas City while I was stationed at an air corps school near there. Great place with great music. Of course, it wasn't my mother's classical favorites that I heard there. Jazz and blues, mostly, although I went to a concert by Stan Kenton's Orchestra. I guess there is a Kansas City Symphony, too. Didn't have time to check that out."

"That sounds like fun," said the young woman. "My husband filled in on a record date back in the city – New York, that is – when we needed the

92

cash for rent, for one of those big swing bands. Was it Stan Kenton, honey? Somebody like that." She turned to her husband.

"No, dear. Woody Herman," he answered, "They needed a bass player for a recording gig and I can do that as well as the cello. It was a one-shot deal. On the other hand, I've played in theater pit orchestras when in need. Weird experience, actually, hidden down there while things you can't see go on above your head, up on stage. Union scale, not bad in an emergency. That Petrillo knows how to look out for his musicians."

"Not exactly your kind of music, I guess," said the young soldier, "How about Glenn Miller?"

"No, never. Too bad about Miller, down into the Channel and never found."

"Jerry likes all music," said his wife, "Or nearly all music. Maybe not Guy Lombardo, or Kay Kyser, and he really does prefer the classics."

This discussion was interrupted by the little girl who began to make whimpering noises.

"Potty," she said.

"Here, let me take her. You handled it in the Chicago terminal." The young father stood up and took his daughter by the hand. "Watch the cello," he said over his shoulder, as the two of them inched down the aisle, past a few people who were actually sitting on their luggage.

The young soldier and the woman sat quietly for a few moments, looking out of the windows at the country side along the right-of-way and fields beyond. Finally, she broke the silence. "He envies you, you know," she said, obviously speaking of her husband, "He tried to get into one of the military band units, but couldn't pass the physical. Besides, we were married and already had a child and I really didn't want him to go. I don't know why I have to say so, but I know people look at him with suspicion, thinking why he isn't fighting for his country. He would like to be you at some level."

"That's okay with me. Not everybody has to fight," the soldier said, "People have to do what they have to do." He stopped for a moment, "But I would switch with him in a minute, when you come right down to it." He turned in the seat to look at the woman. She suddenly blushed.

Then the two lapsed into silence again, until the man and his daughter reappeared. "Wow, how crowded it is in here," he said as they sat down.

The little girl was quiet. Her eyelids started to droop. She put her head down in her mother's lap, her feet in the young soldier's lap and fell asleep.

Darkness began to turn the car windows into mirrors. The adults fell silent. The musician cradled his cello against his shoulder, as if it were a person sharing the seat. The young wife dozed and then she too seemed to fall deeply asleep. Her head rolled inevitably against the young soldier's shoulder.

He remained still and quiet, watching the reflections of himself, the woman and the child in the glass. He did not want to move and wake her. At times, the mirror images were pierced by lights beyond, from the passing countryside. Farm houses, diners at crossroads, car headlights, would intrude briefly and vanish behind as the train rushed on through the night. At times, the passing lights seemed to be moving back, as had the walls of the terminal. At other times, he could destroy that illusion and feel the train and its occupants moving forward through the night. Sometimes delusion took command about the speed and direction, and sometimes it seemed as if his brain asserted itself and knew the truth of movement.

Like life, he supposed. *Hardly profound*, he thought. *What do I know at eighteen?*

What did he know? He imagined he could hear the opening bars of Shostakovich's Seventh in the rhythm of the train wheels, but then it was gone. Only in his head. Not going to hear much of the music outside his mind where he was going, he thought. Nor did he know where he was going from Utah.

What he did know was this singular moment, was the warm pressure of the woman against his shoulder, a woman he would know only in this part of his journey, and never again. Unconscious in sleep, he felt her warm breath and the weight of the child's feet supported by his lap, as the train and its passengers plunged into the future. Or stood still as the land sped into the past.

That would have to be enough for now.

EIGHTEEN

1948

"What's with Demi anyway, Gussie?" Rebia confronted her brother after dinner at the Karras house.

"Nothing that I know of, Sis. What exactly are you asking?" Gussy looked up from the copy of Time Magazine that he had been leafing through.

"You know, Gussie. When Demi first got home we seemed to want to connect. Movies together, seeing one another a lot. I thought we had become a hot item by the end of that summer. Now I hardly see him except on the street when he is coming or going to the campus. What happened?" Rebia looked down at her hands clasped over her waist.

"Come on, Sis. You're asking your brother about the condition of your love life? Give me a break," Gussie groaned, "And keep me out of it."

"So? I don't have a sister and Mom is no help in these matters. She just remembers what it was like when she was a girl back in Greece. Besides, you must see Demi every day, practically, out there on Raymond Avenue, and talk to him about things, like maybe me or – other girls." Rebia waited for her brother to answer.

He did not.

"There he is, surrounded by these high class girls from expensive prep schools, with families with scads of money, social position I can only dream of. Smart, sophisticated girls with interesting lives, who can talk about stuff I just read about in the society sections of the newspapers like the Herald Tribune or the New York Times. And they have these classes in common where they talk about literature, politics." Rebia might have had tears glistening in her dark eyes."Big ideas that I know nothing about."

Gussie did not really want to know all this, or to watch his sister melt down in their parlor.

"Look, Sis, Demi is working his ass off at his school work, just like most of the vets. I can count on the fingers of both hands the number of men there who planned to go to college when they were in high school. We all have to run like hell to stay in place, you know, and that does not give us a lot of down time to play socialite with the girls you talk of, that actually exist mostly in your imagination." Gussie nearly shook a peremptory finger at his sister. "There are a few snobs, I suppose, but overall I think they are not really interested in Vassar men, not us working class former G.I.s, not when there are the Yale blue-bloods and the gentlemen of Princeton sniffing around the bait."

Rebia dabbed at her eyes.

"There are really interesting young women there, well-read and bright, who want to explore intellectual matters, and to go from Vassar to intelligent careers in science, in theater, in journalism, in college teaching. Ted Collins told me about one who is a lab assistant with him, the only Astronomy major at the college apparently, who is the pride and joy of the chair of the department. This girl is going to make a life career of studying the stars and planets, in the tradition of Maria Mitchell. Hard to compete with that kind of person with that kind of ambition, if that is your aim."

Rebia sniffled audibly.

"If you really want my advice, it would be to get on with your own life. I don't want to be cruel, and I love my sister, but Demi is going to be out of your league when he finishes, or you are going to be out of his, I suppose. Find a nice local boy with good prospects, hook up with him, and have the babies and the kitchen you want. Maybe a house in the suburbs." Gussie took a breath. Listening to his own words, he thought he was beginning to talk like Jack, much to his horror.

"And get the required dog or two, or maybe a cat," snapped Rebia, "Thanks for the candid explanation of my flaws and thanks for planning my life for me."

"You asked," said Gussie.

***

"Haven't seen much of you lately, except coming and going from across the street," said Rebia, "College work keeping you busy?" She leaned against the porch railing with her back to Conklin Street and watched Demi as he put his hand on the door knob of his front door.

"Right," Demi said, "Finals coming up and I want to get good grades. They don't put vets on a Dean's list, that is discrimination, but I want to get the kind of grades that would put me there if I was a regular student."

"Well, good for you," Rebia said, "But I hate to be forgotten, you know." "I haven't forgotten about you, Reb, but I do have a lot of research and writing to do, along with helping out here with Corry. Hardly have time to breathe. Serious studying required, you know. I got ambitious and signed up for a double major and I find that I may have gotten myself in, I hope not, over my head."

"Yes, I can tell you are a serious student, a very serious student." Rebia pouted.

"Look, I am trying to catch up with life. I was on hold for three years, and don't want to waste any more time. I have an education to get. You have to understand that. Now, you have not really begun, still being just out of high school, in fact."

"I think I have begun," Rebia said, "And I am through with school even if you are not. I want to get on with my life, too. I intend to get a good job like Helena in a professional office, law or accounting, and live a good life. I am not some dummy."

"Fine," Demi said, "On the other hand, I don't think you should count so much on me for your social life. Look around at the guys from your high school class. Find a football star and bat your eyes at him. You won't have any trouble collaring a date, I am sure. Branch out."

"Now you are getting mean," Rebia protested, "They are all such kids, you know. Girls mature faster than boys, you know. We learned that in the Senior Problems class."

"The infantry matures you pretty quickly, too, I guess," Demi said, "I suppose that evens it out in the long run."

"You know what I think? I think that being out there on the campus with all those sophisticated girls has made you look at the people like me on Conklin Street with scorn. We are all such small town hicks." Rebia was getting worked up. Sweat glistened on her upper lip.

"All those sophisticated girls? Hardly. I took an art history class with one, Jackie Bouvier her name was, and I remember it because she had these really big eyes and this little tiny voice, who happened to tell me she was going to have to transfer to some college in a big city or go to some European University because the rest of the girls at Vassar were so protected and provincial, and Poughkeepsie was some upstate backwater. So, in her eyes, we were surrounded by girls too parochial for her taste. Those others she felt disdain for? They are the sophisticated girls you are talking about, I suppose."

"Oh, you are going to find answers to all my arguments. You are too smart for me, I can tell." Rebia's eyes glistened with unwept tears. "Too smart for me."

"Just give me some space here, Reb. With Corry to take care of, with my mother run ragged and worn out, with my father roaming the downtown streets of Poughkeepsie or talking to his Greek buddies when he isn't slaving away in the Acropolis Diner because he can't bear to come home and be reminded about Corry, with Cleo and Helena's life on hold while they work at monotonous jobs, dirty and hard for Cleo and not the glamorous ones you imagine Helena has. I have got to get out!"

"That sounds awfully selfish, Demi."

"Probably, and I will feel guilty when I leave. Do I feel guilty just contemplating escape? Yes. But I learned in a sociology course that you cannot let victims victimize you."

"Maybe too much learning is not a good thing," Rebia said, "Makes you hard."

"No, it makes you rational and informed, able to act reasonably."

"Would Timi have been preparing for his life this way, if he had not gotten killed? And had gone to college as your family planned."

"Who knows what Timi would have done? Law? Medicine? Business? Journalism? His plans got cut short in the Ardennes Mountains. If we had both come back, if there had been no G.I. Bill educational benefits, I would probably be either working alongside Cleo in the machine shop at Federal Bearings or flipping hamburgers next to Pop in the Acropolis. But that is not the way it is, and playing the 'what if' game has no point. Or maybe you tell me – what I should do?" Demi patted Rebia on the shoulder.

She shrugged away from his touch. "You can just go to hell, then," she said.

***

"I have been thinking about it," Jack Wyzinsky said while sitting in the veterans' lounge, "Maybe I should change my last name. Make it waspier, you know, or Irish. The law firms around here that have made it seem to suggest that it might be important to have a 'came over on the Mayflower' connection, went to Princeton on a legacy, or else be a combination of Jewish or Irish names. Look at the yellow pages, no Polish names, even though there is a Pulaski Park down near the river. He was a Revolutionary hero, did you know that? People living in the Eighth Ward out on the edge of town most likely never see it unless they are catching a train to the city."

Ted Collins looked up from his book. "Any particular name you have in mind?"

"I thought one beginning with a W so I would not have to change my initials. I have some Arrow shirts with a monogram, so that seems an economical thing to do."

"You already dressing for a court appearance and you haven't even gone through law school or passed the bar exams?" Ted shook his head in wonder.

"How about Wilson? Sort of echo Woodrow Wilson. Or Wentworth? That sounds British enough."

"Why don't you look up the ship's log for the Mayflower. Maybe there was a W on board." Ted smiled. "I would suggest White but my family already has a lock on that one."

"I am not kidding," Jack protested, "It would be a practical career move."

"Jack, I thought your career plans started with staying in your home town, working up in local Republican politics, based on how your outstanding success in high school was rewarded by becoming class president, with some possible sinecure position, perhaps even a local judgeship." Ted closed his book, keeping one finger between pages to keep his place.

"Right. Exactly right. That is my game plan. Be a good party worker, grease the rails to the top, using my war hero status when necessary. I have some medals for the Fourth of July or for Memorial Day parades. Get the local news rag on my side. That should be easy if I join the Elks, and the American Legion for example, or use my Masonic connection. I belonged to the DeMolay chapter in school and that is a feeder league for the Masons. I should have lunch with the hack who is the publisher or with the editor of the local rag. I can be likable when I have to. Butter them up. They want to be stroked like everyone else, and to believe that they are opinion molders." Jack sat back with satisfaction and folded his arms over his chest.

"DeMolay? What is that, exactly?" Ted wrinkled his forehead in a parody of deep thought. "The Elks, I know, as well as the Moose and the Lions. Seem to like those big alpha animals, as do the local business types. Do you know the Lions actually roar before lunch? I wonder what the Elks do to solidify brotherhood, lock horns? Or do the alpha males lock horns politely, of course, although I think for actual elks it is over a nubile female elks."

"Not a joking matter. Those groups have an important function, and how could you get through high school without knowing about DeMolay International? Building leaders since 1919, is their slogan. Hey, Walt Disney was a member when he was young. You had to be asked to join. It was an honor and I belonged."

"The real Walt himself. Now, that's reassuring to know that the creator of Mickey Mouse and Donald Duck was part of the illustrious group. And for what purpose?"

"It was for making life-long connections with like-minded people, and you learned how to lead others successfully and to have a happy, productive life. Belonging opened doors by cultivating civic awareness in the members, developing the concept of personal responsibility and leadership skills. It is a very serious group that mixes a fun approach to life with building important bonds of friendship among young members. You could go to any new place and having been a member of DeMolay would give you a ready-made collection of important civic leaders. You stepped into an important support group."

"Sort of like what the Junior League does for young women. I presume, from your description, which you seem to have memorized from some brochure. There are no females in DeMolay?"

"Any young women would be lucky and honored to be the wife of a DeMolay member and mother his children, but they could not join themselves," Jack noted, "Yes, all males."

"How blessed for the fortunate few women who marry into that group, then. Any mention in all that party line about the intellectual life?"

"Of course, you are expected to do well in your studies and in extra-curricular activities, as well. Sort of like preparing for a Rhodes Scholarship. That is a given, but the emphasis is on the brotherhood and not just a grind. Being well-rounded." Jack looked satisfied with his explanations. "I am getting okay grades here at Vassar. Nothing spectacular, but passing. Maybe I need to go out for play parts, like Rich, to give me a more well-rounded educational career. He said they always need men."

"Except for some of your odd metaphors, greasing the rails doesn't exactly work there, I think, your plan seems quite reasonable if a bit ethically questionable, but have you really thought through how a name change would fit into the scenario?"

"What do you mean?" Jack asked, "What would that have to do with it?"

"You were born in Vassar Brothers Hospital as John Wyzinsky of the local Wyzinsky clan. You went through the local school system as John (Jack) Wyzinsky. Belonged to this DeMolay as John Wyzinsky. Was elected our class president at Poughkeepsie High School as John Wyzinsky. Did your Army duty as John Wyzinsky. Came home with your medal as John Wyzinsky. Plan to get your law degree and go into practice in Poughkeepsie with an eye on an eventual judgeship. Are you suddenly going to appear as John Wilson or Jack Wentworth? What happens to all that careful preparation? All along the way you have been a Wyzinsky. Think about it." Ted sat back.

"Oh, I didn't consider all that. You could be right." Jack frowned. "I did like the sound of John Wilson, though." In a sudden burst of honesty, he added, "If you had had to deal with people calling you a dumb Pollack behind your back and sometimes to your face, you might consider a name change yourself."

"Jack, calling people ugly ethnic nicknames is the great American custom we like to ignore. Think of them. Kike, Heeb, Spic, Paki, Canuck, Nigger, Kraut, Bohunk, Gook, Coon, Frog, Greaser, Gringo, Nip, and on

100

and on. No escape, apparently, from the need of some unhappy people to identity others with derogatory names so that they can feel superior. Even Wasp can be seen that way." Ted shook his head. "What can you do, but look forward to that time when things will change. People will get educated, we hope. As an educated Polish American you can do your part."

"I know you're right," Jack agreed, "Still, it is hard to take."

"I recommend that you stick with your birth name." Ted nodded. "The Poles will rise in the Hudson Valley as many try to escape from behind the iron curtain, and you could cash in. Maybe become an immigration lawyer, for example. And remember Poughkeepsie has honored that great Revolutionary hero, Casimir Pulaski with a park, as you said, and a statue. Perhaps you can incorporate that history into your grand political plan. If you want something less political, think Kim Novak, Chicago born polish movie star. She believed she could succeed with a Polish name, and she refused to change even after the Hollywood opinion molders told her she could not become a big star with a 'pollack' name. You could turn the name to your advantage. Think about it."

"I suppose," Jack grudgingly admitted.

"Have you met the foreign student in our class from Poland. Nice girl, not exactly Kim Novak, I am afraid, although I think her father may have been a German sympathizer in our late lamented war, based on the dictum that an enemy of my enemy is my friend. For Poles, that enemy is always Russia, considering the history of national bigotry, even if that means aligning oneself with the Nazis. Although I suppose he was de-Nazi-fied if his daughter could get in here."

"Didn't know there was such a person in our class," Jack said, "I think I would be especially careful if there was a Nazi connection."

"You could ask about her from Demi. I believe that his friend, Nancy Coffin, may have adopted the girl. Miss Coffin seems to be the sort of kind soul who adopts strays and this Polish girl seems to qualify as a stray, or at least she has not accumulated a wide circle of Vassar friends."

"I think I will pass. Didn't I tell you my advice about steering clear of entanglements with Vassar girls, and sticking with the locals. I suppose a real Polish wife could be an advantage in my career plans for Poughkeepsie, or maybe she would be too worldly to live in the Hudson Valley with a small town lawyer."

"Good Lord, Jack, who said anything about a wife! I just thought you might be curious about such a person. Explore your roots. Expand your world view a bit." Ted shook his head at Jack's observations. "Her name is Blanka Pavlik, in case you change your mind."

"I most likely won't. Polish Jew, by any chance? If there are any left. Got to think about getting into law school, anyway, and the kind of planning that will take. I am settling on either Fordham or St. John's. Kind of lean a bit more toward Fordham, actually. Either one would be okay." Jack looked down at his hands. "Sort of embarrassed to say it, but going down to the city and finding my way to either of them gives me the jitters."

Ted looked at Jack's clasped hands. "Haven't you ever been to New York City?"

"No."

"But you have been to other big cities. Maybe not as large as New York, but big enough while in the service. How about Kansas City when you were stationed in the middle of the country. Great place for jazz. Foreign cities, too, in fact. So what is the big deal?"

"I usually stayed on the base unless I went with an army buddy, even in Europe and England. Little towns near the base were not so bad. I knew I could not get lost, but the big cities, no way." Jack colored as he made these admissions. "And when there was a troop movement we all went as a bunch and were shepherded like so many cattle from place to place. No danger of getting lost that way."

"Jeez, Jack, what did you do on leave and have to go it alone? That is some kind of phobia. Maybe therapy would help. Have the problem in the service?"

"That is when it first began. I was okay before," Jack looked embarrassed. "In high school. Of course, I stayed mostly in Poughkeepsie and Duchess County anyway. New York City never seemed to be attractive to me. Everything I needed was right here. The idea of subways seemed a bit scary."

"Good thing General Patton did not know all about your phobia when you were serving under him. If he had gotten that close to you in combat, he might have pistol-whipped you," Ted was serious. "Tough hombre, that Patton. Wouldn't put up with all that battle fatigue shit."

"I knew you would kid me about this if I told you, but my palms get sweaty and I feel as if my heart is racing. I jump if I hear loud noises. Wasn't always this bad, not in school anyway, but since I was drafted, more or less, it has been a problem. And I am not going to tell my personal problems to some stranger shrink, nor to the Chaplain when I was overseas."

"That's what they are for, to deal with personal problems, but that sort of thing is your choice. I tell you what. I will go down with you to visit Fordham, and then we can take in a Yankees' game. Both are in the Bronx so it would be an easy jaunt. I have been wanting to see a game and I would like to see Vic Raschi pitching to Yogi Berra just once. Maybe we can pick a day game when that will be the battery. What say?" Ted waited.

"Would you do that, Ted? That would be great."

"After Fordham lets you in, you will have to handle the trips down on your own." Ted laughed.

"I can do that," Jack said, "I will know the way. Let's just hope they let me in."

"We can pick a date in the spring," Ted answered, "That should be soon enough. After the baseball season starts."

NINETEEN

1948

"Gee—zus! You mean no more opera and no more bridge games? What the fuck? Who says so, anyway?" Phil Costello looked up from his book. "What will Rodolpho Fanelli do, our sing-along king, our own Italian tenor, who thinks he could have been a Caruso?"

"Poor Rudy," said Chris.

"Who do you think? Dean Winifred in her inimitable southern accent. At least I assume so. It might have been President Bloomer, of course, but Dean Thomas delivered the news." Richard Forrest sat forward on the worn leather coach against the Vet's lounge wall.

"Opera? Bridge?" The list raised Jack from a semi-doze in the corner. "Who the hell wants to listen to opera or to play bridge? You raise your pinky when you say those words?"

"Just because you are a Philistine, Jack, it does not mean we all are. Some of us like good singing. I sing in my church choir," answered Richard. "I enjoy vocal music."

"And we mathematically and logically inclined enjoy the science of Bridge," said Leroy, "So don't knock it."

"Okay, okay." Jack retreated.

"We managed to get through all of last year without a screw up so what happened now?" asked Demi.

"Well, the scuttlebutt has it that a female student and one of us, a specimen of the dangerous males on campus got caught *in flagrante*, as one says in the law," explained Ted Collins, "Out they both went, probably escorted off campus without a chance to pack, before they infected the rest of the student body. Unfortunate, but not surprising, given the concerns that will be raised by any of the parents."

104

"I heard that one of the White Angels caught the vet trying to get out of a first floor window in Main building after the lock-down hours," Dom reported, "I guess those women take the nick name seriously. Angelic as all get out."

"Just doing her moral duty," commented Demi, "Right up to the Hudson Valley middle class standard of responsibility. *In loco parentis.* That is also probably what they pay the Angels for."

Ted laughed. "Not really funny, of course," he said, "More of a damn shame, since it only confirms the worst fears of some members of the college staff, expressed when the one hundred plus of us appeared like magic in this sanctuary for virgins, which is probably a public illusion supported by college and in all actuality, it's a latent parental myth here in the late nineteen forties. Whatever happened to the standards, or lack thereof, from the Jazz Age? Where is F. Scott when we need him!"

"So, what about the threat that was made early on in that wonderful greeting by Dean Thomas that if there were any 'male-female problems,' the perpetrators of the 'blazing offense' would be summarily kicked out and the vets' program terminated forthwith?" Demi spoke the question that every man in the lounge had begun to think about.

"That is the sixty-four-dollar question," said Ted.

"Well, actually, I nosed around when I first heard the report of this event," said Dom, "I was in the library, so it was whispered to me, of course. So I called on my special I.R.A. connection in the Dean's outer office and she said, not for attribution, that because there are now a lot of local vet students taking classes, to terminate the program would not be in 'the best interests' of either the men or the college. Think of the nasty publicity over the missteps of just two sexed-up young people. A P.R. disaster in the making, not to mention a town-gown catastrophe, and a failure to live up to the Vassar pledge to do its bit for the heroic returning war heroes, as asked for by the State University of New York."

"So, what are you saying, Dom?" asked Chris, "We go on as if nothing had happened?"

"No, I didn't say that. Just a tightening up of the hospitality rules. That is why our little Saturday afternoon recreational sessions in the Dexter suite will be forbidden henceforth. Off limits," said Dom, "According to my informed source."

"What do you mean? Males have been allowed in girl's rooms during specified times of the day, as long as they sign-in with the 'White Angel' on duty, and get out when the free time is over. You stumble over Yale so-called men all the time, availing themselves of that right. They banned, too?" Phil looked aggrieved.

"Apparently not," said Dom.

"You mean two sets of rules? One for vets and one for visiting firemen from acceptable elite schools like Yale, Harvard, Columbia, Texas Christian?" Chris was looking more outraged at each revelation.

"We see the administration separating the sheep from goats, here, and in the process they are fulfilling the *in loco parentis* expectations of the prosperous parents who have sent their innocent darlings to this institution and are paying big bucks to see that the college does its duty," Leroy finally added his commentary, "What do you expect?"

"What I want to know is who is the schmuck who has queered it for the rest of us, anyway?" Phil looked very angry.

"My informant said it was Ben Meyers," Dom said, "Back to Wappinger Falls for him, pronto."

"Ben?" said Phil, "The quiet guy who never spoke in class? Never caused waves? So we have seen the last of Ben. He most likely won't be missed, but what a shame. And the girl?"

"Betsy Muntz. A sophomore from somewhere in the middle west, like Kansas or Iowa or Wisconsin. Wealthy boondocks."

"The revenge of the M and M's," joked Ted, "Hard and crunchy on the outside and sweet and soft on the inside."

"'Taint funny, McGee," said Chris, "Nor is it fair, to make a distinction between men from other colleges and men from here. We should protest or something."

"How about organizing first?" Ted offered, "Then with the power of a group we can ask for parity. Why should one bad apple jeopardize the future of a group as large as ours, I would ask."

"I don't usually like to make waves," said Jack, "but I agree that organizing is a good idea, and I volunteer to organize the organizing."

"I watched him organize his campaign for class president in high school," Jack informed the others, gesturing at his old schoolmate.

"Right up his alley," agreed Ted.

"Right. We will write a brief constitution for a Veterans Association and apply for club status on campus. Lots of clubs here, with administrative support, even budgets, in fact." Jack could not conceal his enthusiasm.

"See," Ted pointed out, "Politics in his blood."

"And then we take a group protest to Dean Thomas and President Bloomer about the unfairness of the double standard." Jack sounded gleeful. "Okay, boys?"

"I suggest we call in the Dexter sisters, since it is in their suite where our nefarious activities might take place," Demi smiled.

"Our very own Babes in the Woods. Who could ever think that they could be involved in some kind of Saturday afternoon orgy. And their eagerness for justice and equality will not be denied, you bethcha," Phil agreed, "Their strength is the strength of ten because their hearts are pure," He paused and then added, "And Baptist from Oklahoma."

"You guys are something else," said Leroy.

And so it came to pass that the ban lasted only two weeks and fell before the onslaught of the Dexter sisters and the newly formed Veterans Association. As Demi said, it was a problem inherent in the original rules that an all-female college would put in place to protect the young women as their parents would expect. The college was just having difficulty adjusting to co-education.

"It is not really that the administration is out to get us," Demi said, "They are learning about co-education along with the students, both the women and the men. Can't be easy."

***

"You remember my story concerning that instructor of German I told you about back when I first took the class? The young one that taught sitting on the edge of the desk and wore really short shorts on some days?" Phil asked Demi out of the blue one day while they were sitting in the vet's lounge. The two were alone for that moment and Phil seemed to want an audience of only one, since he had been waiting for others to leave. "Fraulein Sander?"

"Sure," said Demi, "You still taking German with her now? Guess you got over seeing her as some transvestite SS officer."

"Oh, I was wrong about that. She just had a very stiff and formal way about her at the beginning of that first semester. You know, really young instructor establishing decorum and hierarchy in the opening days of class, I guess, although she now seems to encourage lots of class participation, in German, of course. Anyway, she has loosened up by now. Actually, I am now taking a more advanced course with her."

"Really," said Demi.

"Yeah. When I got an A for the introductory year, she told me I had a real aptitude for languages and she hoped she would see me in another class so I signed up for more German, including literature, and that is where we are at the moment."

"Goes better with the short shorts?" Demi snorted, "Sure she isn't from the Island of Lesbos appearing like that in a class full of young girls and you?"

"What?" said Phil.

"Sorry," Demi said, "Greek reference. Sappho and all that."

"I get it, and no, not at all. That's what I want to ask you about." Phil reddened and looked at his hands. "By the way, turns out she and I are about the same age. She was getting her formal education while I was getting my informal education in drills, gun fire, and mud."

"So, ask away. You can lie down there on the couch because the Doctor is in and ready to listen. Cheap. Nothing an hour." Demi first decided to make a joke of this, but he realized quickly that that was a mistake. Phil was obviously very earnest about whatever it was that was bothering him about Fraulein Sander.

"I had a short late paper to turn in for her class. Something about Hermann Hesse that she had me do, since, as she said, I really have an aptitude for languages and could do reading that the girls were not yet capable of. In fact, she said I could bring it around to her apartment in the faculty housing below the Alumnae House. Hesse won the Nobel in literature a short time ago, you know, important German guy, and she said I would be interested in his take on seeking spirituality outside of society."

"Bare thighs and spirituality outside of society? Intriguing mix, I would say," Demi commented.

"Come on, cut it out. I am serious here," Phil protested.

"Sorry, sorry, I will curb my quips. But sounds like you are really into this German, the author, the lit, I mean. Sorry, couldn't help myself. I will shut up and just listen."

"She asks me in. Small apartment, full of books. But with that temporary look, you know. Cement blocks and boards to hold the books. Bricks for book-ends. Asks if I would like a cup of coffee or tea while she just sort of skims my paper. See if it seems to be on the right track. Does this seem unusual to you, Demi?"

Demi shrugged. "I would not know what is usual or unusual in these circumstances, what with no experience in the matter. What did you think?"

"Well, I didn't want to appear to be some kind of a schmuck, in case she was just being hospitable, so I took a cup of coffee. Boy, was it strong. She looked over my paper and I waited." Phil cracked his knuckles.

"Don't do that," Demi said, "It always gives me the creeps."

"Sorry. Do it when I get nervous. So, after a while she says that a cursory skim tells her that I have given a perceptive reading of the book and, with a little editing, I – 'we,' she said – could submit it to an undergraduate critical journal. Isn't that something? It seems the college has one. Some geography professor advises for it, supposedly for outstanding undergraduate work."

"All this sounds harmless enough so far," commented Demi, "Even an expression of praise, I would say."

"I thought that, too, and thanked her for the laudatory comments and then she said that it could use just a little editing, sort of tighten up the prose, and perhaps get a few more references that she could recommend, and that although she had to run or she would be late to a class she said why

108

didn't I come by some evening in the very near future, very near, and work on it with her."

Demi widen his eyes in make-believe shock. "Well!" he said.

"There is my dilemma," Phil said.

"You mean you have not availed yourself of this opportunity as yet?"

"Don't kid around here, Demi. "What do you think I should do?' Phil cracked his knuckles again.

"It sounds like, just sounds like the sort of gambit male faculty, if my reading is any indication, have often used. Maybe turn-about is fair play, or maybe it is all very innocent."

"What do you mean about a gambit?" Phil started to crack his knuckles but stopped in time.

"If you could find it, you might read a novel about Vassar that came out about 1941, *Consider the Daisies*. Somehow, I doubt it is in the Vassar Library fiction section, but it might be. The acquisitions librarian could be open-minded. There is talk in it of intimate student-faculty relationships, although not exactly what you seem to be alluding to, but relevant. Background material, I guess you could call it. Other than that, I have no advice." Demi shook his head, then added, "Get over that knuckle cracking," he said. "Although I suppose it is better than biting your nails. At least more macho."

"You are not much help, you know," Phil complained, "I thought you wanted to go into psychotherapy as a social worker."

"Best I can do, given my limited experience so far in the matter. But I could use it in creative writing class if I pretend it is fiction. I need stuff like that, racy, to support my double major," Demi shrugged. "Therefore, you are on your own and we are talking about consenting adults here."

"Anything I should know about?" asked Richard Forrest, coming in just at the moment to hear the final remark, "Consenting adults?"

"Nothing of importance, not really," Phil said and scuttled out the door to leave Demi to deal with the question.

"So?" Rich continued.

"Just as Phil said, nothing of importance. So, how are doing with your thespian extra-curricular activates? Turn out to be fun?"

"Yes. I think I told you that I have sung in a men's chorus connected to my church for quite a while, and that is a kind of acting performance, but this play stuff is a whole different thing. Really challenging, inhabiting the character of a character and telling a story while you are doing it with a bunch of people all doing the same kind of thing. And it all has to fit together." Rich shook his head in wonderment.

"So you religious or just like to sing?" asked Demi.

"Normal, as to religion, I suppose. That came with my family, but I do like to sing, there is a kind of comradeship in the group and the chorus sometimes travels to places I would not ordinarily go, so I like the experiences. And I sort of feel the same way about the theater kids and the few faculty who join in." Rich looked a bit embarrassed about the admissions.

"Maybe you have found a whole new career," Demi said.

"I don't think so. Economics and business is more to my interests, just as it is for Professor Ellsworth who talked me into this, but it is important for some of the women and some are really very good at it. This Harriet Snyderman, who is the horse loving girl I mentioned earlier. Now, she is definitely dedicated to an acting career. Talking about Yale School of Drama after Vassar, or someplace like that, and eventually legitimate theater, maybe Broadway in her future or off-Broadway at first. Got to admire that kind of ambition, grit and determination, particularly if one also has the kind of talent she obviously has."

"Sounds like you have developed an admiration, may I say, interest in this Miss Snyderman?" Demi looked at Rich.

"I guess you could say that," acknowledged Rich, "It's funny, I sort of forget that she has a long nose and not one of the cute buttons the girls of my uninformed youth had. I can even say that she has a long sort of horsey face, and still feel attracted because it is an interesting face, you know, and she is really smart. And she does clean up well after the riding to the hounds, or whatever it is she does at the Greenvale Farms with her Eastern Shore horse."

"That last item is really important, Rich. Glad you mentioned it." Demi laughed.

"Oh, you know what I mean," Rich protested, "Anyway, I really feel that doing this theater thing has given me the sense of what it is to be a real college student. Professor Ellsworth is a fount of economic knowledge as well as acting technique, and doesn't feel that there is anything odd in the combination. The female students have begun to treat me as just one of the guys who have this problem to solve, which is how to put on this Aeschylus thing and make it as authentic as we can. They have this classics professor giving us advice, for example. He has kind of affected mannerisms, in fact, with an eye for the pretty girls, but is also very knowledgeable."

"Now, believe it or not, Aeschylus is someone I know something about. Greek guy, influenced by the Persians who invaded Greece. The Greeks won, of course, against all odds! Really big deal for my father who replays the battles over and over again in his spare time." Demi laughed, but he was obviously proud of his father's acquaintance with his national artistic and military history. "Maybe you need my father to give you some insights into the spear carrier you are playing. Drop around at the diner some time. Free cup of coffee on the house. And a *loukoumades*. That's the Greek version of the doughnut, but a million times better that the usual American diner

110

variety. Mom really knows how to make 'em and we bring them to the Acropolis. And you know what? The cops really love them. They take their doughnut break at the one and only Acropolis Diner."

"Sounds good. Maybe I will, and bring along Harriet. She said she would like to get to know what authentic Poughkeepsie is actually like. Could use knowledge like that in theater. She said all she ever sees of the town is the bus stop outside of Main Gate, glimpses of Main Street from grimy bus windows, and the tacky railroad station, dark and sooty."

"Or the bus out of town to New Haven, I would bet. So give her something new at the Acropolis," urged Demi, "Won't be exactly exiting but it certainly will be authentic."

"I may just take you up on that," said Rich.

***

"Mr. Christopoulos, I want you to meet my classmate and fellow performer in Greek tragedy, Harriet Snyderman, Hattie to her friends." Rich sat down on one of the counter stools and waved Hattie to the next one. "I brought her in to let her see the authentic Poughkeepsie, and have a cup of hot coffee and one of your wicked Greek pastries."

Hattie stood up to lean over the counter and extend her hand to Mr. Christopoulos. She was the best-dressed person in the Acropolis Diner, wearing a light lavender sweater set, the cardigan unbuttoned over the mock turtleneck sweater beneath it. A simple single strand of pearls glistened in the florescent light. She had on a glen plaid skirt, nylon stockings, and penny loafers. Slightly shorter than Rich, she was relatively tall, thin in body and face, with the prominent nose that Rich had mentioned to his fellow student veterans. She had an air of self-confidence mixed with the puppyish air of youth.

"So glad to meet you," she said quite formally.

She had dressed up for her foray into the genuine town, Rich had realized when he picked her up. Kind of naive but charming, Rich thought.

Mr. Christopoulos turned from the grill, wiped his hands on his apron, and reached out to shake her hand. "Well, I don't know how authentic Poughkeepsie it is here, but it is certainly an authentic Greek diner. You know what they say, put two Greeks together and they open a diner." He laughed.

"Oh, Mr. Christopoulos, Rich has had nothing but praise for your coffee and the Greek pastries you prepare, not to mention other authentic dishes. I love lamb, you know, and Rich says you make the most delicious baked lamb with yogurt sauce. They all sounded so delightful when he described them. They would be wonderful after the dull meals the Vassar dorm dining rooms offer, and certainly not anything like what we eat on the

Eastern Shore in Maryland. One can even get tired of crab cakes." Hattie sounded so enthusiastic that Rich could not help but smile.

"We will have to come back, then, at lunch or dinner time, Hat," he said, "How about it?"

"Absolutely," she answered, "Just say when. Maybe after a matinee performance, to celebrate."

"You say you two are acting in a Greek play?" Mr. Christopoulos asked.

"Yes," they both said in unison. Rich waved Hattie on and remained silent.

"We first did a Shakespeare together and now the drama department is working on *The Persians* by Aeschylus," Hattie explained.

"They are always desperate for men to take a male part which explains why they tolerate such a klutz as me, but I find it great fun and challenging," Rich said modestly.

"You are really good, Richard," his companion protested, "You get right into the part."

"Well, I just follow directions and see what Professor Ellsworth is doing, since he has the experience."

"The Persians," replied Mr. Christopoulos, "The Greeks win. Nice play. I have read it a number of times, as has my son, Demi, but he is not someone who would feel comfortable on the stage, I believe. At least, that is something he has never tried in school, to the best of my knowledge. And you, young lady, theater is going to be a career for you?"

"Yes," said Hattie, "I just love it. I want to be in serious plays eventually in New York City, with a stop first in some really topnotch graduate program in theater. Maybe even work myself into directing, eventually. I just lose myself in drama."

"Well, be sure you find yourself later," said Mr. Christopoulos, "It sounds like quite an investment you are making in the future. Marriage and children, too?"

Hattie laughed, "Oh yes, eventually, of course, but at first one has to establish oneself."

"I imagine so," agreed Rich rather somberly.

"My father says he will subsidize me along the way, if necessary, although I think budding actors are waiting on tables in all the restaurants in the city and I am not too proud. I can do that for my art. He says he is not a Medici, though, and if I have not made it by thirty it will be law school for me. I think he would actually like me to join him in his practice in Maryland, when it comes right down to it, but he has never discouraged me. My mother is a support, too. She wanted to be an actress herself, she said, but taught in the grade schools before and after she married. Her parents who had to deal with the Great Depression said teaching was always secure, particularly for a single woman, and that is the way she went. But she hasn't been the cartoonish stage mother one hears about, not a Mrs. Temple. She has just been encouraging."

"Here you go," said Mr. Christopoulos, putting coffee and pastry in front of each, "Sugared Almond Cookies – *Kourabiethes* – light, goes well with Greek coffee. *Bon appétit*, as we Greeks would say -- if we were French, of course," Demi's father laughed, enjoying his own little joke.

"Looks delicious, Mr. Christopoulos," Rich said.

"Yum," said Hattie, taking a bite.

TWENTY

1948

"Reading a book for a class assignment?" asked Mr. Christopoulos of his younger son, who was sitting in the corner of the couch under the brightest lamp in the room.

"Sort of, for a Philosophy course." Demi responded.

"Sort of?" his father said.

"Well, it is not on the reading list because it is actually more theology than philosophy, but this girl in the class suggested I might find it interesting given what we were studying in ethics."

"Religion is not about philosophy, son?" Mr. Christopoulos looked inquiringly at his son.

"Not in a Vassar philosophy course, Pop. For theology you got to take a religion course and the philosophers at Vassar do not seem to regard offerings in the Religion Department rigorous enough. Theology isn't rational because it is faith rather than reason, at least that is what my professor said. But this girl was so enthusiastic about the book, I thought I would give it a whirl." Demi closed the book, but kept one finger between the pages to save his place.

"What is it about exactly? Something I could understand, you think?"

"*The Nature and Destiny of Man* is the title. Some lectures he gave in 1940. That is, the writer, Reinhold Niebuhr, is professor at Union Theological Seminary."

"That is a big topic, I would say," noted Mr. Christopoulos, "Your philosophers don't think that sort of thing is exact enough? And how does this Niebuhr get that down in one series of lectures? I would think it would take a lifetime to address all that. So, if you can explain some of the points

114

to a Greek diner owner, why don't you tell me why it is important to read this book."

"I was interested because he takes on the morality of war and since I have recently been saturated with war, I wanted to see what a big thinker like this man would have to say. I want to think I was doing a noble thing, and that, incidentally, Tim lost his life for a noble cause."

"Of course, he did," said Mr. Christopoulos, "They are planning to put up a large marble memorial in Arlington with all the names of the men who gave their lives to defend our nation. Timi's name will be there for everyone to see for as long as that marble lasts."

"I know we all want to believe that this war was the 'good war' and certainly all rational people will say that Hitler was a kind of monster and that his treatment of thousands and thousands of people was morally repugnant, even hideous and gruesome, to put it mildly," Demi said, "But there is something to be said for examining the reasoning, or lack of it, behind the decision to go to war. Stalin was instrumental in killing more people than Hitler but he was our ally. So it seems our decisions are often not ethical but political."

"I think you are getting too deep for me, but go ahead until I ask for mercy. I always like to learn new things when I can." Demi's father settled back in his chair.

"Well, for starters, this Niebuhr said that the surprise bombings of Hiroshima and Nagasaki were morally indefensible, as he put it. I wonder if I should tell Ted that. Anyway, he says that while patriotism is advanced as a good thing, it changes individual unselfishness into national egoism, not a good thing. No one really sits down to talk. Even talks usually have to do with nationalistic ego and individual power. Someone said that war is diplomacy by other means. Something like that, anyway."

"This explanation is full of two dollar, maybe ten dollar, words, Demi. Can't you make it a little simpler?" asked his father.

"Well, you see, Pop, according to this theologian, the projection of generous instincts of self-sacrifice from the individual to a collective object is a psychological jump that contributes a new and unnecessary evil to the life of the group or society." Demi paused. "See?"

"Not exactly," shrugged his father, "Still too many of those ten dollar words for a simple Greek diner owner."

Demi tried again. "The unselfishness of the individual makes for the selfishness of nations. Think Greeks and Persians, Pop. That should be familiar. Consider your favorite topic, the Peloponnesian War. All those heroic Greeks and Persian doing and dying out of a sense of individual self-sacrifice and instead what you get is hordes of Greeks and Persians dead or maimed in order to prove the Greek nation is are more powerful than Persia. By now, who cares?"

"We Greeks do, Demi, and probably the Persians, but I do get your point. Individual self-sacrifice feeds into power plays over which nation is the winner. Everything is about power, isn't it?" He paused. "We do live in a winner takes all society. In the original Olympics, you know, no one bothered to keep track of who came in second or third, the way they do now. No silver or bronze medals."

"Alpha male leaders vying for power, Pop, and the general population takes the rap. Young men fight old men's wars," said Demi, "Masking reality with definitions of 'good wars' and 'bad wars.' No one really sits down to talk, really talk, about conflicting issues or there might be no proving ground for national ego or the power of individual leaders. What was Hitler but an egomaniac? Maybe Winston Churchill was one too, but he was on our side. We talk about these things at the American Veterans' Committee meetings over Brad's Bakery and what it means for the future. We wonder if they talk about such concepts at the American Legion Hall on New Market Street. Some of our guys who tried out the Legion just to see what was up with them say that mostly they talk over beer about World War One as if it were some big Boy Scout Jamboree or high school sports."

"Don't be too harsh on the old boys, Demi," admonished his father, "I talk to some of those men in the diner or walking on Main Street, and they are okay people at heart. The first World War was the only big thing in their lives. It was the event that got them away from Poughkeepsie and they came back, forgetting the bad times and remembering the wonder of foreign countries, even if it was only being stationed in Texas at the Mexican border."

"True," offered Demi.

"None of them is Alexander the Great," added his father, "On the other hand, Sophocles, over two thousand years ago, did dramatize the evils of war, you must admit, so we are not dealing with new ideas here. And none of this belongs in a Philosophy course, but in a Religion course at your college? Sounds like philosophy to me and something the great Greek philosophers would be tussling over."

"Me, too," said Demi, "and I will have to see if Bernie Black can tell me, if he will, why there is this condescension to religion courses in the Philosophy Department. He is one of the vets, although his father teaches in Religion. On the other hand, I do know that religion is never really reasonable, the way logic and philosophy is, and true believers often want to impose their faith on others because they think it is the absolute word of their god. Then if that happens, democracy becomes extinct."

"You are turning out to be a born-again skeptic, Demi," his father said, "Probably a very good stance to take in this all or nothing society. You are a new Pyrrho of Elis, I guess."

"Guess you are right, Pop," Demi said.

116

Demi wondered to himself if he could get the straight dope from such an interested party as Black, and whether it was worth the effort to address Bernard Black at all, since he seemed to mock the low cultural level of the other veterans. *Funny guy,* he thought, *I wonder why he decided to be a student at his father's college.*

"And you are reading this weighty book because some girl told you too? What influence she must have on you! Really some girl, I take it."

"Aw, Pop, don't make a big deal out it. She just said it had been important to her and she was thinking of taking graduate courses at Union with this theologian. She is interesting and passionate about ideas and doesn't seem to mind I am Greek, the way some of the other girls do. In fact, she seems very interested in the ancient Greek culture, as she puts it, although also with the cuisine, oddly enough. She asked about what kinds of food Ma cooks and whether the Acropolis serves genuine Greek dishes."

"You can tell her the diner, when it serves Greek, it is genuine, but that Philly cheese steaks and Reuben sandwiches are genuine American diner food and that is mostly what is in demand in Poughkeepsie, on Main Street in the Hudson Valley." Mr. Christopoulos laughed. "If she wants a genuine Greek menu from soup to dessert, she will have to come to our house."

"What would you think if I invited her, then, Pop? "

"It would be a family meal. No putting on the Ritz, and Corry would be there, you know. No hiding her in the attic. Also, did you think what Rebia will say or think if she finds out?"

"Rebia will just have to adjust to change. She's got a life and needs to get on with it." Demi frowned. "Never any commitments there. Just recreation."

"Maybe that is how you see or saw it, but the female perspective could have been different, you know. There may be rough seas ahead with the Karras clan."

"Gussie gets it, Pop, in fact he and I already had a talk about it. He understands the adjustment necessary when people grow apart. College has changed him, too. Rebia is still a kid. Plenty of time ahead for her."

"I don't think that Gussie is the last word on the subject, even if he is her brother." Mr. Christopoulos shook his head. "You don't know how strong the convictions of a woman can be when she thinks something is so. It becomes so. I found that out with your mother and me and Corry."

"That is different, I think, but I will keep this conversation in mind when I deal with Rebia, if I have to deal with her. Maybe as time goes by the connection will just vanish into the past as she gets involved in her secretarial job with that law firm or finds another boyfriend. At least, I can hope so."

"You may be too optimistic, son, but we shall see. And I would like to meet this marvelous young lady of theology that you are so taken with. I don't know about your mother who feels loyalty to her female neighbors. She will be courteous, I know, and if the young lady is as personable as you say, and as interested in Greek culture, your mother may warm up." Mr. Christopoulos placed his hand on Demi's shoulder. "You are good boy, a good man. This college experience is the very best thing in your life so far."

For Demi, what was left unsaid was that Tim would have had this chance if he had survived. The G.I. Bill would have let both of them go to college, although Demi wondered if he actually would have gone or if he would have just accepted the jobs that his shop-kid status in school would have directed as his fate, as had happened for Cleo Junior and his sister Helena.

Put those questions aside, he told himself. Get on with his education – and with a life with Rebia – no, probably not. The two paths were clearly diverging. With Nancy Coffin, now that was the intriguing question. Was he aiming too high, was he kidding himself, just racing his motor like some kid, or was this all a mature choice he was thinking of making? For when he became that rarity, a Vassar Man, B.A. certified college grad, even if the degree would say, University of New York State – what would his life really be like, after that?

***

"The lieutenant will find some patsy hero to take you up to the woods where the tank appears. It's just a dirt track through the trees, in order to get a clear view for firing. About every half hour it shows up and fires four, five rounds, and pulls back again. It's about seventy-five yards where you guys should dig in, fast. We need two foxholes on each side of the road about twenty-five yards spaced. You got less than thirty minutes, maybe. You got all this, you guys?" the sergeant waited.

"Got it," the corporal said.

The sergeant went on, "When the tank comes through, the first guys drag the chain of anti-tank mines across the road behind it, quick as a friggin' bunny. You guys in the two foxholes ahead draw your chain in front of it just as quick. Remember, if you got it right, you will catch the tank between two strings of mines and you should be too close for them to use the 88 on you all."

"Oh Christ," said the youngest soldier.

"When the krauts stop, don't waste time." The sergeant ignored the comment. He had heard it before. "Fucking thing is too big to maneuver easily, remember that. You will have the two bazookas, one for each hole in the front of the tank. Let fly as soon as you've got the bugger stopped. No time to reload, so each of you carry a couple or three grenades. Use 'em.

You have a better than fifty-fifty chance, if you don't screw up. So don't screw up like the high command did that got us into this mess."

TWENTY-ONE

1948

"Well, I did it," Richard Forrest proclaimed as he came into the Vet's Lounge.

"And what is that exactly?" asked Ted Collins, "The play open to raves for your spear carrying performance?"

"No, not that, although the rehearsals are going well. I mean I convinced the powers-that-be that the Vets should be sponsored for a basketball team. I found out that if we could put five guys on the court, we could schedule a game with the men at Skidmore up in Saratoga for starters. The College will purchase us uniforms, actually. In pink and grey, I am afraid, but what the hell, maybe we can get the pink toned down a bit to light maroon or something." Rich looked pleased with himself. "Maybe because it turns out that we men will be here for longer than two years after all."

"You know, Rich, you have morphed into some kind of belated gung-ho college boy, if I may be frank, but I guess it is natural to want to experience all those things marginal to getting an education that you thought you were going to miss." Ted smiled. "But I guess – why not go for it if they turn you on. Chance of a lifetime. For me, I think I will stick to the education part."

"I won't let myself get diverted, Ted. I am doing well in my classes, on track to get that degree in Economics that is going to make IBM management value me even more, and along the way I get the pleasure of these other things. All work makes Jack a dull boy, as they say. Come on, you guys, sign up. I need at least four more for a team, plus a couple for the bench, just in case." Richard turned to the others lounging in the couches.

120

"I could squeeze it in," said Chris, "Wake up the basketball muscles I haven't used since high school. Hope the coordination still works."

"You make it sound like you have become decrepit since your discharge. You can do it, and that's an okay for me, too," said Phil.

"Count me in," said Dominic Calenti, "It's not playing fullback on a football team, which was my thing, but it will do."

"I guess I could use a little exercise," put in Jack, "and an extra-curricular activity might look good on a C.V."

"I'll do it," said Gussie Karras, "How about you, Demi? A Greek one-two punch for the good old Pink and Grey? It will be like old times."

"I guess I can spare the time for a little muscle-eye coordination," Demi answered, "Better make me a fast forward. At my height, guarding the basket might be a bit outlandish."

"I could be a bit over the hill for college basketball," said Leroy, "but I think I could survive, with a little basket shooting practice. I was second string center at Highland High."

"Not me," said Evi, "Too light and too short. I will get knocked all over the court, even if basketball is not a contact sport."

"Okay," said Rich, "We have clearly more than the minimum five, anyway. Maybe I can scare up a couple more reserves. I'll beat the bushes, and you guys can talk it up, too. Then we have to arrange practice time. The Physical Education ladies, I assume they are, say we have to reserve the gym in Kenyon so as not to conflict with the female use of the facilities, if I may quote the head honcho in charge of that place of girlish sweat and tears."

"There is an irony here, of course. Vassar exempts us vets from the physical education requirement for graduation, including the dreaded swimming test, if you can believe that cartoon book they sell in the college bookstore, and here you guys seek out an alternative." Ted shook his head, chuckling. "Hmm. Could always play Poughkeepsie High School, if they are not too young and energetic for us older men, or maybe some of the younger faculty or alumnae."

"Sound mind in a sound body," said Demi, "An old Greek saying, I think. Or it should be. Maybe you could get Bernie to sit on the bench since he is one of the taller vets, and make his comments. He would be good at that. A loud and sarcastic bench is always a good weapon."

"That might not be a bad idea. At the beginning of this semester, when the weather was still warm, I saw him playing tennis with someone and he seemed quite athletic, at least at tennis. Maybe he would like to be one of the guys, even if it is only sitting most of the time on the bench," Phil suggested.

"Actually, maybe he can play," said Rich.

"How about one of the WACs or WAVEs, if we could find them," Jack said.

"Don't be absurd," Rich said, "Or you were just joking, right?"

"I was joking, but on second thought it could be a good idea. Show these women who volunteered to serve their country that we honor them as comrades-in-arms, or something like that," Jack was not laughing.

"Forget it, Jack. You will have to find your Vassar girl in some other way," Rich said.

"I told you people I was sticking with the local offerings, so I am not looking for ways to connect with Vassar women for any reason other than the educational," Jack looked offended.

"Have it your way, Jack," said Phil, closing down that aspect of the conversation, "Go to the library and work on your assignments! How will you ever become a local big shot if you don't excel or at least get that gentleman's C?"

***

Nancy Coffin turned to Mrs. Christopoulos. "That was delicious soup," she said. "What goes into it, besides a lot of care and experience?"

"It is just chicken soup," protested Mrs. Christopoulos.

"It's the lemon and egg addition that gives it the special taste," explained Demi, "The rest is a good chicken stock, which Ma makes, but it is the combination of the lemon and egg that gives it the individual flavor. Maybe the touch of vinegar."

"Good for an upset stomach, too," said Mrs. Christopoulos.

"Oh, Ma," said Helena.

"The Greek name is *avgolemono* soup," said Demi, "I like it because it doesn't have the ever-present garlic."

"And is that gorgeous looking dish that you have there for the next course?" asked Nancy.

"*Moussaka*," said Demi, "Sort of like lasagna without the lasagna noodles but with eggplant slices instead, layered with meat and cheese. You have to like eggplant to be Greek; it is big in that part of the world. Persians love them, and so do Greeks and Turks. I heard someone say that to be a Greek bride you have to know at least two dozen recipes for eggplant, just for starters."

"Well, I love eggplant, even if it is not a New England thing, and I could certainly find more than a dozen recipes," Nancy said enthusiastically. Then she blushed.

Mr. Christopoulos filled in the sudden silence. "Coffin is a different kind of last name. Not unattractive, but different. It comes from?"

122

"It is one of those old New England Puritan names," said Nancy, "Lots of them around in Cape Cod and Nantucket, Massachusetts, Connecticut, and Rhode Island. Preachers, poets, politicians, the three Ps. It never dawned on me it was odd until I went to a prep school near Albany. Someone in the family once looked it up. Found it probably came from the Welsh. Means the high ridge of a hill, apparently. Nothing to do with burials and that kind of coffins, it seems."

"Interesting. Not odd," assured Mrs. Christopoulos, "Just different to Greek ears. And have some of the *moussaka*, please."

"Leave some room for a serving of Ma's desert," Demi urged. "It will be magnificent."

"Oh, Demi, don't exaggerate," protested his mother.

"Who's exaggerating? You do fabulous deserts. Tough for the blood sugar and the calories but delicious," laughed her son, "Wait until you taste her *baklava*!" He turned to Nancy. "It is wickedly delicious."

"Perhaps I could copy out some of your favorite recipes," said Nancy, "I have actually started a notebook of authentic Greek recipes. I only hope that eventually I will be able to find the right ingredients."

"I can help," said Demi. Nancy blushed again.

"Just need to go light on the garlic for Demi," smiled his father.

***

He became aware of a buzzing drone coming from a horizon he could barely see. It sounded like a thousand wasps in flight, looking for some new place. *To sting*, he thought. Following the queen? He could begin to see black winged silhouettes against the white sky. They slid into his vision. B-17s. *Flying fortresses*, they called them.

Cleaner up there, he thought. For a while anyway, until flak began and took some down. The smaller soldier flinched at each distant explosion. He watched the bright bursts and thought about Fourth of July fireworks over the Hudson River. These were deadly fireworks. There was an occasional parachute, but not many.

No place to hide. In the air. On the ground. No fortresses in this war. All the same in the end. No escape.

TWENTY-TWO

1949

"What class are you going to, if I may ask?" Ted pulled alongside Demi as the two walked across the campus toward Blodget.

"*The Family*. Sociology 305, Dr. Fulsome's specialty." Demi slowed down. "Thought I should get the latest poop on such matters if I plan to be a social worker in real life after Vassar."

"I guess you could say that," answered Ted, "I understand he is on his third wife. The last one drowned in a boating accident at the Cape. This one is a lot younger and a former student."

"I wonder what happened to the first one. Maybe he bored her to death," Demi laughed. "He is the most lethargic teacher I have had here. It is supposed to be an upper level seminar, you know. We, all ten of us, are around a large conference table and Fulsome sits at the head, like the daddy of us all, and lectures from there."

"Not exactly the give and take of a seminar then," commented Ted, "But with three wives, think of the family experience he can import to all you beginners."

"Well, actually, I am not sure the ten of us are really listening, since everything he says is right out of his textbook that we all had to purchase, and since we have already spent a relatively large sum for the info, why bother." Demi shrugged.

"Well, he might slip in a new insight just gathered from young Mrs. Fulsome, who might have a different perspective from that juvenile, shall we say, post-adolescent, viewpoint." Ted laughed. "You might miss it, you know, if you nod off."

"Not much of what he says seems to be from the female angle, I am afraid," replied Demi, "He seems like a gentleman of the old school, or something like that. My father, ancient as he seems to me, is more *au courant* with the post-war world than Dr. Fulsome. You learn what the world is like and what both men and women think when you hear them open up in the diner."

"*Au courant*, huh? Vassar seems to be expanding your vocabulary, my friend. Sorry, did not mean to make that sound condescending." Ted looked embarrassed.

"That's okay," reassured Demi, "I actually knew that expression before I got on campus."

"Anyway, being behind the counter at the diner sounds sort of like being a bartender," continued Ted, "I didn't know coffee and a sweet roll loosened the tongue like a double Scotch with a beer chaser."

"Yeah, funny how people reveal the most intimate things in the friendly atmosphere of the Acropolis, seven days a week, twenty-four hours a day. Of course," Demi winked, "What happens in the Acropolis stays in the Acropolis."

"Naturally," Ted agreed, "Any juicy bits about people we know?" he joked. "Or local big-wigs?"

"I wouldn't tell you, at least not here in the open."

"So, is this class a waste then?" Ted inquired.

"Not a waste, actually. Nothing learned is ever a waste. The book says some important things about family structure and the interactions of parents and children, even if it all does smell a bit of the past. You can learn from the past, after all. I will be able to use a lot of it if I get my M.S.W. What good Greek would not agree with that, as my father would be happy to point out," Demi nodded.

"Glad to hear you aren't wasting the government's money then," Ted joked.

"I am listening, most of time, unlike Rich, who has a beer with lunch at the Log Cabin, and then tends to doze during the afternoon session. Of course, this is only an advanced elective for him anyway, and as long as he gets his gentleman's C in it he will be content. Playing his part in the student theater productions naturally seems to be his major preoccupation at the moment."

"Ah well, all the world's a stage and all the men and women are but players," Ted responded.

"You English majors are always ready with a pertinent quotation," said Demi.

"Beats having to be original on short notice," answered Ted.

"Funny thing about college," said Demi as they turned up the walk to Blodget. "It is both what I expected, and not what I expected. I guess I had some notion of the lofty nature of higher education and its practitioners, and that belief has been largely borne out. At the same time, I have run into

125

pedestrian thinkers here and there, as well as some misfits cranky about their existences, who are not exactly admirable people in their personal lives."

"And so it goes, as Kurt Vonnegut would say," Ted commented as the two men pulled open the door to the building and entered the venerable hall of human relations.

***

"You all right, son?" Professor Black came into the living room of the Black house, located in what was a kind of faculty row. The sounds of traffic on Raymond Avenue, just beyond the living room window and the lawn that ended where the street began, could be heard, muffled by the drapes pulled against the night.

"Fine, fine," said Bernard, "Just thinking, you know. Here I am at twenty-five, back home living with my parents. In my third year at my Dad's college. What a joke."

"So are a lot of your peers as they adjust returning to civilian life. Nothing demeaning about it," Professor Black said.

"Perhaps," said Bernard, "but it just throws you back into some kind of arrested childhood. The old bedroom. The adolescent posters. The saved academic reports from prep school. Childish clothes hanging in the closet. A bunch of crap, actually, if you will pardon my language. Guess hanging out with the vets has roughed up the Lawrenceville polish. Hard to escape."

"Takes time, I am afraid, and all the old stuff is still here because your mother did not want to disturb anything since it reminded her of happier times." Professor Black patted his son on the shoulder. "It will work out," he added.

"I suppose so," said Bernard, "Just – I felt really grown-up, with responsibilities serving in the army – and then to be thrown back into my teens is a wrench. I suppose it would have been the same if I had gone to party Princeton instead of coming here, anyway."

"Humor your mother, son. Hard for her when you are the only child, and the focus of much of her early adult life. Having you back here safe and in one piece is a gift of sorts. Soon enough you will be off to graduate school and freedom. Humor her, and me. I like having you around, too, you know."

Bernard looked at his hands. "Right," he said.

"I am sorry you are not happy as a student at your old man's college," said his father, "You could have gone somewhere else. You did extremely well at school and there was always, as you say, Princeton."

"Well, it is kind of hard to take classes from the same people who come to your cocktail parties and who talk about what I was like as a kid and as a pain-in-the-ass teenager home from school, you have to admit. Although they would never use a term like 'pain in the ass,' of course. Too polite and circumspect."

"We have had this talk before," said his father, "First, right after you got discharged and were floundering around about what next, as if college was not always the 'what next,' in this family. Princeton was ready to take you, or the University of Chicago, if you wanted to get away from the East, as you said."

"Right, right," said Bernard, "So I picked good old Vassar when it went nominally coed. Not rational, I know. Therefore, here I am and I don't seem to fit in. I sort of thought at the time that maybe I'd do two years here, and then finish up somewhere in the west. I applied to Southern Methodist but didn't tell you. Just got the school guidance person to send my transcripts off to Texas."

"Southern Methodist, Bernie? We are not even Methodists. Why there, for heaven's sake?" Professor Black looked confused as his eyebrows elevated, his forehead wrinkled to his hair line. "And the wild west of Texas. You might have chosen Austin, at least, where the city and college is a bit more cognizant of the cultural nuances. Austin is hardly Texas at all."

"I know. Irrational. You don't have to tell me. I know." He paused, searching for words. "Dad, I don't fit in. I thought maybe being a fellow veteran and someone who knew what the European theater was like, I would feel as if I belong, but I can't seem to talk the same language as the guys, and 'guys' they are, in the vet's lounge." Bernard rubbed his eyes, frustration evident in his taut fingers. "Maybe I thought it was more real there in the lone star state."

"Real? What kind of a concept is that? More real with Texas long horns and swaggering oil millionaires? Some sort of nineteenth-century notion about the effete east, I suppose." Professor Black snorted.

Bernard pressed the heels of both hands into his eye sockets and rubbed again, harder this time. "Well, I even thought about art school and a B.F.A. without telling anyone, but deep-sixed that stupid idea."

"Getting a migraine, son?" asked his father, ignoring the art school revelation. "Why don't you go lie down?"

"No migraine, Dad. Just depressed."

"Look, Bernie, you did your duty. Being a medic in a battle zone was not easy, but you saved lives, and came home in one piece to be rewarded. The 'guys' as you call them, are mostly rough diamonds and we are trying to both educate them and polish them as much as we can. You are already educated and quite polished. Lawrenceville saw to that. You will meet all kinds of people for the rest of your life, just as you must have in the service, and you will have to take the bitter with the better. Excuse the cliché. Some good men there, your fellow vets. Eventually most, if not all of them, will certainly accept you as an equal, or not," the professor shrugged lightly.

"Hidden away in some of them is probably envy for the kind of life you had as a youngster before the war." Professor Black halted. "I think I have been preaching, Bernie. You will have to forgive me. It comes with the territory."

"It is okay, Dad." Bernard sat up from his slump against the back of the easy chair. "Think I will go over to the library. Got some research to do on a paper for my Philosophy course. It is on Wittgenstein and Logical Positivism."

"Then you should also take a look at A. J. Ayer's work. Freddie has written more than Wittgenstein did and is more lucid. I remember talking to him about Wittgenstein when I went to that symposium at University College London during the fall that I went to the U.K."

"Thanks, *Pater*, I will do just that." Bernard stood up and slipped on his Harris tweed jacket, which he had been sitting on. He did not bother to shake out the wrinkles. "I knew I could get a hot academic tip from you."

"Anytime, son," said Professor Black.

***

"What do you mean, that's it?" Carmen slid off the bed, the condom hanging from his now flaccid penis. "What do you mean, exactly, Kitty? Wasn't that okay?"

"First just take off that thing, it is grotesque, and flush it, or something. Then put on your pants. And keep your voice down. You know you aren't supposed to be in my room. You would think you went to Columbia or some such. I don't want to get thrown out just over a bit of a ride on the D train."

"Okay, okay, but I thought…" Carmen swept the limp condom away with a Kleenex and pulled up his trousers. "I thought we had something really good going here."

"For the moment, buster, and I think the moment is now over." Kitty put on her black panties and slid into her matching lace bra. Nonchalantly, she reached for the blouse that was hanging on the edge of the bed, where Carmen had dropped it sometime before, when clothes were being dispensed with in a hurry.

"What do you mean *over*? Over for just now? Or *over* over?" Carmen buckled his belt and looked at his bare feet. *Ugly,* he thought, suddenly and inappropriately. He should cut his toenails more often.

"I mean that is really it. I thought one more ride for old time sake and then break it off. Got better plans, in fact." Kitty pulled on her skirt. "You can just go back to your grocery, because I won't need any more of your salami."

"Come on, Kit, you don't have to get mean and nasty. Not after all we have meant to each other over the past months." Carmen looked stunned. He

128

heard the whine in his voice and was sickened by it. He did not plead. That would be out of character. He was a war hero. Bronze Star.

"Let's be real here, Carmen. Nothing long-lasting is going to come from a few times of screwing around. It was pleasant enough, but I have other plans." Kitty was fully dressed now, and handed Carmen his sweater and his tie. "No doubt you will need both of these."

Carmen took the objects from Kitty, and looked at them as if they were strange artifacts that he did not really recognize.

"And now, Carmen, I think, I think you are leaving, are you not?" Kitty stood by the dorm room door, with her hand on the knob. She seemed to be listening for any sounds in the hallway.

"So, you found someone better?" Carmen said.

"That would not be hard to do, I think," answered Kitty, "But yes, someone with more potential, shall we say. Sabbaticals to Cambridge, perhaps, or Conferences where Bertrand Russell might be in attendance, if we are lucky. We could meet George Bernard Shaw. Think of the level of the conversation. He and I will sparkle. Or we may even go to Paris in the spring."

"I have seen Paris in the spring," said Carmen.

"Wearing your combat boots, no doubt," said Kitty, "Making out with the locals for some gum and chocolate, perhaps." Her laughter trickled like a slow drain down at the bottom of a well. "Well, that is not me. Larger fish to fry, thank you. Someone already on the way up, who just needs the bit of social register for the final touch. He knows it, and I know it. Realists, we are. I predict the sky is the limit – and you barely reach the horizon, I am afraid."

"Okay, then," said Carmen.

Kitty opened the door. "Coast is clear, hall empty, so you can go quietly."

"Quietly, it will be," said Carmen, "Good luck with the rest of your life. It should be exciting."

TWENTY-THREE

1949

"Anyone seen Carmen lately?" Demi looked around at several of the veterans sitting in the men's lounge.

Some were reading text books, some were flipping through the *Vassar Miscellany*, some were smoking and staring into the middle distance as if watching some inner scene of great import.

"What?" finally responded Dominic, who had been buried in his history book. "Who?"

"Carmen," repeated Demi, "You know, and I don't mean the singer with outrageous hats. Our very own Carmen with the fixation on the glamour girl of the upper west side. I haven't seen him lately."

"You're right," said Dominic. "He has not been in History class for a couple of meetings, and he was very conscientious about class attendance. I wonder what happened. History is his major."

"Maybe something has gone awry in his pursuit of Kitty," put in Ted who lowered his copy of the *Misc.* in order to look over it at his fellow vets. "I figured that was doomed from the start. He was aiming too high. Italian grocery moving on up to the upper west side."

"Right," said Richard Forrest.

"Stick with the local females. That is what I have said all along," added Jack from behind his book.

"We know, we know," responded Gussie, chiming in, "You have sung that song before." He lifted his fingers and mimed playing a violin.

"So, that doesn't make it any less true," said Jack, nodding knowingly, "Besides, I have seen that blond Kitty person who has been Carmen's fixation actually in hot pursuit of Professor Katzenbaum. I recognize the signs. Waiting after class to ask Katzenbaum questions about the material.

Leaning over his desk so that he can get a good look down her blouse at what appear to be minuscule boobs, sitting in the front row with legs akimbo so he can check out her lingerie, if he is so inclined. Poor sucker doesn't have a prayer, unless he is a fag, and I doubt that."

"I would say 'poor sucker' is more fitting for Carmen in that case," said Leroy, getting into the conversation for the first time, "What chance does a poor grocery clerk slob, even the owner's son, have with that kind of competition, particularly one named Carmen whose family owns a grocery even if he escapes eventually with his degree."

"Kitty Katzenbaum-to-be, then, or Kitty *Katz* for short," Ted laughed. "Why would she even give the time of day to someone like Carmen?" he continued. "What attractive qualities does Carmen possess? Besides persistence, of course, and dog-like devotion. Must be something there for this Kitty to spend time on seducing our poor slob of a fellow student?"

"Here Kitty Katz, here pussy cat," joked Jack, and he made a yowling noise in the back of his throat.

"Always in the gutter, eh, Jack?" said Ted.

"That's where the fertile dirt is, after all," said Leroy.

"Oh, I don't know exactly what someone like Kitty wants," said Demi, "Maybe the challenge of the chase, although there can't be much of a challenge to arouse the interest in our pal Carmen. He is a sitting duck, you might say, racing his motor, if you will pardon the mixed metaphors."

"A beer at the Log Cabin with an 'older man' who has seen and survived battle – and has the medals to prove it. I suppose that has some attraction, particularly if other female students are envious of your success," Gussie argued in favor of their friend. "On the other hand, gaming an attractive handsome brilliant young professor with an assured intellectual academic future – if that works out for this Kitty, Carmen is not only a sitting duck, but a dead one."

"On the other hand, all this analysis does not really address our original question of – has any one seen Carmen lately?" Leroy brought the group back to the earlier query.

"He has dropped out," said Bernard Black who had come into the lounge in the middle of the conversation, "My father told me. He got an official withdrawal form from the recorder's office. Carmen was taking one of my father's courses. In his third year, too. Dumb thing to do. He was passing, plenty of gentleman's Cs and often better, according to Dad. What a waste."

"Well, what do you know. A late fatality of the Great War, that is, the great war of the dating game known as the college years." Ted shook his head. "Some of us are still the walking wounded – and some of us are the dead."

"I keep telling you guys, stick with the locals. They are so grateful, and their expectations are not as elevated as those of our fellow female classmates." Jack looked around with satisfaction.

"Oh, shove it, Jack," Ted responded, "This is someone's life here. But to quit over that sort of thing. Just rejection by a pretty face or change to a now unwilling body. Not a sign of good mental health, I suppose."

"Probably better off, actually," added Demi, "Kitty Katzenbaum, nee Brown, if our suppositions are correct, would never have been available to the likes of Carmen Dalio, I am afraid I have to admit. He was just aiming for a fall and that Infantryman's Badge and the Bronze Star did not protect him from this other life."

"But to be toward the end of his third year," repeated Bernard, "When success is in your sights, and the finish line is really right over the horizon. He could do it. I don't get it."

"Didn't have the self-confidence that you have, Bernie. We envy you that quality," said Demi.

"Little you know, Demi," Bernard said, "Little you know about that."

"Maybe he just needed General Patton redux to give him a few slaps around the chops to tell him to shape up – as would have happened over there on the battle grounds," Gussie added.

"I am afraid it was the second part of that famous advice to shape up or ship out that Carmen chose to follow." Ted shook his head. "As I said, another battle casualty, I guess, at a distance. For some, war never ends once you have absorbed the ethic of battle. There are only winners and losers, the alive and the dead."

"Anyway, Carmen won't need a purple heart from the Battle of Vassar, since he already has one," said Jack.

"Why don't you just shut the hell up," said Demi.

"Why, for Christ sake?" replied Jack, "Survival of the fittest, as you Darwinians would say. The weak fall by the wayside."

"Just button up, you insensitive creep," Gussie finished the conversation.

***

"Ha," said Demi, as he dropped into one of the leather chairs in the Vets' lounge few days later, "Vindication at last."

"Vindication of what sort, exactly?" asked Ted.

"I got an A in Psych. Social Psych, to match my As in Soc and Anthro from one of the young women in the department. I could never get better than a B- from the Psych Department's Three Witches of Elsinore and mostly C or C+. Glad I don't need to take any more from them."

"The three witches from Macbeth?" Ted asked.

"Right," said Demi, "You must have seen the senior three man-haters who believe male students are incapable louts for whom a C minus grade is a gift There is the little scrawny one who looks sort of like a malnourished monkey, there is the pudgy one with the short Gertrude Stein hair-do – a rose is a rose is a psych teacher – and the self-hating Greek lady who is sure no W.A.S.P wants to live next door to her."

"I think that you may be exaggerating out of irritation at what you think of as unfair treatment, when it could be simply that in their view, the upholding of Vassar standards is as they see them. Can't be as bad as all that since these women are scholars, after all." said Ted thoughtfully. "Although, I have run into a couple of English faculty who seem very uncomfortable around males. Fair, but uncomfortable. There was one woman teaching a lit course who could not look at me, even when I was either asking a question, or answering one. Sort of weird, actually. I always had the impulses to swing around and stare where she was looking, usually somewhere in a corner of the ceiling, like those people who look up at the tall buildings in the City when they see others looking up. Of course, otherwise it was an okay class, and I got an A in it, so there was no discrimination. She was a 'Miss,' and I figured that for her, perhaps teaching at Vassar had been an escape from a reality where she dealt with men, at least in class. I felt sort of sorry for her, in fact."

"Like the Academic Dean who welcomed us, if welcome is what you call it, back at the beginning – when we all thought this situation was only for two years. From her demeanor, she probably believed we males were intruders into their special world. And I can understand that," said Demi, "but to stereotype us, and then judge according to those false expectations – it is like expecting every African male in New York to be a mugger waiting to attack with a box-cutter in hand."

"On the other hand, I took a course from a Foster woman who turned out to be a distant relative from New England – Providence, in fact – and she was just great with everyone. Very encouraging of my writing. Wrote me a letter of recommendation for graduate work at Minnesota and Stanford not very long ago, in fact," Ted said.

"Is that some kind of nepotism?" asked Demi.

"If it is, three cheers for nepotism," Ted laughed. "Could be it was in the Foster/Collins genes – to be fair-minded," commented Ted. "On the other other hand, the second semester of my English 105 section in Freshman year was taught by a visiting male professor from N. Y. U. who was really something else. The class was assigned to read any worthy contemporary novel, and write a critical review of it. As the class was filing out after he made the assignment, he stopped me and suggested that I read a book entitled *End as a Man*, by someone I had never heard of, Calder Willingham, up-and-coming writer. He said he would be interested in my reactions. He said this writer would eventually be big, and that he, the instructor, knew him and expected great things of him in the future. Then he patted my shoulder in a friendly manner and said he would be waiting to read the paper, which he expected to be perceptive."

"And?" asked Demi.

"Turned out to be largely about homosexual activity amongst some lonely isolated boys in a prep school, a military prep school, in fact. Sort of like one of those single sex English public schools. Boys with raging testosterone poisoning, you might say. Eton or something, you know, except with the added sadomasochism of the junior military. Dumb little book that some young writer had to get out of his system, I am sure. Not badly written, but a bit lurid, smug and self-satisfied. Then I had a Joycean epiphany. I suddenly recognized the visiting professor from N.Y.U," Ted shook his head and lifted his eyebrows in a knowing manner. "I don't mean that literally, I just mean I was enlightened as to his motives. He reminded me of a Staff Sergeant I worked under in the 20th Air Force who was quite obviously a closeted homosexual. Had to be, in the service, of course – in the closet, I mean. I learned how to steer clear of him except on the flight line, where if he trapped me into a conversation, I would talk about my serious girlfriend back home, even though I did not have one at the time, and escape to live another heterosexual day and ultimately get my discharge from the Army Air Corps. I was sorry for him and his dilemma, but I did not want to play."

"So, what did you do about this New York guy?" asked Demi.

"Well, I wrote the paper, expressing my fervent dislike, using the words I just used. He gave me an A and wrote a comment on the paper that said it was very well written, that I had a way with words and no doubt had a future as an English major and perhaps even as a literary critic."

"That was nice," said Demi.

"It was also at the end of the semester and of the class. I think he went back to N.Y.U., but Sara and I did see him one more time at Morrison's Grill downtown one evening when I took her to dinner. He was bumping shoulders with another one of the faculty members, both sitting on the same side of the booth, giggling, and studiously ignoring us. I guess if my paper had not done the trick, seeing the two of us, Sara and me, having a date together would have been the clincher. But he was too busy with his companion of the moment, so I never had to worry about it."

"Poor sucker," said Demi, "I guess. Or maybe not."

"Probably both as happy as clams," said Ted, "Not necessarily a poor sucker. Why be sorry? To each his own, as they say."

"I suppose you are right. Just think about that ancient and honored Greek tradition; although I would rather not. Right now, my biggest worry is getting that friggin' creative senior thesis for Mrs. Nadeau in shape."

"Well, she is looking for publishable quality, she says, given her professional success writing for *The Atlantic* and other such highbrow magazines," Ted said, "She said that she would like to show some finished work by her more mature male students to some editors she knows."

"Listen, I am just an undergraduate," protested Demi, "Not one of her writer colleagues. This double major is turning into a real bitch, particularly with the English department requirement of a senior thesis. For Sociology, you just take courses and write individual research papers. No problem. Piece of cake. But this creative small book I have to get together is another matter. Besides, Mrs. Nadeau wants me to write about my battle experiences, yet I just want to forget it, which is one good reason that I am in college. But then I wonder what my subject matter will be, if not the war."

"All in the same boat, Demi, we vets. Different battles," Ted responded.

"And then she tells me I can be the Greek Saroyan. *Saroyan*, would you believe it! Besides I do not want to be 'the Greek anything'. I want to be me. In addition, I think that Saroyan writes 'cute' and I avoid 'cute' at all costs."

"Everybody is looking for gimmicks, Demi, to sell a book or a story. She may be a creative artist, but you gotta market yourself and your stuff, as she has done, even though it looks as if her work and style has outlived the current push for the new. As Elliot, I think, said, when the culture says your work must be new and different, that can lead to greater and greater eccentricity, until nobody knows what the hell you are talking about or what is your point. 'Make it new' as Pound said, can be the final trap."

"I know, and then you get the dead end of *Finnegan's Wake*, but I have all this war stuff in my mind only as chaotic details, and I need to get them into shape and find meaning in them and I simply can't seem to do it. I was just too close to it all to find meaning in the chaos. Going back over it all just makes me have nightmares," Demi shuddered.

"You should read her non-fiction book, *The Secured Heart*, about the Brittany coast during the German occupation if you want a clue to her style, and what she probably wants to see in your work."

"Who has time to read one extra more book right now?" Demi complained, "I will put it on my 'to do' list for after I get my M.S.W."

"Tell you what, then," replied Ted, "Why don't you let me help? I can be your Maxwell Perkins; you know, the editor who helped Tom Wolfe shape his novels. I can find the time, since I am not playing basketball or acting in some student production. What do you say?"

"Would that be kosher?" questioned Demi.

"It will all be your stuff, my friend. I will just tweak the language and the focus. I would not do anything you did not feel is what you want said. It will be yours," Ted reassured his friend, even though he did not feel all that confident he was really offering to do the right thing.

But Demi seemed desperate, and Ted considered what a waste it would be for Demi to blow it all like Carmen, merely because of one requirement. He had done so well at all else that the College had asked of him, this Greek shop kid that circumstances and a benevolent government had propelled into higher education. And it was probably just because he had the serious hang-up about appearing brave, or heroic, or God forbid, a braggart. He deserved it.

He deserved it all. So Ted smiled, confidently, brightly, one eyebrow lifted at his friend, who sighed audibly. Perhaps in relief, perhaps for some other reason known only to himself.

"Okay," said Demi, "Let's do it."

***

He heard the buzzing Tiger's engine mutter before he was really aware of it.

It was coming from beyond the horizon, which he could barely see through the mist filtering past the trees. A thousand insects on the move.

The sound became louder and louder, bees looking for some new place. To sting. The black winged silhouettes that became silvery as they slid into his vision. B-17s. Big birds of prey. Ready for flight and fight.

Cleaner up there, he first thought. For a while anyway, until flak began and took some down. Into the mud with him. Bodies as torn there in the metal, torn as the ones he had seen and held.

No place to hide. In the air. On the ground. All the same in the end.

No escape.

Tiger, tiger, burning bright. Funny thing to come to mind here from high school English class. Why was this shop kid remembering that line, he thought?

Hurry up and wait, he thought. The unofficial military motto. Funny time to think of it. Waiting for life, or death.

Life and death.

He waited.

TWENTY-FOUR

1949

"Hey, Mom, where do you keep the old copies of *Punch*? I want to show the guys some British humor, if you can call it that." Evelyn Smith, with a long E, was looking through a pile of old New Yorkers, Atlantic Monthlies and Harpers.

"What did you say?" Mrs. Smith came through the kitchen. "I was out in the garden and didn't hear what you said. I was busy digging around the snapdragons and staking up the Jacob's ladder. That plant really is trying to reach heaven, and it keeps falling to earth!" She laughed bemusedly at her own sharp-witted commentary.

Mrs. Smith was English, and gardens were a necessity in her life now that she was an American married to an American engineer. Actually, she liked to think her married name was not just plain Smith but could be Cottle-Smith; since her maiden name meant something to her, she wished to preserve it somehow. Her husband, the American engineer, and her son, as well as her two older step- sons by her husband's dead first wife, did not share her pleasure in the format.

They all considered it both humorous and pretentious, and did not want to be ridiculed by their American friends. A combined name would remind her of her home in the Cotswolds, as did the formal garden and the subscription to *Punch*, but it was not to be.

Simplicity was the American way. Nothing pretentious, her American husband had warned.

Evi had actually tried his mother's name on once when he went to a new school. He thought it might make the little shrimp he felt himself to be different, but the other children made his life miserable, referring to him as Evelyn Cuttlefish Smith. It was bad enough being smaller than the other boys his age, and having what his contemporaries considered a girl's first name, but that label was too cruel and he abandoned the use of the hyphenated moniker, although it took a while for the other children to forget about it. His efforts to explain about Evelyn Waugh and the British tradition of naming interested only his teachers and not his childish peers. Evi finally got his reprieve when a new German boy entered his class, wearing lederhosen with suspenders against the North American winter cold, and there was, for a while, a new focus for cruel boyish mockery.

At this school, being a local public school located in the "best neighborhood," where adults and children knew the proper social code, such treatment had to go underground, of course, but Evi did not enter into the savage mistreatment given his new school mate. He knew the anguish such trivialities could produce.

And he'd found that interests in common things often started a way forward in the ways of social interaction. "I wanted to find the old copies of *Punch*, and maybe *TLS* for the literary guys at school." Evi stood up over the pile of slick publications. "I know you keep them and I will get them back home to you, Mother, after the guys look them over."

"They are in that box in the master bedroom," she said, "You can take them from there as long as you promise to bring them back eventually." Mrs. Smith would pore over old copies while drinking a cup of tea with milk when she was feeling nostalgic for Cornwall.

"And I do," said Evi. He knew how his mother clung to objects that reminded her of home and flower shows where her own mother won prizes for arranging. *Punch* and *TLS* had always been in the Cottle's parlor, and his mother had grown up giggling at the jokes and cartoons in Punch and then graduating to the reviews and commentary in the *Times Literary Supplement*. But when he was young and invited friends from elementary school over to his house to play, he had felt embarrassed by his mother's accent."

"Why does your mother have that hoity-toity way of speaking?" one of his school mates had asked.

He had really not been aware that his mother did not talk exactly the way other mothers did. When he later went to play in the yard of the Cough Drop Smiths with Ginny and a couple of other classmates from Governor George Clinton Elementary School on Montgomery Street, he heard the difference when Ginny's mother brought out juice and cookies. There were the flat nasal short As, the pronunciation of tomato, and the references to the Wappingers Crick, instead of Creek.

He never knew whether he should feel superior or inferior because of these differences, and in the effort to fit in, learned to speak both British English and American English, depending upon the circumstances. In the Navy during the war, he first shifted completely to the American pronunciation, but when he was finally stationed in England he found himself reverting to his Mother Tongue, as he thought of it. Kismet. Dating English girls, when he worked up the nerve, helped re-enforce the language of his mother. He did not want to fit the British crack about American service men – over-paid, over-sexed, and over *here*.

He wished to be the gentleman his mother would have wanted him to be.

When he returned to the States and was mustered out, he found that he had to drop the accent because some people found it effeminate or worse, as affected as the Trans-Atlantic Buckleys, and as a small man, only five feet five, he had a horror of not being seen as manly. Worse, his two much older half-brothers were tall like their engineer father, were civil engineers themselves and often appeared in muddy rugged boots and blue jeans with corduroy shirts or lumber jackets from their place of employment. In addition, they had served with the Seabees in dangerous military areas, while he had spent most of his sea time on vessels guarding convoys across the Atlantic. Not that that could not be quite as dangerous with U-boat activity, but somehow in Evelyn's mind, it did not measure up to the sort of things his half-brothers were doing in the war effort.

It was after he was mustered out, that he bought himself a couple of pairs of Adler's Elevator Shoes, without telling anyone in his family.

"I found them, Mom," he said, holding a small number of the magazines in his hands. "I'll just take six for the moment."

"You really think the other veterans will be interested in British humor?" Mrs. Smith asked.

"Oh, some of the guys served in England during the war and will find the jokes fun. No one talks about the war much, with study as the first priority, but I am sure a little kidding around after the war experience is not a bad response to the grimness of that chunk of life."

"Makes sense, I suppose," said his mother.

"Got to go," said Evi, "Or I will be late to class." *Sort of a high school moment*, he thought to himself. *Funny how we fall back into the old routine* – as if, at such times, he was still a sixteen- year old leaving for school.

Of course, he was not.

He was a sailor, standing watch in the North Atlantic, peering into the midnight darkness where the darkened convoy of merchant ships, some carrying supplies, others carrying stacked men in bunks over bunks; sleeping or seasick soldiers sailing to Europe to fight. The night was only lightened at times by fluorescence in the sea waves.

Were there U-boats below? Would he know it before it was too late?

He was both of those young men, as well now also the college student, carrying the books, studying in the library, going to classes, eyeing the shapely girls in and out of class, trying to make out in as normal a way as possible, but then coming home to his parents' house and his old bedroom, and hoping to fit back into a civilian life after the military time-out.

It was schizophrenic.

It did not make it better that some of the guys, such as Bernie Black, complained of the same thing; he envied Leroy Freer. He went on being an old married man with an independent life in spite of being an academic re-tread student again.

Leroy had permanently escaped from kid-hood.

Evi sighed, shifted the packet of magazines he carried carefully in his two hands to a nonchalant location against one hip, and took the stairs up to the lounge two at a time.

***

"Hey, Ted," Evi said in a stage whisper as he came up to the library table where Ted was surrounded by a few stacks of books and bent over a bunch of note cards. Across from him, Rich was also deep into a book with a like stack of cards.

"Quiet, Evi." Ted looked up. "This is the sacred inner sanctum of scholarship. You will disturb the brain cells which are firing away here."

"Go away, Ev," said Rich without looking up.

"Okay. Okay. I'll try to keep it low, but I need some immediate help. Can't just go away at this moment. You guys each got a car, right?" Evelyn looked desperate.

"Sure. Post war. Plymouth. Latest 1946 model punched out of the last 1941 dies, I think. Just bragging. Why?" Ted looked suspicious. Evelyn was the accident-prone classmate of the group, often needing bailing out of self-inflicted difficulties. He often seemed childish to others in the group. Was it his slight stature and baby face?

"I'm stuck in the mud in the orchard on the other side of Raymond Avenue. You know, just across from Skinner Hall and south of Vassar Lake."

"Hell of a place to be," said Ted, "What did you go there for? Sounds kind of dumb, if you will pardon me saying so."

"When did something being dumb ever stop our friend here?" Rich still did not look up, but obviously he was tuned in. "Got a girl in that car, right, Evelyn Smith?" Rich finally raised his eyes from the book.

"Yes, and I got to get her back to the dorm before the doors are locked. You know about the shutdown time for the dorms." Evelyn's voice began to rise again. "We don't have that much time."

"Shish! Well, tell her to walk back. It is not very far," said Rich.

"She can't do that. She has on high heeled shoes and the mud is really deep where we parked."

140

"Why do you do these things, Ev? If you don't have good sense, you should pick girls who do. Who is this one?" Ted sounded very exasperated.

"It was her idea to go into the orchard," Evelyn protested, "I guess she had parked there before with someone else. It is remote, or at least hidden by the trees from Raymond Avenue."

"No doubt with one or more of those mythic Ivy League men with a car! Aren't you the lucky one to make that kind of choice." Ted snorted. "Or did she pick you? If she is so experienced in parking, why was she wearing those kind of shoes?"

"Didn't expect to have to walk home, I would suspect," put in Rich.

"Come on, you guys. Time's a-wasting and I have to get the car out, and back home and... uh, erm – Wendy back to the dorm."

"I am not going to risk getting my car mired in the muck with you," said Ted, "No way."

"I have some flattened cartons in the trunk of my car," said Rich, "Maybe putting them under the rear wheels and with us pushing, you can back out."

"Sound good," said Ted, "What one has to do to get a higher education when you are stuck with low brows like Evi here."

"My brow is as high as yours," said Evelyn.

When the three men got there, they found the girl slumped down in the passenger seat of Evi's car, her head barely visible over the seat back, her knees up against the dashboard. They were white and bare. The three men went to work with the flattened cardboard. She remained mostly hidden below the side window while they worked, and never spoke. The dark car hood and roof were both patterned with fallen pink and white blossoms from the fruit trees.

"How romantic," Ted noted to Rich as they pushed the cartons under the rear wheels.

"Ah, young love in Springtime," answered Rich.

"Shut up and just do it," said Evi, "She probably can hear you."

Rich and Ted pushed at the front of the car and Evi put it into reverse. He gunned it.

"Slow and easy, pal," directed Ted, "or you will just throw the cardboard under the car."

As Evi's headlights retreated before them, Ted and Rich walked slowly back toward Raymond Avenue and Ted's car parked on the gravel road above Vassar Lake, near the caretaker's house.

"Another good deed done, my friend," said Rich, "Did you see who the girl actually was?"

"Not clearly with her scrunched down like that, but I think it was that infamous hot and hungry child study major," Ted answered. "Did Evi say Wendy? She seems to be testing all the available vets, I am afraid, but who really cares? Actually, if it was *the* Wendy, that is, Wendy Baker, I feel kind of sorry for her. Someone told me she was from a parochial school in Queens or Long Island somewhere and really was interested in science, but her father wouldn't pay for Vassar unless she prepared for sensible grade school teaching. Along with the fact that the freedom of college with men on campus, and a predictable hormonal surge, has totally undermined the nuns' teaching. Might also be the shock of reading D. H. Lawrence in an English class without any preparation. Sex and confession and then more heavy petting and more confession. Seems to be the *modus operandi* for such protected girls. Wild and wooly, she has become, and there are always the Evelyns of the world ready to go along. Besides, with Evi it is always game today and gone tomorrow. He wears Adler Elevator Shoes, poor guy, working out some kind of need to be the taller, macho male. He will be lucky if he doesn't screw up his academics and get busted out. Another Carmen in the making, maybe?

Rich nodded in the dark. "There is always Champlain College as a fallback. Gussie tells me that they are still taking students, according to some guys he knows who went up there to check it out when he did, before deciding on Vassar. They are students there now, he says."

"I hate to see someone like Evi give us all another bad rap. Ben Meyer did that and one is one too many, anyway. It is tough enough being here without some screw-up like Evi getting us all tarred with the same brush." Ted groaned.

"Oh, I think the aware faculty and students can make a distinction. We don't all look alike to them, I am sure. Besides, Evi isn't all that bad. At other institutions – Yale, Dartmouth, Williams, Amherst, or Princeton maybe – his occasional goofing-up would be taken for granted. Undergraduate monkey-shines, that's all, such as putting a cow in the chapel tower in some southern Baptist college, a story my brother told me about. Goes with the territory. There are always that kind in every college, even in the prestigious schools and the lower tiers, too. Hey, don't worry too much about it," advised Rich.

"You do have to feel sorry for the poor girl, though," Ted remarked. "It's all a part of the self-discovery of growing up, particularly when there has been an unnatural protection, such as we think she probably experienced," said Rich.

"Right. I wonder if we have any time left to work in the library." Ted tried to look at his watch. "I was going to meet Sara on the steps after we finished studying."

"Don't worry, you can make it," assured Rich, "Carry on, buddy."

***

142

The black bulk of the tank blotted out the space between the trees. The grinding sound became louder, as guttural as the Jerries' speech. The hoarse noise seemed to press him against the side of the foxhole the two of them had dug thirty minutes before. The shadow took on substance, looming over them.

"Now! Now!" A husky cry came from somewhere and he pulled the chain, hand over hand. It was like dragging up an anchor, he thought.

"Enough!" He was aware it was the young soldier who spoke. He sensed rather than heard the 'whoosh' of the bazooka. The exploding shell rang against the steel. There came a second more distant 'whoosh' from the other foxhole. He saw the youngest soldier, with his mouth open and his teeth bared like some animal, his hand fumbling for a grenade. He made himself seize a grenade. He rose in the hole. The tank had stopped.

"Throw for the tracks, the *tracks*," someone shouted.

He heard the punch of exploding grenade, and then another. The tank turret whirred and turned toward them. *Crack-crack-crack-crack*. The turret gun fired over the foxhole into the woods. Sarge had been right, and then it stopped.

"It's burning! They're burning!" One of the other guys from behind the stalled mass of steel yelled. The tank unbuttoned. Smoke belched out of the hatch. He saw the blushing light of fire against a dark screaming form that heaved itself out of the turret. Another shape climbed even more slowly from the bowels of the machine and fell forward, only half outside, uniform smoldering. There was a sweet, hot smell floating toward and around them, a mixture of metal, oil, and meat.

TWENTY-FIVE

1949

Demi was walking down Conklin Street, coming home from the campus, when he saw Rebia standing on her porch with her hand on the front door knob. She was dressed in her clerk's office outfit. Should he stop and talk or just pretend he was so filled with academic thought that he did not see her? *Better to be honest*, he thought.

"Hi Rebia, how have you been?" he said as he paused at his own front steps.

"I have been just dandy," Rebia answered, "I have a steady right now. Someone I knew in high school, in fact. I ran into him again when he delivered some forms and stationery to the law office where I work now. Followed Helena's advice about looking for good clean positions as assistants for lawyers, you see. Use my shorthand and typing skills. And my bosses are very smart, not ambulance chasers. Jimmy works for Fitchett's Stationery on Main Street. They supply legal forms to all the high class law offices in the city. He hopes to learn the business and work up. He is *very* ambitious." She stopped as though she had run out of steam, or story.

"Sounds great for you. Congratulations." Demi did not know what else to say. He could see that Rebia was recapturing her sense of self-worth. He knew that was important, and he was also very grateful to hear it.

"Thanks," she said, and then laughed, "Jimmy is just my speed and you are off the hook."

"Off the hook?" Demi said.

"Of course, I might have sued you for breach of promise and I could have used one of the lawyers in my office, *pro bono* or on a contingency basis or something."

"Come on. You must be joking. That sort of thing is only for millionaires and show girls and the like, as reported in the *New York Daily Mirror* for the salacious benefit of the fifth grade level readers who buy that newspaper."

"I know that," Rebia protested, "I was only kidding. Don't worry about it. You have your plans and I have my plans. Don't be so serious. I am over you and you are over me. Good luck in California with your society girl."

There still seemed an edge to her words, but Demi decided to ignore it. "Thanks," he said, as he mounted his front steps. Rebia gave a casual wave of her hand, opened the door to the Karras house and disappeared inside.

The door was shut behind her very carefully.

"There," said his mother who had been watching from the slit of a window that edged the front door. "Over with in a civilized manner."

"I have invited Nancy for dinner tomorrow evening," said Demi, "That all right?"

"Of course," said Mrs. Christopoulos, "Such a dear girl."

***

"Did you win?" asked Ted Collins.

"Did we win? We slaughtered them. Just shows what practice and determination will do for a bunch of over-age undergrads." Richard Forrest hooked his thumbs in his armpits and struck a cocky pose. The other men in the lounge laughed.

"Skidmore guys just weren't up to speed. Maybe it's the colder weather up there," said Demi.

"Oh, come on. You guys haven't even reached middle age by a long shot so don't play that older guy game with me. I am one of you, after all," Ted mocked.

"The other guys were of the same vintage," said Dominic Calenti, "And it wasn't like Basic Training. Just a game."

"You looked a little winded at half-time, actually," Demi pointed out.

"Well, so I am not in as great shape as I was in the Army. None of those push-ups or jumping jacks in the morning, or running in place, thank God. And if you remember, I did have one season with the high school track team as star shot-putter. Just to stay in shape for fall football." Dominic patted his stomach. "Still pretty flat, nevertheless."

"So, cut down on the beer then," warned Gussie, "Hard to do, I know, after drinking that three point two swill in the PX."

"You know, they set up a Coke bottling plant in the Western Pacific to handle all the Coca Cola kiddies drafted into the military. Nothing too good for our boys at the front, or at least near it," said Ted Collins, "Actually, I used to drink it instead of coffee for breakfast, since the mess hall coffee was invariably awful, at least in the 313th Wing, and that stuff felt like it would take the enamel off your teeth."

"Ah, fond memories of the Pacific paradise, eh, Ted?" Gussie laughed, "Way back from the real fighting when you got to those islands. Wasn't the real war the way it was in Europe."

"I don't know about Europe, but being in a blacked-out convoy of Liberty ships outfitted to carry a bunch of G.I.s, like it was some slave ship from Acra, was unnerving enough. I could imagine the conditions as being sort of like what my friend Nan described from her reading, even though we were not actually shackled to the cots. No lights on as we zigged-zagged across the Pacific. Sometimes in good weather we could make out the destroyers riding herd on us, sitting ducks out at the edge of the flotilla. I can still recall the mixed smells below decks where the men slept, a combination of body odor, vomit from the poor bastards who were sea sick, some nearly all the way across to Tinian, and shaving lotion as some guys tried to escape their own stink, or the smell of peppermint from the life savers you could buy in the ship's store."

"Sounds like fun," said Gussie, "At least it wasn't front line battle, but it is a war story."

"The beat-up merchant ship we went over on was the *Mormac Hawk*. What an ironic name. We came back on the *Marine Dragon*. More ironies. I had a camera all through the affair. Cheap little Kodak I picked up from the PX at Kearns in Utah as we waited for the troop train to Vancouver. My prize picture is of the *Enola Gay* parked on the hard stand on Tinian. Good old number 82. It was in Bomb Group 509. Or maybe the cloud of smoke from the end of the runway on Tinian where an unlucky B-29 did not quite make it and crashed and burned. That was the closest I got to combat, I am glad to say. My particular B-29 was number 48. 505th Bomb Group –Very Heavy, 313th Wing, 20th Air Force. Hard for me to forget those numbers. My machine guns, my computerized gun sights, my canon, my bombsights, my General Curtis LeMay, a real killer. What an ego driven guy he was. Made Patton seem like a shrinking violet," Ted laughed.

"Yours?" asked Demi.

"I was Armament Crew. Just outlasted the others as their discharge numbers were higher than mine. Getting there before the *Enola Gay* blew up the enemy and ended the war, you see, gave me a low discharge number; late comers like me had to stay around and mothball the armament. Another smell I can conjure up is the smell of Cosmoline, the greasy coating that prevented rust. I wonder if it was cancer producing. We worked with that stuff for weeks. Guess no point in worrying about that now. We did have time on our hands. Some of the guys started making jewelry out of welding rods. A couple of cooks in the mess tried to make a sort of brandy out of the fruit bars in K-rations. Awful stuff. Lots of fun and games, though, to use up the hours."

"Grist for your Stanford mill, Ted. Write it up," advised Dom.

"No, real men don't dance and real men don't tell heroic war tales, unless forced to by Mrs. Nadeau," said Ted, adding that comment quickly for Demi's benefit. "Or unless you're Norman Mailer, the brief army chef, who seems to have testosterone poisoning. I suppose I could write comedy about the time my crew forgot to secure the turret dome cover on one of our B-29s when I was at Barksdale Field in Louisiana. The cover flipped off on a training flight to Cuba and banged the length of the fuselage and bounced off the stabilizer. The whole armament crew lost weekend pass privileges for two weeks, along with getting a reaming out by the Squadron Commander. Good thing that S.N.A.F.U. was not made on a combat mission. I suppose it might have damaged the plane, but it didn't."

"With that kind of stuff, it was a wonder we won the air war in the Pacific. Bad as you paint it, I think I would have traded it for one of my foxholes. But let's get back to the next game," put in Richard Forrest, "And not re-fight the war. We need to work out some pre-arranged moves to make our way down court and to the basket. We were just winging it in that first game."

"War strategy," said Gussie, "Think of it as the second front."

"Okay, give me a piece of paper," said Demi.

"You going to diagram some slick maneuvers?" asked Ted, "I thought baseball was your sport. Second base. Shortstop. Scooping up grounders, throwing people out at first. Working double plays. That kind of thing."

"I have some playground time at basketball. Played during the baseball off-season in high school. I know what I am doing," Demi said, "You saw me fake out some of those bigger guys in our winning game. Give me a break. Besides, I have watched the pros play."

"Me, too," said Dom, "You have seen the Knicks?"

"Why do you go?" asked Ted.

"They are New York, you know. The home team and all that." Dom seemed surprised at the question.

"They are a bunch of hired hands," said Ted, "They get big bucks for what they do and tomorrow for bigger bucks they will be in Toronto or Philadelphia. What's with the home team stuff? Now, if you want home team, let me tell you. When I was a kid in grade school, my father used to take me to watch the Poughkeepsie All-Stars, a semi-pro team that played at Riverview Field on the same diamond I played on in the Poughkeepsie Grade School league. The star pitcher was a local cop, the catcher – big guy – was a local plumber. The clean-up hitter was an insurance salesman. Now there was a local team. And cold Cokes for a nickel a bottle."

"So, what was the quality of the play for these bozos?" Jack asked.

"Good enough," said Ted, "for a Sunday afternoon at the park. I remember watching them with my father when they played a team called 'House of David.' Bunch of guys, wearing big beards, who were just amazing with the tricks they could play with the ball. A double play was not just a double play for them but a kind of ballet – dancing and flipping the ball around."

"That I could identify with," said Demi.

"Funny thing how so many guys get hooked on watching professional sports these days," observed Ted, "Sort of bread and circuses, but without the bread, unless a ball park hot dog and sauerkraut with a beer is the bread. Somebody said that you have to be smart enough to understand the rules of the game and dumb enough to think it's important."

"I don't know," said Demi, "As my former psych teacher, Professor Labropoulos – may she remain healthy and prosper – might say, these games are sublimated war, and the audience can get the thrill of combat without the dangers. Maybe pro football is the most extreme example, but even basketball is getting more physical, and have you ever watched some of these base stealers slide into second when safe by a mile with cleats up? Mayhem is often on their mind. Or see a pitcher brush back the hitter? Give him a concussion if he isn't fast enough, or break his nose."

"Good grief, is that how you guys are playing vets' basketball?" Ted asked.

"Not us," said Rich, "We are gentlemen to the core. Officers and gentlemen, I was going to say, even the former non-coms amongst us. And there is always Major Berg to set an example."

"Speaking of sublimated combat, went to your student production of *Aeschylus* with Nancy," Demi said, "I wanted to make sure that the Persians still lost to the Greeks. Glad to say, they did, with multiple Persian deaths. How is it going with you and Harriet Snyderman, the embryonic Broadway star?"

"Well, she calls me Rich and I call her Hattie by now, and we have shared a beer or two at the Log Cabin after library and before she has to be locked in her dorm in the evening. They sure do protect the young ladies here. *In loco parentis* and they really mean it."

"Maybe the good beer king, Matthew Vassar, thought he was creating a kind of intellectual nunnery for the protected young ladies of his day, particularly with those reverends who helped him set up the place," Gussie put in, "Remember the warm, perhaps even 'hot' Vassar welcome from that hard-nosed Dean back at the beginning?"

"The way they celebrate Founder's Day, you would think that they were paying tribute to God, the Father, although by now he is the Holy Ghost." Ted laughed. "I wonder who was the Messiah. My sister, who went here before me, always seemed to think it was President Henry Noble

MacCracken. According to her, he was the one who really established the academic tone for the Ivy League status Vassar now has, killing off an early misconception of the school as a place to prepare pure young ladies for an intellectual and artistic but married life. The way my father's cousin Blanche Merrill was a special music student here, studying piano. MacCracken actually taught, it seems. My sister took his course on Shakespeare and said it was inspiring, and that is a word she seldom used."

"You think spinster President Sarah Bloomer is the current stand-in for the Virgin Mother?" asked Gussie.

"Don't be blasphemous," interjected Jack.

"What, bad luck?" countered Gussie.

"I am just careful," answered Jack.

"Well, a pure life in a women's college it was supposed to be. When my mother, who was a member of the class of 1916, got married and pregnant, she had to leave and was not allowed to return to campus. Although, we have noticed that when the school now asks alums for money, it seems to have found her again." Ted laughed.

"Boy, you have turned out to be from a real Vassar family," Jack exclaimed.

"Don't hold it against me," said Ted, "My sister came because she could live at home and it was good education, cheaper than some alternatives. In addition, the National Youth Administration paid her to work while she was a student. The NYA was part of the WPA that our local hero, FDR, set up during the great depression. She worked in the library, I think, or in some administrative office. Good deal."

"I read somewhere that FDR was on the Vassar Board of Trustees," Demi put in.

"Yeah, my sister said that once Eleanor sent her car to the campus and took some of the NYA students up to Hyde Park for tea. Haven't noticed anything like that these days," said Ted, "Of course, they still do have after-dinner demitasse coffee in the dorms. So very civilized."

"Speaking of the Holy Trinity, as we were a minute ago, you guys been following the big ruckus over some story in the *Vassar Review* that offers an alternative version of the immaculate conception?" Jack asked.

"Made the local paper, in fact, with quotes from the complaining Reverend Pike, who is Pastor at a local Episcopal Church and also, apparently, the Episcopal chaplain here at VC," Ted explained.

"I thought John McGiffin was the college chaplain," said Gussie, "That is how he was labeled when they told me he would be my academic advisor. A Unitarian minister."

"That seemed to be part of the Vassar problem according to this Reverend Pike. I read an account in the *New York Times* where a small article also appeared. This Pike fellow, who is some sort of publicity hound, it appears, has claimed that having an official chaplain who was Unitarian was non-Christian since Unitarians do not believe in the divinity of Jesus. Anyway, so Pike is some kind of alternate part-time chaplain for the Church of England true-believers." Phil laughed. "They even have some Rabbi in reserve on the holiest of benches and a Catholic priest ready to give religious ministration to those who belong to that Mother Church."

"An editor of the *Vassar Review* that I know from my classes told me about the story," Ted explained. "Actually, she was first in my Freshman English class, and we seem to have coincidently been in several other classes since."

"And she is?" asked Phil, leaning forward with some interest.

Ted huffed out a breath, whether from annoyance or embarrassment it was hard to tell. "Doesn't really matter, but, okay, it's Sara. Likes to write fiction. Friendly from the get-go, not like some of the patronizing types we have talked about," he explained. "Anyway, she said that the literary magazine published a short piece of work by some rather eccentric little student who proposed a story that went something like this: A pregnant innocent young Mary more or less shot-gun wedded Joseph, because in her simple gullibility she had been exploring sex with a 'mountain man' or a real nature boy. Then she found out she was with-child, putting a lie to the biblical notion of the immaculate conception and a virgin birth. Just a poor naïve late teenager, who may have been pure before, but turned out not to be afterwards, with parents who engineered a reputation-saving marriage to this slightly older carpenter, who himself may have been a bit simple, but willing to go along with the public story and get himself a sexy young bride," Ted smiled at the assembled vets. "I do believe Jesus was supposed to have had a number of siblings. There you have the whole calamity in a nutshell."

"I don't think there are any real mountains in Israel, from my limited knowledge of geography," said Phil, "but I suppose reality is not a requirement when you are creating myths, or rather anti-myths. Big hills, I suppose, would do. Or maybe this student writer had been listening to Nat King Cole's recording of *Nature Boy*."

"Whatever," Ted answered, "Anyway, the story has made a large stink, conflict between town and gown, so to speak, with a self-promoting, big-mouthed, ambitious local preacher carrying on like Vassar and its godless, liberal students have pushed us toward Armageddon or something. Unfortunately, bad publicity in the press could enrage some of the funds-giving conventional old-girl alums or their conservative, wealthy husbands, who might withhold contributions."

"I don't think that Armageddon is exactly the right image," noted Phil, "Maybe urging us toward a reborn Sodom would be more fitting. That would equally outrage those graduates of which you speak, however. So, who exactly is this Reverend Pike?"

"Minister at Christ Episcopal Church. The social church of Poughkeepsie. I spent Sundays there for nearly twelve years at their Sunday School; my mother expected it. She went to services on the big holidays like Christmas and Easter. My father never bothered; one of those classic gender divides, I think," Ted said, "This Pike, though, is a strange bird. Started out as a Catholic, apparently, with a desire to become a priest, and then shifted gears into the Church of England and has become a kind of pseudo Brit. Walks his two Dalmatians around the neighborhood. Wears English tweeds with his turned collar. You could call this contretemps the consequences of Pike's pique."

"Oh, please – resist those puns, Ted, but that was a good one," Demi laughed. "And you continue at this place of worship?"

"Not me. I opted out just before Bible study class leading to confirmation, which is a big deal for the Episcopals, sort of like a high church *bar mitzvah*. Looking around the place, I realized that there was little separation of church and state in Poughkeepsie. The Sunday school teachers were nearly all teachers in the public school system. The Sunday school superintendent was also the Superintendent of the City School System. The secular head of the church body that ran things was some big deal at the Poughkeepsie Tennis Club, a sanctimonious place where no Jews had ever darkened the door or threw unwelcome shadows on their courts. My fellow students were the spawn of Poughkeepsie's small town oligarchs, the socially elite that ran the law firms, the local hotel, the medical practices, some connecting to the original Dutch settlers who had converted from the Dutch Reform church in town, and so on and on. Wasn't for me," Ted shook his head.

"Hey, I used to play with the spawn, as you put it, of some of them. I lived nearby and Ginny Smith sometimes invited me over to play in the Smith back yard," Evi laughed. "They had a big swing and slide set, with sand box and play house before anyone else. Ginny sometimes wanted to play doctor in that playhouse. I could oblige. Only thing, Mrs. Smith would never let us smelly little kids from grade school actually into the real house, although on hot days a maid would come out with lemonade and cookies. I did get to see how the other half lived, I guess, but from a safe, antiseptic distance. You know, they named a new grade school after her grandfather. Somehow I have never been able to believe that family actually gave money to the city to get that honor."

"I think you told us that story, or at least part of it before. You getting prematurely senile, Evi?" asked Demi.

"Sorry," apologized Evi.

"Yeah, right," Ted went on, "Anyway, these types seldom actually run for public office, but they put forward the puppets that looked as if they were the political honchos. An illusion, of course. I just woke up in my teens. Of course, I was also a self-righteous teenager, as many are, although in retrospect, I still believe I was probably right, " Ted shook his head in wonder at his own childish unawareness before his epiphany. "The capper for me was when my school guidance counselor, who also taught at the Sunday School, called me down to his office from study hall and told me I should return to bible class because, and I quote his exact words, *I was just as good as they were*. The matter of principle seemed to escape him entirely."

"Wow," said Phil. "What an asshole."

"He really was," continued Ted. "His personality fit his almost comically tragic appearance. The kids used to call him Ichabod Crane because his coat sleeves never covered his wrists and his pants always were too short and revealed his socks, which were also white, no matter what else he wore. He looked like an illustration from our American Lit text where the dopey school teacher is being chased by Brom Bones as the headless horseman."

"You sound like you don't like your home town," said Demi.

"Oh, I like certain aspects of it, particularly its geography, if not its politics, but as Sherwood Anderson says, the caring that is supposedly part of the small town myth may also be just snooping, and really hides grotesquely warped lives. The parochial limitations and the stultifying existence of the inhabitants deform their character, he said. Just read Anderson's *Winesburg, Ohio*, if you want to see a literary depiction of the condition," Ted grimaced. "There are good people here. I know some of them, honest people doing the best they can, having fought through the First World War, the flu epidemic that killed my Aunt, the great depression, the last 'Good War,' and survived. But I know lives that are severely limited because, well, now you know."

"You are really on a soap box there, Ted," said Demi.

"You try living in Highland if you are looking for provincial and narrow-minded," said Leroy. "New Paltz, village that it is, is miles ahead in sophistication compared to Highland. That town is as close to being redneck as you can get along the mighty Hudson. The teachers' college does bring more enlightened faculty into the community, even if some of them are intellectually limited, as compared to Vassar, hold-overs of the teacher Normal School days."

"Duchess County is not all that bad," put in Jack, "If you know how to play the system. I told you, I plan to stay in the good old home town, the Queen City of the Hudson, and do my thing, and I won't be a puppet, believe me, because I know how to massage the egos of those W.A.S.P.s you were talking about. I expect to pull the strings. I got elected class president in high school, as you know, running against some proper tweedy kid whose father went to Williams and had a good law practice, which he was going to hand on to his son, naturally. I intend to do exactly the same things when I am a local lawyer. Times are changing. I may even get into the Tennis Club, or the Amrita down on Market Street. Those buggers are going to need people like me as their blue blood starts to thin out. Just you watch."

"The Amrita Club?" asked Gussie, "What is that? Never heard of it."

"I have," said Rich, "Some of the upper management at IBM are members. I believe the company pays the dues. Good for the company to be part of the Duchess County business world and cozy up to the local bigwigs. In fact, apparently it is company policy to pick someone as the fall guy, usually one who is not particularly effective at his IBM paying job, and it is his function to get out of the way at the office and join local organizations. He even gets time off to do that. I heard about it when I was there full-time. Apparently, the name, Amrita, comes from Sanskrit and has something to do with immortality, knowledge, and the gods. I guess the local bigwigs wanted a men's club where they could hide from the women, sit in large arm chairs, smoke their Cuban cigars, and look out over their feudal domain of Market Street, and gave it this pretentious name. Sounds perfectly Victorian. The Immortals of Duchess County!"

"That is really neat," said Gussie, "Sounds like the anti-Vassar in its way. Men only."

"I know about it because I was a waiter there at a part-time job after school," Jack said. "They tipped reasonably well, or most of them did, as I recall. Lots of dark wood, plush carpets, leather chairs. In the best of taste. Although, I remember waiting on some Smith guy without the Smith name, married into the cough drop dynasty you guys talked about, and he was no gentleman. S.O.B. stiff-the-waiter kind of guy. in fact, who spent a lot of his time complaining about F.D.R. and talking up Ham Fish, Joe Martin, and Bruce Barton."

"If all that was to your taste," said Ted.

"It wouldn't be mine," put in Demi.

"Nor mine," said Ted, "And all of the above is why when I finish here at Vassar I was for making tracks to the University of Minnesota for graduate study. Out of here like a shot. I thought I could study with Robert Penn Warren but he has just moved on to Yale, I have discovered, and Yale is not for me, anyway, having snatched Sara from the jaws of the eastern elite. My dream place now is Stanford, though, and I have applied there for a graduate fellowship to supplement the last of my G.I. Bill money since it won't take me all the way through the Creative Writing Program. I do think California is preferable to cold and snowy Minneapolis where Billy Graham is currently deep into some Christian crusade to save the middle West. There was a narrative writing teacher during my second year whose husband is going to be second in command to Wallace Stegner at Stanford, and she was the one first urging me to go there. Great place, Palo Alto, from what I hear and Sara and I would love it, she says."

"Leave your parents and the old homestead behind?" asked Gussie.

"My brother, who works for IBM in Kingston, and his wife and kids can take up the family slack," Ted said, "But to get back to the *Vassar Review*, the Right Reverend Pike, and undergraduate blasphemy, you might have noticed how President Bloomer stood up for the free speech rights of her students in public. She became a stalwart supporter of the Fourth Amendment; although Sara tells me she did call together the editorial board of the magazine to tell that they also should always consider the possible adverse reactions of the various communities involved, and plan for the kind of responses that might be required. It was a very cordial meeting, Sara said, but there was a message there in the President's little educational exchange with the students."

"So, like all Presidents, Miss Bloomer is handling a hot potato as diplomatically as possible. Nothing new in that," said Phil, "Got to keep the influential wealthy donating alums happy, or at least reconciled, without appearing to sacrifice academic freedom. What a dance!"

"Although, as they say in the advertising circles, all news is good news, on the other hand," commented Jack.

"Most of the time," Phil contributed, "It certainly leaves the Reverend with nowhere to go but up. He has made his point for the devout in his heavenly political base, as they say, and the more open minded free-thinkers have been appeased with the official stand of the College. What more could you ask?"

"Right," said Ted, "Or left as the case may be. Just what I told Sara."

TWENTY-SIX

1949

"You are just going to have to meet them sooner or later, Ted," Sara said, pushing back from him in the passenger's seat of his car, "They aren't ogres, you know, just rather conservative, at least my father is. Business executive that he is, and all that. Mom is probably less so, maybe even voted Democratic without telling Dad, I wouldn't be surprised. She paints in water colors, volunteers for worthy causes like eye glasses for the indigent. Things like that. They do belong to the local Golf and Tennis Club, of course, and that is important for Mom. A place to have the mass cocktail party to pay off dinner invitations from people you don't really like, or don't want extended conversations with."

"I know. I know. But if your father thinks that sending you to Vassar is the sort of thing that turns nice young ladies from the suburbs into communists, what is he going to think of a veteran who belongs to the American Veterans' Committee with all those left-wing founders and members? Oh, the horror!" Ted tried pulling her over against him and she did not resist.

"Okay, Conrad, or is it Kurtz? We shall just face the horror until they figure out the whole thing isn't really horrible, and that we know what we are doing and where we are going. They have typecast you as an 'older man' as if three years' difference in age is a major problem. Actually, I think that is about their own age difference." She laughed. "Besides, they will come to admire you, if not right away, then eventually, as a person of talent and principles."

"What exactly does your father do, being a vice-president for Union Carbide? Or rather what does vice-president-ing consist of?" Ted seemed genuinely curious.

"That is really funny, since for so long what it meant to me was that he got up reasonably early and drove to the train station and took the commuter train into the city with a horde of other men in dark suits reading the *New York Times* or the *Wall Street Journal*, never a prole tabloid for the masses, of course. Then my father vanished from our lives until he came home and sat down in his easy chair with his old-fashioned, made with genuine Jim Beam bourbon, and we had dinner prepared by the cook." She laughed. "At first my brother and I, as little children, ate earlier and separately. It sort of reminded me of living in a Mary Poppins world, only we had a cook instead of a nanny. In fact, I think I maybe knew the cook better than I did my mother for a while. Mom was that glamorous person dressed up for a night on the town or a party with friends. Right out of *The Great Gatsby*."

"Not something out of my experience," acknowledged Ted.

"Eventually we two children grew into an acceptable pre-adult condition that allowed us to participate in the grown-up meals. So that is what I knew about being a vice-president. It was having the ability to make a really strong old-fashioned with great fruit in it. He always gave me the maraschino cherry. I did not even have to ask," She laughed again. "Of course, with the war and all the hired help disappearing into well-paying industrial jobs, Rosie-The-Riveter stuff, Mom and I had to take over the housekeeping and the food preparation. What a shock for a lady who could absurdly imagine herself one of the FFVs. Not a nice scene, but we adjusted."

"FFVs? What exactly is that?" Ted asked.

"Stands for 'First Families of Virginia' and is a big thing for some Virginians. Actually, Mom's family had the connections but not the funding, you might say. In Virginia, sometimes the family was the more important thing, since that was sometimes all you had left to cling to, rather than lots of money. Civil War did that, I guess. Money came with Dad's family and with his Cornell pedigree and, of course, his chemistry degree."

"Well, I am afraid all I can counter with is my connection with the original Eddie Collins from Millerton in Duchess County, the only honest player on the Chicago White Sox team caught in the 'Black Sox' scandal of game-throwing and the greatest second baseman of all times, according to some. That, and the fact that he and Lou Gehrig were the only Columbia graduates to make it into the big leagues, at least so far. Small potatoes, I guess, in the face of FFVs. How about the fact that my mother's father was a school superintendent? That carry any weight?"

"Oh, Ted. Such a joker, you are," Sara ruffled his hair. "I didn't know you cared about big league baseball."

"I don't, actually, although it gave me something to talk about with Demi when we first started in here as veteran students. Now we have other topics, of course," Ted grinned. "Like Vassar girls."

156

"Vassar women," corrected Sara.

"Whatever you say," answered Ted, "By the way, how about going with me to a Martha Graham dance company performance here in Poughkeepsie? This guy who runs the Arts and Gifts shop, Merle Ettinger, is trying to bring high culture to the area, and he is starting with Martha Graham. Going to put her and her dance troupe on at the High School. Should be interesting to see if there is an audience in the old home town."

"That would be wonderful, Ted. Did I ever tell you that I danced, briefly, with Merce Cunningham?"

"No. Didn't know I was acquainted with a famous young modern dancer who danced in the big leagues."

"Oh, he had been invited to visit our modern dance class here at Vassar, and he performed with the students in a master class. It was great fun. But I intend to be a great philosopher, instead."

"You will have to grab every dancing moment you can get, Sara, since I don't dance. So I take that your response to my invitation is a 'yes, I would love to go'?" Ted waited expectantly.

"Of course, and don't you worry, I will get you dancing yet, sometime in our long life together. You just wait." Sara smiled. "I am a very determined person. You will see."

***

"Very nice, your young lady, this Miss Coffin," Mr. Christopoulos said.

"Yes," agreed Mrs. Christopoulos, "She even offered to help feed Corry when I had to go to the kitchen."

"She told me that she had a couple of much younger sisters, and that as a teenager she used to take care of them when her parents were busy, so I guess it involved feeding babies at times," Demi explained, "as a homegrown baby sitter, I guess, so she has that experience."

"Quite maternal, then," commented Mr. Christopoulos.

"I guess," said Demi, "Haven't given it that much thought."

"Make a man a good wife," said his mother.

"I don't believe she is going to Vassar to prepare herself to be a good wife, Ma. Not with her interest in Union Theological for graduate work after Vassar."

"That would be a nice interest, but marriage is what is important, and children," Demi's mother stated a fact of life as far as she was concerned, "And who is going to want a woman minister?"

"Someday they might, Ma."

"Not in my lifetime," Mrs. Christopoulos said, "But she is a very nice, considerate girl anyway. I am afraid that Rebia is not even a close contest, sweet as she is."

"Rebia is a nice girl, too," commented Mr. Christopoulos, "but I agree that she is not likely to fit into the world where you seem to be going."

"I am sorry about that," said Demi, "particularly if she thinks I led her along, but, you know, I had really just come back to civilian life and did not know exactly which end was up. I couldn't talk about it then, but when I first came back to Conklin Street I felt both like I was still in high school and not in high school. Like maybe the Battle of the Bulge and the war was a nightmare. I found all those newspaper clippings, Ma, that you must have cut out of the local paper, about Tim and me and baseball, and had saved like it was just that spring. And there were our old report cards, Tim's and mine, stacked in a bureau drawer. It was weird. Then Rebia presented herself, and it was like having a girlfriend back in school, but it was summer vacation and time on my hands, with some work at the Acropolis." Demi looked up from staring at his hands in his lap. "You see that?"

"We knew you were kind of mixed-up and at loose ends," said his mother, "but you would work it out. We have confidence in your good sense."

"Sometimes you don't want to grow up, and then you realize that while you weren't looking, you have had to. Grow up, I mean. It is too bad about Rebia, but she hasn't quite grown up yet. In fact, I find her kind of silly. To tell the truth, silly and juvenile. Someone like Nancy, not that much older than Rebia, is grown up, with ideas and values and knowledge."

"Agreed, son," said his father, 'You have to do what you have to do, and you still have a long life ahead of you."

"God willing," put in his mother.

"Or good genes and random events willing." Demi could not resist.

"Oh, Democritus, always with the smart wisecrack," his mother protested, "What would your theology girl think of that remark?"

"She's broadminded about that sort of thing, Ma. That is one of the things so great about her."

"Well, if she makes you happy..." his mother's voice trailed off, thoughtfully.

"We wouldn't have it any other way, Demi," said his father.

***

The car was the latest from Detroit, with red paint on the lower half of the body, the fenders, hood, doors and trunk, while the upper part was painted a gleaming white around the windows, the upper half of the doors, the roof.

"So, how is it going now over there with all those highbrows, Roy?" Mr. Freer leaned against the gleaming red fender of the 1948 Chevy in the showroom. He has been polishing it, and the two-toned car shone as if it were costume jewelry in the floodlights, illuminating it smartly for prospective customers.

"Okay, Dad. At first it was hard to get back into the swing of things as a student, because of being out of high school so long, and I felt a bit rusty about the studying thing, but after a couple of years there I have been able to get back into the student routine." Leroy picked up a cloth and polished the chrome bars of the grill.

"Good for you, Roy! Make the Freers proud. Live up to that old French Huguenot heritage," Mr. Freer punched his son playfully in the upper arm. "Your ma and I knew you would be a winner, just like this Chevy Stylemaster." He patted this model's shining red fender.

"Aw. Dad. Don't overdo it with that kind of stuff," Leroy smiled.

"Not at all. Named you Leroy because of our hopes. It means 'The King,' you know, can't deny the spunky Huguenot lineage." Mr. Freer smiled in turn. "They make a big deal here in the Hudson Valley about the Dutch roots and the English roots, but the Huguenots were as tough and as principled at the Pilgrims coming ashore at Plymouth Rock. We settled along the Wallkill, built our stone houses, worshiped our own way, farmed the land. Hardy stock, as they say. You did your duty as a soldier for our country and now you are being rewarded with an education. American aspirations, you know."

"Shit Dad. You make it sound heroic," Leroy protested, "I done my duty, that's all."

"Did, Leroy, did. You are a college man now. So, the old car dealership has been good for me. Tough years during the war with no new models, but the car industry went to war, too. We hung in there with used cars and repairs to keep the old ones going. You know all that. Now, with the war over and new cars coming off the Detroit assembly lines, we are back in business again." Mr. Freer waved at the showroom, with a flick of his fingers acknowledging the full inventory parked in the lot outside.

"Gotta admit, Dad, they don't look all that different from the pre-war models." Leroy continued to polish the chrome, rubbing the hub caps. "No rust, and brighter finish, but they must be using the old pre-war stamping forms."

"Just you wait. The '49 models will be really new. Actually, the first truly postwar Chevy. You could have one for your Vassar graduation in 1950, if you wanted. Then your war will be over." Leroy's father punched his son's arm again.

"Or a different kind of war; job hunting, I suppose," answered Leroy, "I need to get one more year so I can get the teaching credential. Child Study at Vassar doesn't do it, so I guess New Paltz will have to be the grand finale. I hope the wife can continue to balance your books while I put in that last effort."

"No problem, Leroy. In fact, I expect Chevy to be around forever, if it can survive wars, depressions, Plymouths, and Fords." Mr. Freer patted the car they had been working on as if it were a faithful horse.

"I hope so, Dad. Have you seen pictures of the new Kaiser that West Coast guy is beginning to huckster? Should be on the market soon, and it is certainly a modern design, sort of like an old Chrysler Air Stream. Or the revamped Studebaker? Hard to tell which way it is going with that streamlined design."

"Flash in the pan, believe me. People will stick with the old tried and true brands like Chevrolet, Pontiac, Buick. Cadillac, the mark of having made it. Everyone wants to trade up eventually, so that when they park that car in the driveway, the neighbors all know you have arrived. Keeping up with the Joneses is a concept that never dies. And for better or worse, in the Land of the Free, you are your car. I learned that in marketing sessions that GM gives the authorized dealers. You will see."

"Don't be too sure, Dad. Postwar is not pre-war. People may want something really new. Maybe that helps remind them we won," Leroy shook his head. "Maybe not a good way, that is, but one way."

"Don't be such a pessimist when you are on the edge of the big Freer breakthrough with higher ed." His father shook his head.

"Well, when I get into that classroom finally, I am going to make darn sure I prepare students to have an open mind, and be ready for the changes that are certain to come."

"Okay then. That's my boy," said Mr. Freer, "Ready for the future."

TWENTY-SEVEN

1949

"That's another win under the belt," crowed Phil to Rich and Demi, "Your diagrams of plays worked, when I could remember them."

"Slick ball handling," said Gussie, "That's the trick. Fake them out of position and drive for the basket. Works every time."

"Don't get so worked up that you forget your studies," warned Ted, "That is what you all are really here for, I would think."

"Right," responded Jack, "but don't be a spoil sport, Ted. Got to have a little fun mixed in with the serious stuff!" They all laughed in agreement.

"Speaking of fun," Demi said, "Anything new on the German front, Phil?"

"I thought the war was over," said Jack.

"This is a different theater of operations," Demi said.

"Locker room talk coming up?" asked Rich.

"You guys! I thought I told you about my problem in confidence, Demi," Phil complained.

"I apologize, it just slipped out." Demi seemed honestly embarrassed.

"Okay, okay," Phil said, "I believe that."

"Whatever," protested Gussie, "but you just can't leave the mystery hanging there, Phil."

"Yeah," said Dom, "Spill the beans, Phil. We are all warriors together here."

"Right," said Jack, "One for all and all for one."

"I think that was just for the three musketeers or was it four, and we are eight at the moment." Phil noted, "But since Demi has breached my confidence…"

"Inadvertently, I assure you," Demi interrupted.

"I will continue," said Phil, "to reveal the sordid facts of academic life to you innocents. I accepted the good Professor's invitation, although she was only an untenured instructor working on her doctorate in the big city, and went to her faculty apartment, where we discussed language and literature and my facility, in her judgment, in German as well as French and Italian – war and family, you understand – along with the course work in German. She was very complimentary, I must say."

"Way to go, Phil," said Dom, "Going to get you an A there, for certain."

"Oh, this was not this year. This happened during our first Spring semester. I got the A. A lot has happened since then, though."

"Continue. You have us all in suspense," said Gussie.

"Okay. So, we talked. She offered me a beer – German, of course – and then suggested we send out for a pizza to go with it. We ate, and drank more beer; she asked about my war experiences, and then one thing led to another – and I stayed the night." Phil stopped there.

"Whoo-whee, Phil," said Jack, "How about that!"

"Well, I told Demi originally, that Aggie was not really much older than me, maybe a few months, because while I was fighting the Fascists, she was going to school."

"Aggie, already yet, nickname familiar," laughed Jack, "A big change in the teacher-student relationship."

"You can laugh if you want, but she is really a great person and lonely as a junior faculty member without tenure security. Actually, you could say sweet," Phil protested, "She says after I graduate from here that I should go to Teachers' College at Columbia, and get the degree and the state certification to teach foreign languages in a public school. I think it's great idea, and I am just going to do it. Aggie believes I have an aptitude for languages. She thinks I would make a good high school teacher, and that I am good with kids that age. She says she can tell by the way I work in groups in class, the way I explain to the younger students."

"Go for it, Phil," said Ted, "When all these older vets start popping out kids and trying to catch up with life, getting the Rosie-the-Riveters back in the kitchen and the bed rooms from the assembly lines, they are going to need plenty of public school teachers. And what about a future with Aggie?"

Phil reddened. "I don't know. A bridge to cross later, I guess. I wonder how a college professor considers the status involved, if she were to become the partner or wife of a high school teacher. Some kind of intellectual class thing, I would bet."

"Bridge is not the metaphor I would have chosen," said Ted, "But okay. Sounds a lot different from the first description you gave many months ago, about this storm trooper type, in front of that *Intro to German* class."

"So, I was guilty of stereotyping," Phil acknowledged sheepishly, "People are not always what they appear to be. She has had a really tough history. She got very personal that first evening over beer and pizza, maybe too much beer. She said her mother was Jewish and her father was not. Came from some upper class European banking family, it seems. When the going got brutal with the rise of Hitler and storm troopers roaming the street and harassing Jewish people and such, her parents sent her and her older sister to relatives in England for safety. In fact, they were put into the same girls' public prep school that Indira Ghandi had attended, so it was obviously an impressive place. Ghandi was ahead of Aggie. That's how come Aggie speaks such proper British English."

"That is some story," said Ted.

"She considered going to Somerville College at Oxford where Indira Ghandi went, but then her parents got out finally through Spain, apparently, picked up the daughters and came here. Her father had banker connections and could get asylum and a job, and Aggie and her sister went to college in the city, Colombia. And that led to an instructorship at Vassar, while she finishes her PhD."

"Really some story," repeated Ted, "And her sister?"

"She is a social worker in New Jersey," said Phil, "Aggie says she had issues to work out, and becoming a psychotherapist herself seemed to help."

"So, what will become of this torrid soul-match, my friend?" Demi asked, "Any future to it?"

"One day at a time, or one month at a time, or whatever," said Phil, "It is not as though she is still my college teacher, after all. She has to finish her doctorate and maybe get tenure here, and maybe not. I have to work on graduate education myself."

"Sounds long-term to me," said Jack.

"Would you consider her a 'local girl,' Jack?" asked Ted, "By way of explanation, before I met Sara, or rather before I found Sara interesting and interested, I fell into that 'local girl' thing. The daughter of a neighbor was mowing her lawn next to ours and we struck up a conversation. She was a nice girl, obviously, and had not lived there when I went into service. Anyway, her father, a doctor and pathologist at Vassar Brothers Hospital, had moved to Poughkeepsie and she was a day student at Bennett Junior College, that holding tank for young females of the upper classes. To make a long story short, eventually I took her to a football game at West Point and to dinner afterwards and I found upon closer examination that she was nice and sweet but really rather stupid, which is why she was going to Bennett, I guess. In addition, I could not imagine a casual conversation with her father. Perhaps it would be about autopsies and malignant diseases revealed in the cutting room of the morgue. So that was my experience with a 'local girl.'

What will you discuss with the undertaker father-in-law that you said you were contemplating? The most effective embalming fluid?"

"Don't start on me about that again. You know my take on the matter." Jack sounded peevish.

"Sorry, Jack," Ted answered, "But to change the subject, how about that guided New York City tour you wanted to take with the side trip to the Admissions Office at Fordham to investigate the law school? It got postponed when Vassar decided to let those of us who wished, to take the full four-year dose of liberal education on Raymond Avenue. But baseball is upon us again, and we just need to check the Yankee's home game schedule, and you have to contact Fordham about an appointment, I would suppose."

"That's great," Jack said, "I will get right on it. I have all the catalogues about the University and the Law School at home. I should phone their admissions office."

"You two are going together to make this pilgrimage to Yankee Stadium and Fordham University? What has gotten into you, Ted?" Demi asked, "I thought you had little interest in professional sports. Bread and circuses, I think you said some time ago, and these big businesses that pretend to be sporting are not really a 'home' team as they trumpet it."

"Oh, once in a while a few sips of genuine sherry is okay, if you can be disciplined enough to know when enough is just enough. So we will try to see some future Hall of Famer pitcher throw to guaranteed Hall of Famer, Yogi. Something to tell our grandsons, I suppose, when they are young and impressionable and probably in love with America's National Game."

"You make it sound reasonable," said Gussie, "You would not want to be charged with inconsistency, I know."

"Along that sensible line of preparing for the future and life after Vassar, Gussie and I have found a great possibility," Dom broke in, "We have signed up to take the State Department's Foreign Service Officer examination. We checked it out and we seem to be eligible, particularly since I speak Italian – I knew those grandparents would come in handy someday – and Gussie knows Greek. A couple of hot spots in the cold war will be Italy and Greece."

"Particularly Greece," put in Gussie, "what with struggles between the Communist Party and the others for control."

"Same goes for Italy. I understand that there they even elected a Communist mayor of some town," said Dom. "If we make it, we get a free European trip back to the old countries. There will be a mixture of public service and fun. Better than serving in the military in Italy and Greece during the war. The pay is better, too. I just wonder what Mary and her Irish auld sod family will think if I do get a job like that."

"The O'Donnells are flag wavers, if you can get them off 'the troubles' and the IRA back in Ireland. I think they send them money, so I would not worry about their acceptance," said Gussie.

"Sounds like a good career move to me," said Jack.

"I guess," said Demi, "Only some of those leftist parties do have some good ideas about reversing the autocratic systems in both countries, particularly Greece, so I wouldn't want to go there and help undermine democratic processes just because they are left wing and because you get a free trip to the sunny Mediterranean with pay."

"Oh, you American Veterans Committee guys with those liberal thinkers meeting at Brad's Bakery," scoffed Jack, "Be realistic. This country will never be socialistic."

"Like the public school system, the police, the firemen, the roads, the public library, the G.I. Bill, you mean?" Demi asked, "Going to live long enough to get Social Security?"

"You will really fit into the Republican world of Duchess County, Jack. They wear blinders here that lets them see only to the right, not even straight ahead, like the old junk man's horse that used to go past our house on Church Street when I was a really little kid, probably an Ettinger forefather," said Ted.

"Well, anyway, we are signed up, and if we make it, we will go and be patriotic American State Department people," said Gussie, "I would not mind being a C.I.A. agent, either, now that that the O.S.S. has become the C.I.A. Get in on the ground floor, I say. No better time to make that kind of career move."

"Holy smoke, Gussie the spy. Would you believe it?" said Rich.

"Me, too," said Dom, "Spies together. Then we retire and write our fascinating memoirs. Right, Gussie?"

"To Florida? I wasn't thinking so far ahead, but I suppose there are possibilities in that sort of thing. I will worry about that when the time comes; although, I have heard that about agents having to sign agreements not to reveal classified stuff," Gussie responded.

"Well, if you do get the job, don't get yourselves killed by the K.G.B. in some super-secret activities," said Ted, "It won't be all fun and games for either of you."

"Listen," said Dom, "we both made it through World War Two. Though we hate to say it, both of us have killed people, not always at long range, either. We should be able to make it in peace-time, right, Gussie?"

"I think I will go for a less exciting, but more socially useful life with social work in California," said Demi, "I finished with that kind of exciting life when I completed my senior thesis for the English Department."

"We will be highly useful, Demi, if we make the cut," said Gussie, "Just in a different way."

"Not my way," said Demi, "What are you going to do about the 'girl next door' from your High School past, the arty one who went to Skidmore that you have mentioned?"

"It's been fun, as they say," acknowledged Gussie, "But somehow I don't see her fitting in with the life I envision in D.C. or in Athens, if I get this appointment."

"Love 'em and leave 'em, eh, you Greek Romeo. No sad love lost suicides for you, I see?" Demi laughed. "After all, Romeo and Juliet were Italians, more fitting for Dom, and yet he has his Irish future all mapped out."

"Come on, Demi, don't be sarcastic as we get closer to the end of our Vassar career," Gussie said.

"It's the way of the world, as William Congreve might put it," said Ted, "But let's change the focus of this conversation. Stanford has accepted me into the Graduate Writing Program where I can get to work with Wallace Stegner, and the Newhouse Foundation has even given me funds to supplement the rest of my G.I. Bill money. Thank goodness for strong letters of recommendation. Except you know what was funny about the Newhouse Fellowship? There was one non-academic stipulation, it could only go to someone who had never been in a fraternity. Luckily, that was okay with me. No fraternity possibilities here at Vassar, luckily."

"Grades help, too. Great for you, Ted. Palo Alto and Berkeley aren't that far apart, so we four should be able to see one another, at times, when we get there. Say, I wonder if Nancy knows Sara? I'll ask her," said Demi.

TWENTY-EIGHT

1949

"How's it going, Chris?" His uncle Jerry looked up from the menu. "Been three years."

"What, exactly, Uncle Jerry?" Chris fingered his menu and steadily eyed the Chief.

"What but college, of course. What else is there to ask about at the moment?"

"What will it be, gentlemen?" asked Mr. Christopoulos, coming up behind the counter from the grill.

Handing over his menu, Chief Wohl said, "How about some of those Greek doughnuts the boys on the beat tell me about, Chris? And a cup of coffee?"

"Sounds good," agreed Chris.

"Loukoumades," said Mr. Christopoulos, "A plate of loukoumades and two coffees. Coming up."

"So, how is college going as you get to the home stretch?" Chief Wohl swiveled his counter stool to face his nephew and god son. "Figured out what's next, have you?" He scratched his bald scalp and then rubbed it from front to back. "Thought I should work on my godfather role a bit here. Your parents have any suggestions?"

"They pretty much back off and wait for me to say something. Only thing Dad really said was, that since I was a man home from the wars, he was sure I could make my own decisions. He said he felt that way after the first world war when he came back from the Mexican border. Grown up, someone who did not need advice from the nineteenth century. So, I guess I am on my own."

"Have any civilian plans before you went?"

"Oh, I thought about engineering, sort of, in high school, but probably because it seemed like a manly profession to a teenager, but at Vassar I have just been taking the liberal arts courses and majoring in history, since you have to pick something. Not an engineering preparation, I guess you could say." Chris smiled as he bit into one of the honey-drenched Greek pastries. His mouth watered.

"Wow, sweet, Mr. Christopoulos," he called. Demi's father smiled and nodded his head.

"So, not Engineering, then. I seem to remember you talking about Clarkson, what seems like a century ago, before the draft."

The Chief also took a bite of doughnut and them a swig of black coffee to cut the honey. "Mmm. Wonder how many calories in that thing," he mused in appreciation. "A desk job pads the waist so you got to watch the diet. Not like the guys exercising on the street, if you can call patrol physical exercise, but no wonder they sing praises of these things."

Chris nodded. "Yeah, Clarkson in Potsdam, I remember. It seemed close and convenient. Cold up there. Not like MIT, but an okay school," he grimaced. "But all that technical stuff in the army, the schools they sent me to, made me decide I was not cut out for engineering. That's why I picked history, I guess, or it picked me."

"History is good," said his godfather, "I always liked history. My history teacher in high school really loved it. Said if you don't know the past, you are condemned to repeat it, mistakes and all. Good prep for law, he also said. I took that to heart, and if we'd had the money back then, that was my goal."

"Yes, I know. That's family history, I guess," acknowledged Chris, "Actually, I have decided about law school," he admitted. "That's part of the family history, too, I guess, getting a lawyer in the family."

"Really?" said the Chief, "My aborted dream, of course."

"Yep, sent my stuff from Vassar to Albany. What with the building boom going on with the post-war housing springing up, Dad's electrical contracting business is good enough these days that he said he can help me pay, if necessary, even though I still do have some G.I. Bill time to use for study there."

"Why Albany? Not down the river to New York City?"

"Nah. Jack Wyzinsky wants to go to Fordham or St. Johns, but I don't want to go where he goes. I'd find myself lumped together with that super conservative trimmer, as your sister-in-law would call it. I just don't want to risk being known as one of those Vassar guys who are on the make."

"You exaggerate, Chris," protested his Uncle Jerry.

"Not really," said his nephew, "And if you are still chief of police when Jack gets to be a lawyer politician in Poughkeepsie, I recommend you and the D.A. keep an eye on him. I think he is actually capable of 'trimming' the law to his advantage."

"Well, whatever you do, I am happy about your decision, and I am sure your parents must be." The Chief finished his coffee. "I think I will take the rest of these doughnuts to go, unless you want them, Chris."

"Thanks for food and the mid-morning break, Uncle Jerry. Take the doughnuts, they are all yours, and I really wasn't kidding about Jack and his possible future. On the other hand, the law school work may actually change his ethics for the better. I am sure they will try, but as Jimmy Durante says, one never knows, do one?"

***

Mr. Christopoulos wiped his hands and turned away from cleaning the grill. The Acropolis was now empty of customers at four in the afternoon. He poured Demi another cup of coffee as his son sat at the counter. "One of your classmates was in here this morning with his uncle, talking about future plans. Couldn't help overhearing. Going to law school in Albany, it seems."

"Chris Wohl and Chief Jerry. Yeah, I know. Chris has talked about it. Good plan, if you want to stay local, near relatives," Demi shrugged.

"You have absolutely decided, that is not for you, then? We know you have talked of it, but we, your mother and I, thought maybe with the strong interest in Miss Coffin and her interest in graduate studies in New York City, you two might have given staying East some serious thought."

"I know," acknowledged Demi, "We talked about doing that, but then the idea of going West, out to the last frontier on the coast, just seemed too appealing. No old ties there, everything absolutely new, just like us coming together into a new world. Not that we won't miss you all, but we will be totally on our own."

"At least you two didn't decide on Hawaii or Alaska," laughed Mr. Christopoulos, "There would have been the real last frontier. You two will still be able to visit, even at that distance."

"I thought I would tell you before I let Ma in on our decision. She wants the family to stick together, and for me to stay in Poughkeepsie after Vassar, maybe get an advanced degree in the city or something like that. C.U.N.Y. does offer good programs in social work, I suppose, and Nancy could go do her graduate work at Union at the same time, but I have looked into Berkeley and the California state social services, and they seem more advanced in such matters than New York. After all, it was in California that they first floated the old age pension plan proposed by some semi-nutty guy named Townsend. It didn't go, but even considering such a socialist idea shows that ideas do start in California and come back East eventually."

"I don't know about all that, son, but if you believe the University of California graduate program is the one for you, then I think you, and clearly Nancy, should make the move. What will she do about her graduate study?"

"We did some research in the Vassar Library and found a bunch of reasonable places in or around Berkeley where she could go. One is called the Graduate Theological Union, for example. She will find a place."

"Getting married and starting a family while still in college, even though it is graduate school, seems quite a bit different from what we would have thought sensible in the past. The man gets established and then he marries and the wife becomes a mother and homemaker. That is the way we did it, but I guess things and customs change." Mr. Christopoulos shook his head. "You do what you and Nancy think best. We are not in the old country and the depression is over."

Demi sat back and crossed his arms in preparation for his next revelation. "I guess I should tell you I have another reason for getting away, Dad," he began. I found that on the college campus and in my classes, I would not be conscious of Timi's ghost. Ghost isn't exactly right, I know – his presence, maybe – but here on Conklin Street and in the Acropolis Diner, or even playing basketball in the park, I can't get rid of the memories that he and I were there together in great times. The house on Conklin Street is the worst – sorry to have to say that, Pop – but it is a small house, and Timi and I shared a room. There are old unfinished conversations hanging in the air there. It was where we talked all about our adolescent imaginings of the future. Two Greek big leaguers,whizzes of the infield, for example. Ma or you can clean out the material stuff, his varsity letter on his old sweat shirt, his great school report cards, his high school diploma, stuff like that, but you cannot clear out the residue of memories. I need California, Dad," he continued. "New scene. New people, Nancy. I don't want to make this painful for you and Ma, and maybe you should not tell her about this part of our conversation, but it is just something I have to do."

"I understand, Demi," his father nodded. "We have all felt the pain of Timi's absence, and each of us has dealt with it in our individual way. Your mother did it by putting all the hopes she had for you and Timi on you alone. Hard role to play. She would like to have kept all the old ways in this family, but that effort is impossible. I think she expected you to live the life Tim would have lived as she imagined it if he had survived the war." Mr. Christopoulos wiped his eyes in some embarrassment and blew his nose.

"The war made the old way into the old way, Pop. I still have time left on the G.I. Bill, and it will pay tuition and subsistence for another year. Nancy thinks she can get a part-time job, while being a graduate student, and we can probably get some help from her family, which we are definitely not too proud to accept."

"Shall I break the news to your mother, or do you want to do it?"

170

Demi shook his head. "Nancy and I thought we would do it together, maybe after a dinner. Ma always feels good after she puts a good Greek dinner on the table and can see every one appreciating it, and you will be there to lend us moral support, Pop."

"Smart boy, Demi. They teach you that in your Psychology courses at Vassar, or does it come naturally?"

"Maybe I learned how from watching you," Demi smiled.

"Usually things worked out, although I could not budge your mother about poor Corry." Mr. Christopoulos grimaced.

"That is another thing I feel guilty about with this idea of going to California and leaving Corry to the rest of the family. Cleo and Helena have given over so much of their lives to Corry and the family, but I just can't do what they do, or ask Nancy to do that. I feel that I just have to find my own independent way with her and make something real out of my life, particularly after the mess of the Great War. Something good out of the bad." Demi looked down into his coffee cup. "I realize that may sound corny but I can't waste these chances. I know it isn't Greek to say it, but *carpe diem*, Pop. We have to be Latin at this moment."

"I don't know how Cleo or Helena feel about their lives." Mr. Christopoulos shook his head in a characteristic gesture of bewilderment. "They seem content with their lot. Cleo is skilled, has a secure job, and is well-paid. He plays golf with his friends on week-ends. Your mother worries that he doesn't seem involved with any women. Helena has a good job in that law office and has friends, but no eligible boyfriends, either. She may be too old now for the Greek community. With all the good men away in the war, she may have missed her time. Other women may be in the same boat, I don't know. I guess your mother wants grandchildren, and I have the feeling that it could be up to you and Nancy to provide."

"Family of that sort would have to wait for the completion of graduate work and jobs, Pop. We are conventional and sensible enough to make that decision, but in time. Nancy and I have talked it over," Demi was quick to answer, "More Christopouloses in due course, Pop, but not right away."

"Well, go ahead and set up the dinner invitation and the big-time talk with your mother and Nancy."

***

The bazooka rockets had penetrated the tank commander's cupola and exploded inside the vehicle. Smoke began to puff out of this damaged Tiger II. *Aim for the thinner side armor,* a voice seemed to be saying. *Arm the grenades.*

He realized that he had thrown his first grenade without thinking about it. Some belligerent actions had become so automatic that he was often surprised at what he had done, as if something other than his mind was controlling movement. The grenade exploded against the side of the tank. He expelled a long held breath and sucked in more air. He armed his second grenade and threw it, dropping face down across the earthen edge of the hole. Again he heard the 'whump' of the grenade burst.

He heard voices that were faint, as if from far away, although they came from the men on or in the Tiger.

He could not control the violent shaking that suddenly gripped him. "Aboo. Aboo," he heard and then the voice strangled and faded away. *Perhaps it was a name,* he thought. Wondered at it.

He gulped more air into his lungs through an open mouth, and pressed his chin into the soft dirt along the edge of the fox hole. They had done it. Then he felt the warmth of blood spreading over his thigh.

The drizzle had begun again. It felt cool on his face and hands in contrast to the heat in his leg below the hip. Nothing much but that. *When did that happen?*

He felt for it. It was there.

The voices were silenced. They had done it. He closed his eyes in relief.

TWENTY-NINE

1950

Ted, Demi, and Rich were the only vets in the lounge, for a change. Outside it was early Spring. The weather was mild the way it can be in the Hudson Valley. Early blossoming trees were white and pink on the campus hill overlooking Sunset Lake and the Hans Christian Andersen mermaid on her rock, looking out over the ice-free lake, with her eternal innocence, desire, and the wish to be human. The plantings of early jonquils and daffodils were buttery yellow and milk white. The Japanese maples in the quad between the dormitories were just putting out the first rosy buds of leaves.

There was a fragrance in the air, while courageous girls courting Spring colds were sprawled on some of the lawns just becoming green again, seeking an early suntan in abbreviated costumes that may have kept the other vets outside, sitting on the few benches to admire the scenery. After a long cold Hudson Valley winter, everyone was luxuriating in the new warmth of the day.

"In the home stretch, coming down to the wire, and all those clichés of ending," remarked Ted. "How are things with you and Hattie, Rich?"

"Sort-of over," said Rich.

"That is too bad," said Ted. "What happened? You two seemed to share that great interest in theater and acting. You were in more than a couple of college plays together, weren't you?"

"Right. For me it really was extracurricular plus the fact that the theater department desperately needed males for some of the parts, which gave me the in. For her, it was serious preparation for a career in theater. That makes a big difference in how one thinks about the future, you know. I mean, here she is worrying about getting into a prestigious drama graduate program and whether to change her name to a more suitable one for the theater marquee. I am thinking the play acting is fun, but I have to graduate in economics and get back to IBM," Rich laughed. "I live in the real world and she is a kid living in a dream for the future."

"Nothing wrong with that," said Demi, "in the spring of her life, so to speak, but obviously not with a vision that includes amateur theatricals in Poughkeepsie as the wife of a successful middle management IBM'er. Nothing particularly wrong with your less exciting dream, either. Maybe you should take Leroy's version of the American Dream seriously, or take Jack's advice and look for a nice local girl. One who would like to live on Boardman Road and see you off each morning for the walk to the research lab, or where ever IBM puts you upon your triumphant return from Vassar, imbued with left wing economics. How will that fit in with their business model?"

"Not a joking matter to me," Rich said, "I was in the Battle of the Bulge just like you and Tim. I have my two purple hearts, you have your bronze star, and I want a conventional, safe, secure life with a big company that is admittedly paternalistic, but in a way that I like at this stage in my life. The IBM Country Club is a great perk, and I like golf or tennis with my friends. The retirement plan can't be beat. Just don't cash your paycheck in a tavern, they say. IBM and electronics, the wave of the future. Buy their stock when you can." Rich smiled. "So, my choice sounds ordinary and you are flying off to California with your exciting Vassar girl, both of you suffering from an outsize social conscience. I won't knock either option. Variety is the spice of lives, and all that."

"Sorry about the conclusion of the Hattie-Harriet Snyderman college interlude, Rich. Really." Demi sat up on the sofa.

"Right," said Rich, "Maybe I will go backstage sometime when Whatever-She-Calls-Herself-By-Then has a starring role on Broadway and congratulate her for achieving what she set out to do here in good old Poughkeepsie. Did I mention she is thinking of having a nose job after graduation? Her parents said they would give it to her as a graduation gift."

"There you go, Rich. Better out of it all. Think how disenchanted you and she would be if you married, and your girl child came endowed with the unmodified original Snyderman nose. Think of the unhappiness and eventual expense, if that poor girl wanted to identify with the customized nose of her famous mother," Demi laughed.

"Okay, okay, Demi, you can try to laugh me out of it, and thanks, but I think I will go study for my finals at some relaxing table in the library. Good place. Everyone quiet and occupying some individual inner space."

Phil had come into the lounge just in time to hear Rich make his last remarks.

"Laugh what off? "Phil asked.

"Nothing important," said Rich, "Stuff here is only important if you can use it later in real life. It turns out that I am a practical guy at heart."

"Right," Ted agreed, "I think I will join you in the library, Rich, for a bit. I want to polish up my senior thesis for the English Department and my thesis advisor. Later, I'm meeting Sara on the library steps." And then Ted thought that was probably the wrong thing to say since it emphasized his Sara connection and their plans for life after Vassar.

He was sorry about Rich and his disappointments, but it was hard to keep secret these facts of personal life in the small society of the Vassar Veterans. It was too late to take it back, thought Ted, and besides, Rich would just have to cope with life's vicissitude and with other people's plans. *He is a big boy*, Ted said to himself.

***

"Mom, Dad, this is Ted." Sara turned toward Ted. "Ted, my parents." The four were standing in the parking area for the Vassar Alumni House, outside of the Pub. The Bauers had just parked their black Chrysler, understated but expensive and characteristic of the Bauers, Ted learned later.

Mr. Bauer put out his hand for a very firm, corporate handshake. Mrs. Bauer looked Ted up and down first and then put out her hand for a lady-like clasp of the fingers. Ted resisted the impulse to shift for one foot to the other, uncomfortably. He and Sara had walked up the hill from the college campus to meet her parents.

Mr. Bauer said, "I am pleased to meet someone who fought for his country. I was too young for World War One and too old for World War Two, so I guess I envy you for your contribution."

"Happy to meet you both. Didn't really have a choice," Ted answered, "My father thought I could find a gimmick to get out of going. He served in World War One on the Mexican border, but he didn't really want to send his youngest off to do something more in a dangerous place."

"A gimmick?" questioned Mrs. Bauer.

"Well, someone I went to Sunday school with, and whose parents ran a local cider mill with lots of acreage, bought a bunch of sheep for him to herd, and got him a sheepherder's exemption – or a farmer's, I guess, would be the right term."

"Very inventive," commented Mr. Bauer, "if not exactly admirable."

"Good church-going family, nevertheless," responded Ted, and Sara gave him an unobtrusive poke in the arm.

"Ted took me to a Martha Graham dance performance the other night," Sara put in hurriedly, "You would have enjoyed it, Mom."

"On the Vassar Campus?" Mrs. Bauer asked, "Certainly one of the advantages of coming to a school like this, if they bring in programs of culture."

"Yes, when we took in her performance in New York City, it was not cheap. Although I must say sometimes I didn't get it, especially when she got under that blanket or rug or whatever it was as part of the performance." Mr. Bauer shook his head in disbelief. "Your mother said it was experimental with music by that fellow – Cage, was it? Or was it that new one, Copeland? Copeland, I guess, since I could hum the tunes."

"No, Mother, this performance was at a local high school. Put on by a friend of Ted's who runs a book and gift store in town. Harvard graduate and Poughkeepsie native, who likes to bring cultural events to his hometown. Josh White is scheduled to sing in a program next." Sara turned to Ted. "Dad plays the piano and really likes jazz."

"He sounds like a town booster," said Mr. Bauer, "That is a good thing."

"Well, yes, although not exactly like a character out of a Sinclair Lewis. Better, in fact," Ted responded.

"Ah, an English major," laughed Mrs. Bauer, "I read Lewis at Wellesley."

"What?" asked her husband, "Who?"

"A reference to the social criticism in the many novels of Sinclair Lewis. We have some of his books on our shelves, dear; although, I guess you have not read them."

Ted could not tell whether this was said as a joke, or not. "Reading is for retirement," said her husband, "when every day is Saturday. Shall we go in and order lunch? I think the only other time we have been here is when we brought Sara over on one of our college tours."

"I think you are right, dear," said Mrs. Bauer, then she turned to Ted and continued, "You know, Vassar would not have been our first choice, but Sara was insistent. I thought Sweet Briar would be so much more suitable for a young lady with our southern background, or Wellesley, which I attended, and her father was afraid the college's reputation for being ultra-liberal would make it a poor choice for his daughter."

"I am glad, then, that Sara was insistent, or we would never have met," Ted answered.

"You are right about that," said Mrs. Bauer.

Ted was not sure how to interpret that, but decided to let it pass. A future mother-in-law must be dealt with circumspectly,

"Just what is a Vassar Devil?" asked Mr. Bauer, looking over the menu.

"Terrible concoction," said Sara, "You don't want it, I assure you."

"But what is it?" persisted her father, "Some college tradition?"

"A fantastic dessert whose history is unknown," put in Ted., "but definitely a tradition here in the Alumni House Pub. Represents the comfort food for unhappy homesick young students and sentimental alumni. Lots of chocolate in it."

"A square of devil's food cake topped with vanilla ice cream, hot fudge and marshmallow sauce," Sara explained, "Abundance of calories. Not for me or any sane person."

"I think I will finesse it, then, and start with the fish and chips. Good and simple." Mr. Bauer nodded to the waitress. "We will see if they make it as they did in Torquay when we holidayed in England last summer. Business trip about chemicals, combined with a bit of a vacation," he explained to Ted, "Economical that way."

"Crowded but with wonderful beaches, as least for England. It was certainly not the French Rivera, by any means," noted Mrs. Bauer.

"Shingle beaches, a lot of them with big round rocks instead of sand," said Sara.

"Didn't have any business to conduct in France at the time," said Mr. Bauer.

After the others had ordered, there was a silence. Each of the four was unconsciously searching for the next conversational gambit.

"So, what exactly are your plans, then?" Mr. Bauer turned to his daughter.

"Yes, we would like to be let in on this future you are preparing," Mrs. Bauer added.

"I told you in my letter, Daddy. We'll get married after graduation, and after our honeymoon in Maine, we will drive to the West Coast, to Palo Alto. Ted will use the rest of his G. I Bill and a grant from the Newhouse Foundation for the Stanford Writing Program. I have the Vassar Fellowship, which I can take anywhere, and Stanford will let me work on a Masters in Philosophy there." Sara sat back in the booth and looked firmly at her parents on the other side of the table.

"Honeymoon in Maine, you say?" Mr. Bauer replied, "Great fishing in Maine. I don't suppose you fish, do you, young man? Get my gear from L. L. Bean, if not from Abercrombie and Fitch. Did you know that Ernest Hemingway got outfitted for Africa from Abercrombie?"

"Didn't know you knew anything about any writer," said Mrs. Bauer.

"Believe it or not, I've read some of his stuff," Mr. Bauer answered, smartly. "As I was saying, we took Sara's brother up there as he was finishing at Deerfield, to introduce him to hunting. Took to it like a duck to water." Mr. Bauer laughed at his own joke.

"Never took me duck hunting, Daddy," interjected Sara, "A guy thing, I guess."

"Honey, I didn't know you wanted to go duck hunting." Mr. Bauer looked genuinely perplexed.

"I didn't," answered Sara.

"Well, then?" her father replied.

"And you will have enough to live on while you two are doing the academic work?" Mrs. Bauer firmly put the conversation back on track. She seemed to be the ultra-practical one at this moment, with no axes to grind.

"G.I. subsistence payments also continue, as well as the tuition payments, and we have saved enough to supplement. We believe we can get by for the year or year and half it will take," Ted explained soberly.

"I doubt that you can live in a way you have been accustomed to on that, even if it is enough for subsistence," said Mrs. Bauer. "It does sound idyllic, of course, and romantic, but scrimping is not something you, or we, are used to. We could have the wedding at our church, St. John's. Are you Episcopalian, Mr. Collins?"

"Sort of," answered Ted.

"Oh, Mom, I want the wedding in our house or in the garden," protested Sara, "Small would work for us, and I think that kind of ceremony goes with the sort of life we both want. We can do it. Together." Sara patted her mother's arm across the booth table.

"All right. Whatever you two think best," Mrs. Bauer sighed, "I hope the friends we can't get into that space don't feel hurt."

"Not to mention business associates," added Mr. Bauer, "I must say that Roosevelt and Truman have arranged your future with this socialist college plan for veterans. I suppose eventually you can even buy a home with government backing, when your careers in the academic world are established. Certainly not like my preparation for life, when my family expected to ante up the costs. Not that I don't think it is not a good thing. What would the economy be like, if it were flooded with uneducated veterans at loose ends about how to return to some sort of productive civilian life?"

"Just right, Mr. Bauer," agreed Ted, "And what to do with all the women in the work force when the men start looking for those post-war jobs?"

Sara pressed her knee into Ted's leg under the table, and he did not pursue that particular point. "Dad, you are really pushing us too rapidly into the future. Just let us do the graduate study first." Sara smiled. "And maybe leave the politics out of it."

"Oh, Frank, just let the youngsters be independent. Ted has obviously earned the help of the G.I. Bill, and they are clearly level-headed enough to have thought this through. Should I remind you that your mother moved to Ithaca the first year you were at Cornell, to make sure her dear child could make it on his own? How you resented her interference then!" Mrs. Bauer looked at her husband gravely.

He frowned as she continued. "You were really young for college, sixteen, was it? Why yes, of course, and the cherished only child, a son to carry on the family name! But don't you admire your daughter's self-reliance? We could help out in emergencies, of course. There will be the two of them, after all, and both older than sixteen. Although Mr. Collins is not quite the 'older man' I was prepared for from what Sara had written. I somehow expected – oh, I don't know what I expected exactly. A grizzled war veteran, in my innocence, I suppose. Just how old are you, Mr. Collins, if you don't mind my asking?"

"Mom!" Sara said.

"I am three years older than Sara," Ted answered.

"All right, all right, Cecilia." Mr. Bauer had colored at the reference to his mother's concern and wanted to move on from the subject. "No need to drag up that old story. It was another time, you know. I spent my whole life up to that point without friends of my own age, playing alone on the Severn River near our estate, trapping and fishing. I was quite independent, if I do say so. She left in the middle of my sophomore year, you know, and went back to Baltimore. I imagine there will be plenty of time for Ted here to learn the gory details of our family history when he and Sara are married."

"Actually, it sounds idyllic, Mr. Bauer. Trust me, Sara and I will manage quite well," Ted interrupted. "We have really thought it through."

"Call me Frank," said Mr. Bauer.

***

"Sit down at the table, I prepared another real Greek meal and we don't want it to get cold," Mrs. Christopoulos busied herself around the table, moving flatware here and there to line up more perfectly, and moving filled dishes onto bronze trivets in the shape of ancient Greek letters.

"All the food looks so wonderful," said Nancy, "I love the dishes, too."

"Cleo Junior and Helena gave them to me a few Christmases ago. Found them in some little gift shop on Cannon Street." Mrs. Christopoulos picked up one still unused and polished it on her apron. "Caring children, Cleo and Helena, all of them, even Corry in her way."

"That dish in the casserole is chicken with tomatoes and olives. In Greek it is *Kota Yiouvetsi Me Elies*," Mr. Christopoulos spoke quickly into the silence that would have emphasized the omission of Demi's name from his mother's list. "Good Greek olive oil, Greek olives and a fine wine. Not a cooking wine, you see. Always you should cook with a wine that you would not be ashamed to drink with friends, never something labeled cooking wine. That only cheapens the dish and the flavor. Casseroles are not to use up left-over meals. They should be treated with the respect of fresh ingredients."

"Yes, well, let's serve the food before it gets cold," said his wife, reaching for a serving spoon.

They all ate with a small amount of polite conversation. Cleo and Helene were asked about their jobs by Nancy, who seemed genuinely interested. Corry sat in her chair next to her mother and was fed her specially prepared versions of what the others were eating. The answers to Nancy's questions of Demi's siblings were polite and informative, not particularly effusive. Nancy also inquired about the ingredients of the dishes offered and seemed fascinated, even asking if Mrs. Christopoulos could write out directions for their preparation, as if Nancy were compiling a personal collection of recipes. Mrs. Christopoulos seemed flattered by the requests. They finished up with a plate of Greek powdered-sugar butter cookies and Greek coffee.

"After those *Kourambiethes* we need this coffee, strong and black," said Demi. "Lots of real butter in those things. Rich treats."

"Guaranteed to put more flesh on your bones, as well," said Mr. Christopoulos.

"I don't know about me on that score," said Nancy, "I seem to stay the same, no matter what I eat."

"That works when you are young," said Mrs. Christopoulos, "When you get my age and enjoy your own cooking, that is another matter."

"Enough about food and weight," said Demi, "Nancy and I have reached an important decision, finally, and we wanted to let the family know."

"You have completely, absolutely decided to go to California for graduate study," his mother interrupted, "Mrs. Karras told me."

"Mrs. Karras?" said Demi.

"Of course," answered his mother, "You told Gussie. Gussie told his mother. His mother told me over coffee and cookies in this very kitchen. No secrets possible on Conklin Street."

"Sorry, Ma, to have the news come that way. I intended to let you know directly when Nancy and I decided."

"Don't worry yourself, Demi. I knew you two would come to that conclusion. I could see you getting restless for a change of scene." Mrs. Christopoulos reached over and patted his hand, before reaching further and squeezing Nancy's fingers in her own. "Congratulations."

"Oh, Mrs. Christopoulos," Nancy responded.

"We thought we would get married right after commencement, at the County Clerk's office, not in the Orthodox Church," said Demi, "Simple and quick, only family, we think. Afterward, a lunch, but not in the Acropolis, I am afraid."

"I should say not," said his mother. "It will be here, and Christopoulos women will put it together."

"With some important help from the Christopoulos men," said Demi's father.

"And your family, Nancy?" inquired Mrs. Christopoulos.

"My mother, father, and maybe my younger sister. My parents will come for commencement, anyway," Nancy answered. "They really didn't think I would be getting married so soon. I might have used the word 'should.' My parents firmly believe that women should get as much education as men, but Demi and I agree with that, so we will both be taking graduate courses out West."

"I hope it will not all be strange to you out there. You will have to make new friends," said Mrs. Christopoulos.

"Well, you know one of the other vets is going out to Palo Alto with his wife to attend Stanford. Ted and Sara Collins. We are invited to their wedding over in Connecticut in July. So we will have some Poughkeepsie people there with us in the Bay Area." Demi patted his mother's hand. "And I have been in stranger places, believe me."

Then they were all diverted from the celebration when Corry, unattended during this exchange, pushed her plate off the table onto the floor. It broke into china fragments and scattered cookie crumbs under the table. She waved her arms about her head and made her usual noises which her mother always interpreted as signs of unhappiness at being ignored.

That sort of thing I will not miss, Demi thought to himself, with the arrogance of innocence and the guilt of the survivor.

It was important to be the survivor.

***

"You got blood on your shoe, Corporal," the Lieutenant said, "Where is it coming from? Yours?"

"Mine, Sir," he said, "Something got me in the hip, I think. Not bad, I guess. Haven't looked at it. Hole in my fatigues, though."

"Geez," said the other, younger soldier, "PFC, you never said."

"No big deal," he said. Hardly felt anything, except sort of numb.

"It is a big deal when you go on bleeding like that. Get a medic. We need to look at the wound, get some sulfa powder on it. Stop the bleeding. Legs can have arteries as well as veins."

I know my first aid, he thought. *I don't need battlefield instruction. Know anatomy as well.*

"So, a Purple Heart and I am putting you guys in for a unit citation. Good work. Maybe a bronze star. Get that medic, now."

Sarge is the real problem here. The Hero. Medics fix him, not? A citation won't bring him back. None of them. None of them.

"You feel okay?" asked the Lieutenant.

"Okay," he said and thought, *you frigging pompous shavetail.* Then, again, maybe the kid was trying. He was just a kid.

An awful lot of them were just kids.

THIRTY

1950

A snake of folding chairs followed the path under the trees above the Shakespearian Garden, arranged for the beauteous sophomores chosen for the Daisy Chain, the dignitaries, the administration and faculty, the graduates. People were restless, some sitting and some standing, breathing in the pungent odors from the formal garden below, as they waited for the commencement ceremony to begin. If one concentrated on the scent, the sharp tang of thyme, warmed by the sun and redolent of the English countryside, could be detected in the morning air as it drifted up the hill. The little stream, one of the Dutch kills that ran between Skinner Hall and the Garden, made bucolic chortling sounds that became an auditory backdrop for the surf-like murmur of parents and guests already seated in the bowl of the outdoor theater.

The veterans, who had made it through all four years of study, were assembled. Out of the hundred, more or less, who had sat through the lecture on behavior and standards given at the beginning of their college career, twelve men remained.

"Here we are," said Demi, "The dirty dozen."

"Survivors," said Ted, "Benefit of the Vassar faculty and trustees who decided to let us stay on."

"Wonder where Carmen is right now. He was a casualty, although he did make it quite a ways through," said Leroy, "Loved and lost, you could say. Hope he gets it together eventually and tries it again. S.U.N.Y. New Paltz or Champlain are still there and available."

"We are the last men left standing," said Gussie, "And the prize is ..."

"We get to come in at the tail of the procession and get – not a Vassar degree, but a new hybrid – a B.A. from the University of New York State,

183

on the recommendation of the faculty and trustees of Vassar College." Phil laughed. "Good deal after all. Can't complain when a degree is a degree and comes with a genuine leather cover."

"Lots of hard brain work, and reading and typing," said Leroy. "A real challenge after selling used cars to nearly brain-dead Highlanders."

"Don't knock it," said Gussie, "It's worth its weight in gold and we can cash in at the State Department. We got high marks on that Foreign Service exam, and we can thank going to good old V.C. for part of that success, anyway. Dom and I are off to Washington as soon as we celebrate the commencement. Anyone up for a joint celebration?"

"Thanks, but I am going with Sara and her parents to Coppola's in Hyde Park for lunch. I hope the Bauers like Italian," answered Ted. "We need to get 'really acquainted,' as Sara puts it, before she and I get married in Connecticut and drive off to Maine and California. They don't know quite what to make of me yet, and how I will fit in to the Bauer family. They are, after all, United Carbide corporate bigwig types who can fly on company planes, sail in the Caribbean, walk on glaciers in Canada, look into volcanoes on Hawaii, drink Liebfraumilch on the Rhine, water ski and play golf and tennis at The Club. Mr. Bauer even flies his own light plane with Mrs. Bauer as co-pilot."

Demi laughed along with the others. "Sorry, have to miss it. My mother, as we speak, is no doubt whipping up a huge Greek lunch to celebrate with Nancy and me after we go to the Town Clerk's office and get married." Demi grinned. "Simple and straight forward. My brother, Cleo, is standing up with me as best man and Nancy's college roommate is her maid of honor."

"I'm free. I'm with you two for the after-celebration, Gussie," said Rich.

"Me, too," chimed in Jack.

"*Moi aussi*," said Evelyn, "Here I am, much to my surprise and yours, too, I'll bet. I need to celebrate it with a few of my buddies."

"Not with Wendy?" asked Rich.

"Wendy who?" answered Evi with a smirk.

Phil looked a bit embarrassed. "I am going to meet Aggie at the Alumnae House."

"Okay, teacher's pet," Gussie said.

"I am having lunch with my parents," said Bernard Black, "and some of my father's faculty colleagues."

"Good for you," said Phil, "It is nice to fit in. And I mean it. I really mean it, Bernie."

"I would come for one last get together, but my parents are taking my wife and me out in celebration," said Leroy, "My father is really riding high on this. At last someone in the family line who is going to be something other than a salesman, he says. His father was, and so is he. Not that he isn't proud to be a good salesman, but he says it is a strain because you have to keep smiling and be upbeat when you don't feel like it. Be polite to people when they are not polite to you. And you don't make anything. That seems to bug him a lot."

"Don't let him read *Death of a Salesman* then," Ted quipped, "I understand grown men cry in the theater at performances."

"For themselves," said Leroy, "I know."

The faculty were also beginning to turn up, mortar boards in hand and doctoral gowns flying off their shoulders. Aggie Sander breezed by and waved to Phil.

Phil saluted back, a bit of a smile on his lips. "Aggie said that Indira Ghandi was the commencement speaker. I guess I never did note that in the stuff they gave us to prepare for the ceremony. You know, the Indian woman, important in her country, who went to that school in England where Aggie was sent from Nazi Germany. Before Aggies' time, so they never met, even if they do have something in common. Maybe they could talk old school together today."

Aggie was soon followed by a small, round woman who called to Ted as she went by, "A big fat A for Tolstoy, Mr. Collins. Very interesting term paper."

"Now who is a teacher's pet?" said Phil.

"That's the Princess Wolkonsky. She is the Russian department and I just took a course on Tolstoy with her – happy to see she liked my paper. My point was, that Tolstoy's overwhelming Christian impulse ruined his marriage, impoverished his family and ultimately killed him as he wandered around in an irrational search for salvation. I even postulated that perhaps he was a borderline psychopath who could not care for individuals, just humanity as an abstraction. So much for Christianity. Otherwise, he was a great novelist."

"Here we are, the undergraduate world is finished, and you are still giving us summaries of your intellectual theological literary points. Give it up for now, Ted," said Gussie.

"Princess, did you say?" ask Jack, "You took a course from a princess?"

"Thousands of them in Russia, left over from the czarist days, she told us in class. Nothing special," said Ted, "Lots of white Russians running loose in Europe and the U.S.A. She said Tolstoy's daughter actually lives somewhere nearby."

"She certainly did not look like my idea of a princess, at least not from the fairy tales," Jack said.

"Great teacher, though," said Ted. "Interested in having the male perspective in her classes. I took two more of them, besides Tolstoy. One on

Dostoyevsky and one a survey of Russian lit. She was another one of the faculty really supportive of the men here."

"Too bad she couldn't educate some of the old biddies in Psych," said Demi.

"You should forget that, Demi," said Rich, "Water over the dam. You survived, got your As and Bs from more accepting faculty. Move on. Did you ever think that maybe at the beginning when you were adjusting to college work, you might have actually earned those few Cs and C pluses? Berkeley seemed to be happy to accept your total grades for grad study, after all."

"You have to agree that there was mostly plenty of support here when you wanted it," Ted added. "The Chairman of the Astronomy department gave me a job as a lab assistant, for some book money beyond the G.I. Bill, after I took Astronomy as my science. Finally got some real use of the celestial navigation courses from those air corps schools. I can only say it was nice to get the extra cash just for quizzing those girls on the Maria Mitchell Observatory roof about star identification and the constellations and showing them how to read the spectroscope. It was a great student job. I will remember it."

"You are right," acknowledged Demi, "I should know enough at last to live in the now. Very existential. Camus-like. More positive mental health that way, and Nancy would agree as long as the position is also theologically sound as she understands it."

Jack interrupted, "Hey look, the line seems to have finally formed and started to move. Here we go, guys. We've done it. Over the top. Charge."

"Jeez, Jack, you make it sound like some corny war movie. It is just another commencement for most of these jokers," said Leroy.

"Well, maybe, but with a big shot international speaker. Indira Ghandi, yet. We should be honored, of course. That will make the *New York Times*," Ted added.

"Hey, man, not ordinary for most of the young ladies up there in front, Leroy, and certainly not for us survivors," protested Jack, "It is a big deal. It's a life changer."

"Survivors, my ass. Sometimes you are a pompous prick, Jack," said Chris.

"Well, I guess I can agree with both of you or all of you," said Demi, "We are about to graduate from our Acropolis, not the temple to the Goddess of Wisdom in Greece, nor the glorious Greek diner in Poughkeepsie, but the Vassar one by Sunset Hill, overlooking instead of the blue Mediterranean, the muddy Sunset Lake; they both should be named Sunrise as more fitting for our condition, and here *Knowledge,* with a capital K, was the deity."

Now that was pretentious, Demi thought to himself as he finished speaking. Maybe that showy urge was why he had trouble writing simple, realistic fiction. *Got to get over that,* he told himself.

He certainly hoped to be a better social worker than fiction writer.

"Let's cut the gabble and get a move on, gang." The practical Leroy cut through the grandiose talk. "Got a job to do here, get that sheepskin. Save that sort of guff for some future class reunion."

THIRTY-ONE

1950

The two couples did connect that autumn, when they arrived in California for graduate study. Demi and Nancy found a so-called garden apartment in what looked like a motel complex. It was new in a cheap post-war, motel-ish way.

The place Tom and Sara got through graduate housing at Stanford was the ancient guest cottage next to the actual Mr. and Mrs. Stanford's home near "the farm" as the campus was called. In Menlo Park, it was run down, but minimally furnished, and possessed a genuine ice-box rather than a refrigerator that required a fifty-pound chunk of ice, and in which frozen food was a too-modern invention to be stored. No Birdseye held over for the Collins family. Buy it, eat it.

The housing for Demi and Nancy was clearly more up-to-date and had new, if cheap, furnishings. It was surrounded by parking lots and they were pleased with it for the moment. Ted and Sara's cottage was surrounded by bamboo and eucalyptus trees, chickens running wild, a number of white albino cats, and one small boy with an air rifle. Baby chicks appeared regularly from fertile eggs laid about in nests hidden by the underbrush.

"What is missing," said Ted to Sara, "Would be a few Panda bears to feed on the vegetation."

"Maybe we could convince Count Miloradovich to import a few," joked Sara, "I read somewhere that Pandas are actually omnivores but rarely get the chance to eat small beasts in China so have to subsist on huge amounts of vegetation."

"Sounds like graduate students on a limited budget," said Ted.

Their landlord, who was subletting the guest house to them, was a white Russian émigré who was the riding instructor at the University stables. Many Stanford undergrads populating the "farm" seemed to have a need to maintain contact with horses.

Always appearing in jodhpurs, boots and with a riding crop that he would periodically, when talking to his tenants, snap against his right boot, the Count was colorful enough to give some validity to his background. Ted and Sara found him intimidating, like someone out of a Tolstoy novel, or perhaps Turgenev. His wife, who was not a refugee from Lenin's Russia, was an interior decorator and the clearly reluctant mother of a demon male child, about seven or eight, who seemed to spend most of his spare time shooting at and missing the squawking free range chickens. She did seem in great demand by the upper-class residents of such places as Atherton, Hillsborough and Burlingame, all sanctuaries for the well-heeled.

It was far distant from the atmosphere of the Vassar College campus, or the small-town nature of Poughkeepsie, New York.

When they had closed the rental deal with Mrs. Count Miloradovich, she had mentioned that Thorsten Veblen had once occupied that guest cottage while he was writing his classic work *The Theory Of The Leisure Class,* or so was the mythic story on the Stanford campus and in the surrounding area of Palo Alto. In fact, she had said, it seemed he might have died while in residence at Sand Hill Road and Vine, the address of that cottage.

"If that factoid is true, then I doubt he was writing that particular work at the time," Ted noted as they drove to the cottage, "I'm going to wager that the writing of that piece got him a visiting professorship at Stanford. On the other hand, it is kind of quaint to have that story in the history of our first temporary home together, since we will be far removed from the leisure class."

Demi and Nancy did not have that kind of interesting if dramatic residence history, but they moved in comfortably. Demi went to his courses, while Nancy looked for work. She found that her idiosyncratic college classes, undergraduate and graduate, seemed to make her academic record a bit inscrutable, but intriguing to the San Mateo County civil servant who was interviewing applicants for a county social service worker opening. She got the job advising-in-aid to needy children. It turned out she loved the work, particularly the giving of sage advice to single mothers who had botched their lives but needed care from someone, practically anyone, in a position to help. Working closely with, and learning about, these unfortunate young families began to also endow her with a gentle wisdom, or what it appeared to be to these complicated people, but it prepared Nancy in thinking about being a mother herself. And so it was a mutually beneficial arrangement.

The two couples began their lives in periodic tandem with one another. On free weekends, they enjoyed visits to cold and foggy beaches like the one at Half-Moon Bay, across the hills on Sand Hill Road from the Collins' cottage, or drives across the Golden Gate Bridge to Point Reyes or the Redwoods where they marveled at the gigantic trees.

When graduate study was successfully completed, the two men had found appropriate jobs, Ted in teaching English and Demi in social work. The G.I. Bill kicked in again and made it possible for each couple to buy one of the post-war homes sprouting up in the empty spaces where only live oaks, wild orange poppies and purple lupine had grown. The baby boom began to prosper. Sons were born, in that first California decade; two sons to each couple. They shared the exploration of childbearing and child rearing, not always with the same philosophy, although Dr. Spock and his advice became a part of their lives as well, as did shared holiday meals like joint Thanksgivings.

Then as the decade began to draw to a close, Nelson Rockefeller, in his great wisdom and competitiveness, decided to expand a somewhat moribund New York State University system. He wanted it to rival that of the Golden State, California. His administration began building new colleges while turning teacher education institutions into University Centers with doctoral programs and important scholars on board. S.U.N.Y. began scrambling for experienced faculty.

Ted's parents had retired. Their other son had been moved by IBM with his family to Kentucky, and their sister had become involved with her new family in Westchester County and a burgeoning career as a writer of young adult novels. She also worked as an occasional essayist for the Westchester section of the *New York Times*. So the grandparents of Ted and Sara's children made ill-disguised comments on how pleased they would be if the Californians returned and filled the family void, and punctuated these opinions by mailing newspaper clippings about the S.U.N.Y. expansion.

"If I am lucky, I can get an appointment to a S.U.N.Y. unit close enough to my parents to give them some time with their grandchildren. They seem to want that feeling of security that comes with having at least one of their children quickly available," Ted explained to Sara, Demi and Nancy.

"No one, and I mean *no one* who has come to California looking for frontier success ever goes back," Nancy protested, "Everyone says that."

"And I believe it," said Demi, "We love it here and the kids have their California world with schools and play buddies. So do yours. You two have made good friends in eight years."

"Granted," Ted responded, "but there is another more selfish reason. Here I am a junior faculty member, just granted tenure, of course; but given the academic pecking order, I am really low man on the totem pole. In a start-up college, or an expanding one, I will already be further up the ladder." Ted looked over at Sara. "Can't fault that reality."

"True," said his wife. She, too, missed her family, but stayed silent as she knew that Ted, having expressed his feelings, had pretty much already made up his mind to go, and she was happy with this.

"Well, we will absolutely keep in touch," Demi said, "We both still have East coast family and that will require the obligatory visits."

Ted was lucky. One of his former teachers at Vassar turned out to be on the Board of Trustees at the new college, and she gave him high praise in a recommendation. "All very truthful," she had told him, "If the men had been eligible for the Dean's List, you would have been on it."

He also got a good letter from his California English Department Chair, and so off they went, back to Poughkeepsie, to start a new chapter in life in the place that had been the beginning of the one they were leaving. Now, however, they were returning with children and added degrees.

Some people did actually leave California, it turned out, but not Demi and Nancy. They both worked to their retirement. Nancy continued advising unhappy people in San Mateo County, and Demi in San Francisco, where he stayed until his job turned into the sad and negative one of trying to help the poor find a place to live. Urban renewal turned into urban removal when San Francisco began to turn into the upscale real estate market that it would become.

It was not a job for the idealistic.

Demi turned to gardening in his Redwood City backyard where plants were positive and change affirmative as it should be, and summer followed spring, which followed winter, which followed autumn in the certain cycle of time.

There could be a happy logical end to this story, but of course it is not yet to be.

There is always more, until a real conclusion is reached.

2000

The surviving Vassar Veterans sat in a row before the graying women from the class of 1950. There were no longer twelve men there to attend, as had been at their Commencement. They were now down to eight. Some of those present, both men and women, were stooped. Others were as ram-rod straight as they had been when they appeared in Poughkeepsie in 1946.

Some were heavy and lined. Others were thin and tanned. One sat behind a walker and there were a few canes in evidence. A couple of graybeards sat amongst the men. One was wearing the turned-collar of the clergy. Several of the women were holding hats with purple ribbons that proclaimed the class year. All of them were white, of course, but the relatives who had attended with them reflected the multi-cultural panorama of the nation since the civil rights movement had opened doors to many that had been closed when the class of 1950 had been in residence. Some were legacies, having attended Vassar themselves in later years. They had all come to this Sunday morning event that would close the Fiftieth Class Reunion.

At that moment, the actors in *Saving Private Ryan* were fighting World War Two in hundreds of multiplex theaters across the nation, prompting middle-aged Boomer children to ask their fathers if that was really what the war was like, prompting some fathers to shrug and say "maybe," and others to break down in melodramatic responses, as if at last the revealing of ancient post-traumatic syndrome was tolerable. Tom Brokaw had also written his book about *The Greatest Generation,* and in a kind of genuflecting moment, the female class leaders had scheduled this event to honor the World War Two veterans in their class. A bronze plague celebrating their successful attendance had been struck and placed near the circle garden. They had survived the war and their Vassar education. Each man was to speak briefly about his World War II experiences in true "Greatest Generation" mode.

All seemed modest in their accounts. What else could they be, after the accolades from Tom Brokaw, who had praised them in the national media; his work was now on the best sellers list for the *New York Times*. No mere words could really tell others what it was like. But they did their best, it was expected, and the men of the Vassar Dirty Dozen had never liked to disappoint.

Now there was just one to go, Demi Christopoulos, who had continued to do his social work with less and less enthusiasm as California went through its conservative changes, its tax revolts and Governor Reagan, the grade B movie star on his way to becoming the Republican demigod of conservatism, whose way had been paved by that long-ago Yale debate champion, William F. Buckley himself. Not even Ted had foreseen the effects that strong conservatism had shown on modern politics. Not even Jack, in his most careless, self-centered dreams, could have imagined the alarming changes in human rights and fiscal policies that had ultimately resulted.

Demi stood up and looked toward Nancy in her front row chair. Ted and Sara, no longer Californians, watched their California friend, as Demi wet his lips before speaking.

At Conklin Street, Corry had died in her sleep one winter night, after living into her fifties. Cleon Jr. and Helena bought a little house in the Eighth Ward on the better South Side of town, and moved their aging parents into a downstairs bedroom. Mr. Christopoulos did not walk as much except to the public library.

The diner still lived on, but with new owners and a chef from the Culinary Institute north of town. Mrs. Christopoulos cooked whenever Helena let her, or if she was going to be late coming home from her administrative assistant job, which was the new name for clerk-secretary.

Neither Cleon Jr. or Helena had ever married.

"I am Democritus Christopoulos, as most, if not all, of you know. I went from Vassar to the University of California at Berkeley. I was a social worker in California until I retired several years ago. I have the early stages of Alzheimer's, so I had better give you the facts before I forget them; although I am still pretty good on the old stuff." He smiled at the group, some of whom had muffled their gasps at his revelation. "Of course, what I forget so far is important stuff like what I had for breakfast and not what happened in my carefree youthful past. If I do forget something important, I am sure that Nan will remind me. She is good at that."

He continued, "I guess the big war moment for me was the Ardennes Offensive, the Battle of the Bulge, where my brother, Timocrates

Christopoulos, was killed," Demi paused briefly, remembering. *Oh, Tim, why didn't you duck?* He cleared his throat and went on. "They say we won; they write books about us. We certainly did not feel like the greatest generation at the time. I served under General Courtney Hodges in the First Army. People don't know much about him now, because he was eclipsed by the publicity given such warriors as Patten and Bradley. Sometimes it is the modest and quiet who are really the heroes. Anyway, we fell into the trap of the Battle of the Bulge. The Germans really surprised old Ike and us. We fought and won, they say. In his political life later, you may have heard it, quoted quite a bit afterward, Ike acknowledged that he hated war as only a soldier who has seen its brutality, its futility, and its stupidity, can hate it. So, I tell you, not to glamorize battle even though sometimes at the crucial moment war is seen as necessary, after important people have let things go too far. As they say, children fight the old men's battles."

After a pause, Demi said, "I had a great writing teacher here, who told me, in creating a story – never to let a character speak more than three consecutive sentences before giving the floor to someone else. I have violated that rule. It is too easy to do so. She would be displeased that I have forgotten her instructions. I apologize to her memory, and so I should stop."

Demi sat down next to Nancy, took her hand, and closed his eyes.

Ted watched his old friend and tightened his grip on the hand of his wife of fifty years. He looked around at the lecture room where he knew he must have once taken a class, but such rooms in Rockefeller Hall seemed timeless. Even the chairs looked like they had been there in 1946. In his mind, he could hear the chatter that went on in the Vet's lounge, that Vassar had removed from use as the waiting room for Yale or Princeton students passing time before picking up a date for the weekend. It was where the men talked of the future that was to come, and what it was they hoped for out of the life that came after graduation.

He thought how naïve some of that talk had been. He knew of some failures in the after-B.A. years and some successes. As to being the "Greatest Generation" – he knew hype when he saw it, but it had been a really good run, as they say in the theater, and for him and for Sara there were years still to come. He hated to think of how few Demi and Nancy probably had left.

He glanced at Sara sitting next to him, and they both took a deep breath and waited for the meeting to be adjourned so that real life would resume.

***

The air turned gentle as the acrid smoke blew away and the cries receded like some dream that did not include him, as he was now, not this moment, thinking of war. He could imagine with his eyes closed that he was standing on Kaal Rock, overlooking the Hudson River, listening to the calls of lost seagulls that had flown up the estuary to follow the fish that offered fresh-water feeding. The cliffs on the far side of the river above the railroad tracks were gray and black, stained with red and green lichen.

He could hear the sound of a freight train slowly receding up the river on the west side, like distant surf. He could see and hear it all as clearly as if it were happening in that moment. He and Tim were carrying their lovingly oiled baseball gloves, both of them tired from playing at the baseball diamond in Eastman Park with the other Greek kids who shared Conklin Street, but feeling exultant in their exhaustion from the game. Their muscles ached but it was a good ache.

He breathed in the cool river air, spiced with a hint of the salt sea that bathed their sweaty faces.

They were children, together again.

ABOUT THE AUTHOR

HOWARD WINN holds a B. A. from Vassar College, with a major in English. He wrote his senior thesis under the direction of Ida Treat Bergeret, who published extensively in the New Yorker Magazine. He completed additional work at Middlebury College, where he studied with Robert Frost, John Ciardi and A. B. Guthrie, Jr. He has a graduate degree from the Stanford University Writing Program, where he studied with Wallace Stegner and Yvor Winters.

Mr. Winn also completed doctoral level work at New York University and the University of California at San Francisco. His writing has been published in such journals as New York Quarterly, Southern Humanities Review, Raven Chronicles, Beloit Poetry Journal, Descant, Laurel Review, Dalhousie Literary Journal, Galway Review, and many other literary periodicals. A collection of his poetry, *Four Picture Sequence of Desire and Love*, has been published by a now-defunct small press. Mr. Winn's prose writing has been printed in *Water Writes,* an anthology of work by Hudson Valley writers. His poetry was included in *Bridges*, an anthology of Hudson Valley poets, edited with a forward by Mary Gordon. He has also been included in the anthology *Post Beat Poets: Seventy On The Seventies*, published by the Ashland Poetry Press. He has been nominated for a Pushcart prize three times. He is a faculty member at the State University of New York.

Acropolis is his first published novel.

Find more great reads at Propertius Press

Fiction
Non-fiction
Poetry and Verse
Children's Literature
Biography and Memoir
Essays
Anthologies

For the Love of Books
Propertius Press
P. O. Box 55
Boston, VA 22713
www.PropertiusPress.com